I0824016

MARVEL

MS. MARVEL

Don't miss:

White Widow: Secret Sisters
by Tess Sharpe

Agatha Harkness: Fall of the Coven
by Sara Shepard

MARVEL

MS. MARVEL

REMNANTS OF THE PAST

SAADIA FARUQI

Random House New York

Random House Books for Young Readers
An imprint of Random House Children's Books
A division of Penguin Random House LLC
1745 Broadway, New York, NY 10019
penguinrandomhouse.com
rhcbooks.com/disney

Jacket art by Sara Alfageeh
Designed by Emily C. Fisher

Library of Congress Cataloging-in-Publication Data is available upon request.
ISBN 978-1-368-07887-0 (trade) — ISBN 978-0-7364-4792-8 (ebook)

The text of this book is set in Wile Roman Pro.

Manufactured in the United States of America
1st Printing

The authorized representative in the EU for product safety and compliance is Penguin Random House Ireland, Morrison Chambers, 32 Nassau Street, Dublin D02 YH68, Ireland, https://eu-contact.penguin.ie.

Random House Children's Books supports the First Amendment and celebrates the right to read.

For Sitwat and Samar, my partners in crime

People thought patrolling was easy.

How hard could it be, really? You put on your Ms. Marvel costume. Stretched your limbs long, long, long. Climbed on top of a streetlight and viewed your kingdom.

Well, Jersey City. Same thing.

Then you waited for the villains to arrive.

I didn't think it was easy, though. That was the wrong adjective. Some nights it was thrilling, like when a bunch of villains came roaring through the streets thinking they'd cause some mayhem and scare off some civilians.

It was always my extreme pleasure to let them know this was *my* city, *my* streets, and they could just crawl back into whatever sewer they came from.

Of course, patrols could be boring too, if the night was

quiet and nobody came out to play. That's when I tried to get some homework done.

Ugh. I was so not a fan of that. Physics was kicking my ass this semester.

My phone buzzed. It was Bruno Carrelli, my best friend, tech wizard, and maybe, possibly, something more one day in the future. I wasn't sure about that part yet. "You heading downtown, Kamala?"

"That's Ms. Marvel to you," I teased.

"Sorry, Ms. Marvel." I could hear the smile in his voice. "I've intercepted some chatter about villain activity near the museums."

"Villain activity? Are they having a party or something? I knew I should've brought a gift!"

Bruno's sigh was so loud, I heard it clearly through the phone. "Kamala, just get over there. I'll text you the coordinates."

I rolled my eyes. "I know where the museum is, Bruno. No need for coordinates."

"I meant where the chatter is coming from."

"Oh, yeah. That'd be great. Can't wait to protect some innocents!"

Bruno paused. Then: "Be safe, Kamala."

Whoa. What was that voice? And why did the mood of this conversation flip so fast? "Yeah, yeah. Safety is my middle name."

"It really isn't. If you had a middle name, it would be Excitable. Enthusiastic. Dramatic, maybe?"

"Okay . . ."

"Oh, how about Nerdy? That fits you."

"Shut up, doofus." Grinning, I ended the call and walked faster. Tonight, I was patrolling downtown Jersey City, near the art museum. It was one of my favorite places to patrol, because you could see glimpses of the Hudson River from the streets. And if you climbed up a streetlight, like I loved to do, you could see clear across the river to New York City.

My phone buzzed again with the coordinates of whichever villain Bruno had found chattering over the airwaves. The magic my friend could weave using his laptop and brain cells was astounding. I sent back a thumbs-up emoji and hurried to my destination.

Uh, sorry, coordinates.

I was a few blocks from the museum when a deep, gentle vibration shook the ground. "What the . . . ?"

"Aw, did that scare you, Ms. Marvel? I was just getting started."

I looked up. A huge figure dressed in yellow-and-brown armor stood at the end of the street. Its wrists were encased in steel gauntlets that gave off an electrical charge. "Shocker," I muttered in the same tone I'd say *scum of the earth*.

"At your service," he replied, striding closer.

I held my ground. I'd come across Shocker's vibro-shocks plenty of times, and I knew what to expect. Painful shock waves that vibrated the air around him like little earthquakes.

Too bad I was a brave first-gen Pakistani American girl. A little shock wave didn't hurt me. Much.

"What are you doing here?" I asked, eyes narrowed.

He shrugged his giant shoulders. "Got bored. Decided to come outside and check things out."

I took a deep breath. So it was going to be a thrilling kind of evening.

Perfect, just what I needed to get my blood pumping.

"Well, check this out." I clenched my right fist and then yelled, "Embiggen!"

It was more for effect than anything else, because my powers worked just fine without words. My arm elongated like a writhing snake, then shot outward. A second later, my fist went crashing into Shocker's jaw.

He staggered into a big green trash container, grunting. With all that armor, Shocker wasn't exactly light on his feet.

Ha. Dude wasn't expecting my attack, even with all my yelling.

"Are you okay?" I asked with mock concern. "Maybe you need to go home and nurse that wounded ego."

"You think you can defeat me, kid?" He straightened quickly

and held out an arm. A tunnel of air blasted at warp speed, colliding with my entire body and flinging me into the air.

"Oof!" I flew across the street and landed on the pavement.

I didn't stop to think. Still on the ground, I whipped my legs into long ropes and snapped them around Shocker's legs. "Yes, actually, I think I can!"

He tumbled down but threw air blasts at me, again and again.

My legs shrank back. I flew farther down the street like a paper in strong wind. "Is that the best you can do?" I cried, sending a long arm to a streetlight and pulling myself up.

Shocker stood up too. "Oh, no, I'm just getting started!"

I knew what was coming, and I ducked. A blast of air vibrated around me, and a building to the right began to shake.

RRRR-RUMBLE!

Alarmed, I looked to my right. I'd seen Shocker destabilize buildings with his vibro-shocks. My eyes fluttered in relief when I realized it was just a parking garage. At this time of night, there shouldn't be any people inside.

Still, it was time to shut this down. We were too close to the museum to have Shocker shaking things up.

I made both hands big as cars and strong as trees. Then I sent them shooting through the air to pummel Shocker. Once, twice, three times . . . I kept at it, ignoring the air blasts to my skin.

God, those things hurt!

"Gah! Stop!" Shocker grumbled. "I give up! This isn't worth the abuse!"

I panted and grinned. "Not until you tell me what you're doing here this fine evening."

"I heard rumors!"

"Such as . . . ?" I slowed my punches so he'd have a chance to spill the beans.

He groaned. "I heard Kingpin's got some valuable items here, so I thought I'd get them first."

I brought my arms back to my side. "Kingpin? What does he want in Jersey City?"

"I don't know, something legendary." Shocker jumped back so quickly, I didn't have time to blink. In a flash, he'd leapt on top of a building, then another one. "Good luck finding out, Ms. Marvel!" he yelled as he disappeared.

Great! Now I had a dozen questions running through my mind. There was no way I'd get any homework done tonight.

I elongated my legs again and climbed on top of a streetlight, where I had a lovely view of the river. Any villain who got close would have the enthusiastic, excitable, and maybe even dramatic Ms. Marvel to deal with.

It was way too cold for April.

I huddled into my puffy jacket and said as much. Loudly.

"You've lived in Jersey City all your life, Kamala," Bruno said, laughing. "It's not even cold, you know."

"It so is," I grumbled. Maybe it was my Desi roots. I just couldn't stand being cold. Give me warm and balmy any day. Even hot. I was fine with hot. "What is it, like twenty degrees?"

"Forty-five," he replied, checking his phone and laughing even harder. I nudged him—okay, pushed—and he staggered a bit.

"It's all climate change," Nakia said from behind us. Her leather jacket was stylish and matched nicely with her maroon hijab. Even bundled up against the cold, she managed to shine bright. I wasn't even a little bit jealous—Nakia Bahadir was my other best friend since forever—but why couldn't I have some more style? Panache? Elegance?

But nope, all I got was a too-short jacket and a too-big beanie hat with the pom-pom missing. Ugh.

The sidewalk curved, and Bruno stopped. "You've reached your destination," his GPS said cheerfully.

"Here we are," he said, his laugh gone. "Ready for work."

We stared at the building in front of us. Sure, it was the Jersey City Art Museum, but it looked completely different from all the times I'd seen it while patrolling the streets as Ms. Marvel. The old gray stone facade was lit up with colorful strobe lights that waved in the air. People crowded the entrance, wearing tuxedos and ball gowns and brilliant jewelry. "Well, we're underdressed," Nakia muttered.

"Because we're the help," Bruno reminded her.

He was right. Somehow, he'd roped us into joining him as the waitstaff for a stuffy art exhibit for rich people. Not normal rich, but those who fly on private jets and eat caviar and have names ending in Roman numerals.

"Why do you need this job again?" Nakia asked, frowning. She detested elitism and class structure.

He shrugged. "After hours at the museum pays a lot more than Circle Q. I need to save up for summer camp."

He meant Camp TechRo, which stood for *Technology and*

Robotics at some fancy university in Massachusetts. It was exclusive, and therefore expensive. Hence the extra jobs to make some moolah.

"I don't get why *we* have to work too," Nakia grumbled. "All I want is to peek inside, see what the fuss is all about."

I had a suspicion she had more up her sleeve. Nakia was brilliant and always working on some article or another for the school newspaper. I shrugged. "Because we're friends," I whispered, still staring at the scene in front of me. The strobe lights were making my eyes hurt, but I couldn't turn away. They were so, so pretty.

Bruno gave me the side-eye. "Yeah. Friends."

I looked up quickly at the tone of his voice. Was he being sarcastic? He knew we could only be friends, right? Being Muslim meant no dating. Plus, my super hero duties took up way too much time. I had no time for romance, even if I was interested.

Anything else, and my parents would freak the heck out. Seriously.

Bruno looked at me. I looked back, blinking rapidly. *Act cool, Kamala. Act cool.*

"Ahem," Nakia said, and I turned to her. She was biting her lip. I think she was trying not to smile. "Should we go in?"

"Yup," Bruno said loudly, turning away.

Nakia grabbed my hand. "Dude, you were staring at each other like . . . like . . ."

I shook her off. "Like nothing. Don't be stupid." But I knew she was right. My heart was still trying to jump out of my chest.

Bruno seemed to have no such issues. He pointed to the side of the building, away from the crowd. "The staff entrance is over there. Away from the red carpet."

Now my heart thumped for a totally different reason. "Red carpet?" I squeaked. "Are there celebrities here?"

Bruno rolled his eyes and walked to the left. Nakia dragged me after him. "Come on, you can ogle the celebrities inside," she said.

Lucky for me, there were plenty of rich, beautiful, and fabulous types to ogle on the way. We passed some people I'd seen on TV and a few others I'd seen on the big screen. Bollywood, not Hollywood. "This is surreal," I whispered, tripping over my own shoes. "What's that actor doing here? Last I heard, he was filming his latest megahit in Mumbai."

"Dunno," Bruno replied, shrugging.

Nakia's eyes widened. "Isn't that the Pakistani movie producer? Shahana something? Her documentary about divorced women in the Punjab got so many awards."

Bruno shook his head. "I expected this of Kamala, but you too, Nakia?"

"What?" she whined. "That documentary shone a light on women's issues! You know, like poverty and lack of health care."

The movie producer in question was being interviewed by a news crew.

"I don't get it," I said. "Why are there so many famous people here? I mean, it's just a museum exhibit, right? Nothing special?"

Bruno reached the staff entrance first. It was a small door propped open with a rock, a catering van idling right outside. "Come inside," he said. "You'll get your answers."

Inside was a kitchen, one of those big, industrial types that you see in TV shows but never in real life. It was narrow, and everything was metal, and several people in black clothes and white aprons scurried around like their butts were on fire.

"Cool place," Nakia whispered, looking around. "Not too sure about their fashion sense, though."

A red-faced woman, blond hair tied into a tight bun, met us at the lockers. "You're late," she told us, shoving a pile of clothes at Bruno's chest. "Change quickly and take out the appetizers."

"Sorry, ma'am," Bruno said. He waited until she'd scurried away, then handed us our clothes. Black pants, black blouse, white apron.

"I'm rethinking being your friend right now, Bruno," Nakia said, looking at the clothes like they were drenched in poison.

"Yeah, yeah," he replied.

I took my clothes and headed to the staff bathrooms to change. Unlike Nakia, I was glad to be here. I couldn't wait to see what the exhibit was about, drawing rich people from all parts of Jersey City and beyond.

Plus, the job offered free food. Okay, we had to eat in the kitchen, but still. Everything smelled delicious. I changed in record time and tucked my things in a wall of lockers in the hallway outside. Then I headed back in, toward the trays of food on a gleaming metal countertop. "Oooh, salmon bites!"

The countertop rattled a little when I leaned over. I peered down to see it had wheels. *Who puts wheels on counters?*

"Don't touch!" Tight-bun lady picked up a tray and pushed it into Bruno's hands with unnecessary force. Then she did the same with Nakia. "Go—start serving these!"

They scurried away, leaving me blinking at the lady. "What about me?"

She turned to another counter, laden with glasses. The fancy ones, with patterns cut into the glass. "Here, you can pass out drinks."

I gripped the counter with my hands. "Uh, what kind of drinks?" There was no way I was serving alcohol. I was totally against it, on principle. It was technically illegal because I was a minor; also, my parents would probably get some sort of telepathic news alert. *Warning, Kamala Khan touched a glass of whiskey. Alert! Alert! The world is about to end, please send help immediately.*

Of course they had no clue I was actually super hero Ms. Marvel, who helped save the world time and again.

The woman ignored me and started putting glasses on a tray.

"What kind of drinks?" I asked again.

"Cranberry juice, lemonade, and sparkling water."

"No alcohol?" I frowned, confused. "I thought rich people loved their fancy drinks."

She looked up impatiently. "We're not serving pork or alcohol today," she said. "And all the foods are prepared halal."

I took the tray from her and carefully—steadily—made my way out the big doors into the main exhibit area. I took one step, then froze.

Seriously, I needed a breath.

The place was gorgeous. Not the museum itself, because I'd been here plenty of times as a visitor, and it was just okay. But right now it was decorated to high heaven. Rich fabric hung from the walls in pink, purple, and gold cascades. Humongous bouquets of lilies and roses sat on various tables around the room.

And the guests! Oh, their clothes and jewelry made my jaw drop. There was at least a few million dollars' worth of accessories in this room, and that didn't include the actual exhibit, whatever it was.

I roamed around, offering drinks to people. There were a lot of women wearing hijabs, many in saris, a few men in the traditional sherwani. They took the drinks from my tray without making eye contact, which was okay with me. I was too busy making eye contact with all the bling on display.

I crossed paths with Bruno and Nakia more than once. We gave each other winks or smiles, just to say hello. A few times I saw a Black woman dressed in a silver romper talking to groups of people. She had a blond girl my age hanging on her every word.

I stopped to take a breath near a high-top, trying to look busy without moving. Bruno did the same. His tray was laden with the salmon bites I'd seen in the kitchen, and I itched to grab one. He gave me a knowing look and held the tray away from me. He nodded toward the lady in the silver romper. "That's Ms. Natalia Hibbert, the museum curator."

Nakia walked up to us with an admiring sigh. She was holding a tray of bruschetta decorated with sprigs of mint. "She's awesome. Forty Under Forty, three years in a row."

I wasn't sure what that meant. Something competent, no doubt. "And the girl?" I asked.

Bruno shrugged. "An assistant, maybe?"

Said assistant must have heard our whispers. She turned

and gave us a severe *Get back to work* look, which quickly changed to a smile when she spied Bruno.

Nakia nudged Bruno. "Oh, she likey!"

"Come on!" Bruno flushed and walked away with his tray of food.

I gave Nakia a dirty look. Why was she teasing Bruno about girls, for crying out loud? That's not why we were here. Nope, not at all.

"What?" Nakia asked innocently, and walked off in the other direction.

"Drinks Girl!" Ms. Hibbert called, waving to me. "Here, please!"

Ugh, what had I done to deserve this treatment? I stomped over, trying to smooth out my face so it didn't look all irritated.

Close up, Ms. Hibbert didn't seem anything but nice. Very efficient too. "Thank you, dear," she said briskly, then tipped her chin at the guests in front of her.

I offered them my tray, turned to another group, and offered them some drinks too. Anything to make this stupid tray less heavy. Soon, I'd handed out all the drinks, and my load was ten times lighter.

I looked up to find myself close to a big display. People crowded around it, laughing and talking. I couldn't see the exhibit itself, so I satisfied my curiosity by reading the plaque.

Mughal Artifacts.

That was the exhibit. A grouping of paintings and other items straight from the Mughal era of India.

I knew a little about them, of course. Abu sometimes recounted tales from Emperor Babur's memoir—the *Baburnama*—or spoke about Akbar the Great's exploits. They were the coolest thing India had ever produced, way before the British divided the subcontinent and Pakistan was born in 1947. Before that, it was all India, and the Mughals were Muslims who ruled with might and glory.

Well, mostly.

Suddenly, the crowd moved away a little, so I edged closer and peered into one of the glass cabinets. It contained rows of the classic miniature paintings the Mughals are so well known for, some as small as the palm of my hand. The exhibit plaque explained that they were portraits of emperors like Akbar and Humayun as well as detailed scenes from royal life. A group of people sitting around in a garden, a scene of a hunt, women gossiping in a courtyard, and so much more.

I moved to the next cabinet. It showcased coins that glinted serious gold, a tortoise carved in jade, and several rings and bracelets. There were even a couple of jewelry boxes made of gold, with intricate floral designs carved into them.

I sighed. My jewelry box at home was a small plastic container full of trinkets from the mall. The most sparkly gem was cubic zirconia.

The third cabinet contained an entire collection of daggers, ranging from small to dangerously, ferociously large. Like, who needs this many daggers? That last one was almost a sword, for crying out loud. Beautiful but deadly. I wondered how many people had been killed with it.

Knowing the Mughals, a lot.

In the last cabinet, there were booklets with beautiful calligraphy, a couple of rings studded with sparkling jewels, and a delicate but stunning pair of glasses.

Not the ones you drink from, but the ones you wear for your eyes.

"Cool, no?" Nakia said from beside me. Her tray was empty too.

"The glasses?" I asked, looking back at the display. The card next to it read *Gold with emeralds and diamonds.* Wowza.

"I believe the correct name is spectacles," Nakia replied.

"Ooh la la." I sighed, getting serious. "These thingies are gorgeous, though. I get why so many people have shown up to look at them."

"Thingies?" Nakia frowned at me. "They're artifacts, Kamala. Mughal artifacts that have been taken from their countries of origin and displayed in Western countries like spoils of war."

I blinked at the harsh tone of her voice. "Spoils of war? What're you talking about?"

Nakia took a deep breath. People around us were starting to eye her. "Not here." She took my hand and led me away from the exhibit.

Bruno was leaning against the far wall, empty tray under his arm. "Hey, how's it going?" he asked, straightening up.

"Nakia's talking about war or something," I reported.

"Huh?"

"Not real war. Symbolic." Nakia paused. "Well, some of the wars were real. Ugh, forget I said anything."

I felt bad. I didn't mean to shoot her down. She obviously felt strongly about this, whatever it was. "No, tell us," I insisted. "I want to know."

"What's there to say?" She shrugged. "These are all stolen artifacts. They don't belong here. The colonial powers took the wealth of their colonies because they felt it belonged to them. Like—like a prize or something. Might is right, I'll break into your house and steal all your stuff, what're you gonna do, et cetera, et cetera."

I blinked. I'd never really thought about how items in museums got there. Not just this one, but others too. African exhibits. Displays from South America and East Asia. Two weeks ago at breakfast, Abu had read out a news story about the largest display of Ming vases in Europe. "Maybe they borrowed the, uh, artifacts," I said weakly. "Or asked permission or whatever?"

Nakia and Bruno both stared. "Really?" Nakia said.

"I don't know. Seems weird that they'd all be stolen and nobody would say anything. Wouldn't people make noise about it?"

Nakia shook her head. "They do! People write about it all the time. I can bet you anything some of the reporters here are going to talk about it after tonight." She took another deep breath, and her face changed from angry to nervous. "In fact, that's why I'm here too."

"What do you mean?" Bruno asked. "You're here because I asked you to be."

Nakia smiled weakly. "Well, yes. But I had an ulterior motive."

"Wow," I teased. "You mean it's not your lifelong dream to dress up like a server and hand out bruschetta with mint?"

My humor went down like flat soda. "No," Nakia said, her face serious. "I'm writing an article about the exhibit for our school newspaper."

Honestly, I didn't see the big deal. Nakia was the editor of the *Coles Journal*, our school paper. It made sense that she'd want to write something about the exhibit.

Nakia did this all the time. Once, I'd taken her to a new boutique that opened near my house, and she ended up writing a scathing review of the environmental impact of fast fashion.

My heart sank. "Wait, is this article going to bash the exhibit?"

"No, of course not!" Her weak smile was back. "It's gorgeous. How could I write anything negative about it?"

"Then what's the problem?"

She bit her lip. "Uh, it's gonna bash the museum. I'm going to do a deep dive into the debate of who actually owns these pieces. If the museum really has the right to display them."

"Nooooo!" Bruno groaned. "They'll know you're my friend. I vouched for you. You can't say bad stuff about them!"

I scoffed. "It's a school newspaper, Bruno. Not even the students read it."

"Hey!" Nakia protested.

I nudged her with my shoulder to let her know I was kidding. Sorta.

"Can you two keep an ear open for what people are saying?" Nakia asked. "I'd love to get some juicy quotes."

"Sure!" I nodded.

Bruno shook his head. "Listen, we need to go back to the kitchen and get more food and drinks."

I groaned lightly. "Man, I'm so sick of being Drinks Girl. This job sucks."

Then I caught Ms. Hibbert and the flirty blond girl right behind Bruno and zipped my lips. Hopefully they hadn't heard me complaining about my job. Ms. Hibbert was talking to an elderly white couple. The woman had a white beehive, and the man wore a black suit and had a monocle.

I'd never seen a monocle in real life. It was fascinating, but the expressions on the couple's faces were mean and snooty, so I decided I'd rather look elsewhere. Who had time to stare at mean rich people?

I'd rather stare at the exhibit.

I grabbed some more drinks from the kitchen and circulated among the guests again. This time, I kept my eyes and ears open for the types of comments Nakia had mentioned.

"Such beautiful pieces!" someone gushed.

"If only they'd allowed photography inside," said someone else. "I want my jeweler to replicate some of these designs. That bracelet would be perfect at the film awards gala next month."

I kept walking, a polite smile on my face.

"This exhibit is in such poor taste," one woman said, taking an orange juice from me. "Those priceless paintings! And those coins. Wah!"

Okay, now we were talking.

"Yes," the woman's friend agreed. "It would have been

better displayed at the Asia Society or a similar organization. Why should the colonizer get to display their stolen goods like it's something to be proud of?"

"Look at everyone, just lapping it all up like they've no idea what's at stake."

My ears perked. What *was* at stake, exactly? Too bad the group walked away before they could elaborate.

I found myself wandering close to the exhibit again. There was a smaller crowd around the cabinets now.

An elderly uncle tugged at my sleeve. "Where did half of these artifacts even come from?" he asked.

"Uh, I don't know . . ."

He shook his head sadly. "I remember reading about those spectacles in a magazine when I was a young boy in Pakistan," he said, pointing to the piece I'd noticed earlier. It had a diamond frame and emerald lenses, and even through the cabinet glass, they shone with brilliance.

"Aren't they pretty?" I agreed. "All those jewels!"

"Pretty?" He glared at me. "They're legendary. Life-changing."

Wait, hadn't Shocker used that word too? Legendary?

The elderly man was still looking at me, so I tried to lighten the mood. "Uh, do you mean the daggers? Because they could change someone's life entirely, if you know what I mean." I balanced the tray in one hand and pretended to stab in the air with the other. "Haiyya!"

The man's glare intensified. Dude was fierce, even though he must be pushing ninety. He took a glass of sparkling water from me, muttered something about pretentious fools with their bubbly H_2O, and left.

Okay, then.

I agreed about the pretentious part, but did he have to be so abrupt? Although now I was wondering what was so special about the spectacles.

I walked around the room some more. Bruno was doing the same on the other side but with way more smiling and nodding. Nakia was standing next to a couple who looked like they'd robbed a jewelry store on the way here. She'd put her tray of appetizers down and was writing in the little notepad she carried around in her purse.

She looked up at me and smiled.

I smiled back fondly. I had no doubt that girl was going to be president someday. She was going to accomplish some amazing things.

Meanwhile, me: super hero stuck serving drinks to bougie rich people and fighting weirdos in dark alleys.

Don't get me wrong, I loved my Ms. Marvel persona. The work I did was valuable, no question about it. It was only the rest of me—Desi, high schooler, awkward around guys, not sure what I wanted to be when I grew up—that made me sweat buckets.

Although the sweating went with super hero duties in general, so maybe that was okay.

". . . really proud of the work the museum is doing to showcase the culture and history of the immigrants in our communities!" A very loud, very pompous voice interrupted my serious thoughts.

Wait, I knew that voice.

I hated that voice.

I looked up, alarmed. Kingpin—yes, the evil villain Kingpin, A.K.A. Wilson Fisk—stood at a small lectern, giving some sort of speech. Maybe a press conference, since there were mostly reporters with microphones and cameras standing around him. Ms. Hibbert stood on his left, and a tall, lean, dark-haired man on his right. Beehive Lady and Monocle Man were close by.

I stood frozen, trying to make sense of the scene before me.

Kingpin was huge. Big, and round, and bald, with an attitude even a mother couldn't love. I knew, because I'd come across him a few times—or more—since becoming Ms. Marvel. He held a cane in one hand and gripped the lectern with the other. His suit was blindingly white, his tie blindingly pink.

Like Pepto-Bismol on steroids.

Nakia came up behind me, sans tray. "Do you think he wears anything else?"

"Imagine going to the beach in that suit," I joked.

She shuddered. "I'm sorry, but I refuse to have that mental image."

I wasn't surprised that we were both thinking the same thing. It happened a lot. We were soul sisters. Our thoughts and feelings were in sync.

Kingpin droned on and on about the exhibit. How beautiful the items were. How kind the museum staff was to showcase it. "Ugh, his voice is so annoying," Nakia complained.

"Forget his voice," I replied. "Why is he even here?"

She pointed to a sign set up on an easel. It said *Sponsored by*, followed by a bunch of corporate logos. Fisk Industries was right at the top, double the size of all the other logos.

I put my tray on a nearby table and pulled Nakia away from the crowd. "Kingpin usually stays in New York City. That's where his empire is. Why is he here, in Jersey City? At a museum, of all places?"

"He's a sponsor."

My mind took this second to remember Shocker's statement about Kingpin's interest in the museum. Something valuable and legendary. "But why?" I murmured. "I'm pretty sure that guy has never given a cent of his money to anyone without an ulterior motive."

"Well, lots of rich people give to charity. Not because they're good, but because they get tax write-offs. And they get respect from the community."

I turned slightly to stare at Kingpin's bald head. It was shining brightly, thanks to the camera lights. "Eh, not sure he cares about taxes and things."

"Or respect," Nakia added.

"Exactly. So what's his angle?"

She took my hand and pulled me back toward the press conference. "Let's see what he has to say."

We found a gap in the crowd and squeezed through until we found Bruno. "Are you two listening to this?" he whispered angrily. No surprise at this reaction. Bruno despised Kingpin. Something about the big corporate empire versus the small business owner.

"Shhh!" a man in the audience hissed.

"Sorry!" I hissed back. Let's face it, I wasn't sorry at all. But at the last minute I remembered I was wearing a server uniform and should act . . . subservient?

I tried to focus on the scene in front of me. Kingpin was silent now, and a reporter was speaking. She looked Desi, with black hair and an intelligent face. "Mr. Fisk, what are your thoughts about the origins of these artifacts?" she asked. "Many people think they belong to the people of the Indian subcontinent."

Kingpin's sharklike smile grew bigger. "That's not my area of expertise," he replied. "All I know is that the artifacts are fabulous, and we're absolutely delighted to showcase them right here in America."

"Trust him to totally bypass the question," Bruno whispered in my left ear.

"Just like him to take credit for the exhibit like he's in charge," Nakia whispered in my right ear.

I didn't respond. My eyes snagged on the man standing next to Kingpin. Tall, thin, wearing a black sherwani and black shoes. He was definitely Desi, judging from his skin tone and hair color.

It wasn't his ethnicity that made me stare at him, though. It was something about the way he was standing, about his wiry frame and glinting black eyes. He seemed to have unleashed power in his body, something dark and lethal that vibrated all around him like a powerful shield.

I kept staring while Kingpin droned on, answering reporters' questions and laughing big, booming laughs every few minutes like he was having the time of his life.

"I don't trust him," Nakia said to me. "He's got no business being here."

At first, I thought she was talking about the sherwani guy, but then Bruno said mockingly, "Maybe he's got ancient artifacts in his business portfolio."

"Oh, you mean Kingpin?" I murmured.

"Who did you think we were talking about?" Nakia asked. She opened the notes app on her phone and started jotting something down.

Kingpin finished his speech, and the crowd clapped thunderously. He smiled that shark smile again, accepting his due like the king he thought he was. "Enjoy the rest of your evening, ladies and gentlemen," he said before turning away.

I watched as Kingpin shook hands with the rich old couple and the mysterious Desi man. My eyes were bugging out, big-time. They all knew each other. And they were bonding over the Mughal artifacts exhibit.

This was the second evening in a row that I'd gotten a ton of questions in my mind but very few answers.

I hated when that happened. I was an answers girl. I wanted to know the who, what, where, and why of everything. Especially the why.

It was almost midnight before the event wrapped up and the guests finally left. Bruno, Nakia, and I dragged our exhausted selves to the kitchen along with the other servers.

A few dishes of food were still laid out on the counter, this time with a handwritten sign that said *staff*. Perfect. I was starving.

I grabbed a mini spinach quiche in each hand. "Delicious," I muttered as I chomped.

"Glad you came, eh?" Bruno said. He and Nakia started piling food on paper plates like normal people. I took a second to regret my uncivilized eating habits, then shrugged and grabbed another quiche. I'd just served drinks to a hundred snobs. I deserved this.

"Slow down, tiger." Nakia laughed.

"You slow down."

"That doesn't even make sense. . . ."

The door to the alley flew open with a smack, and I looked up. A janitor was dragging a trash bag outside, and behind him in the distance, I could see a giant green trash container. It was dented a little where I'd pushed Shocker into it. Well, shoved, really.

Ahh, good times. I wished I'd encouraged him to talk more instead of letting him walk away.

Bruno came to stand next to me. "What're you looking at?"

"This exhibit is special in some way," I mused quietly.

"Yeah, it's full of stolen stuff that gullible fools are paying money to gawk at," Nakia replied, taking a dainty bite of food from her plate. She picked up her phone and began to walk away. "Gotta check my texts. I'll be right back."

I waited until Nakia went outside into the alley. There were no other servers around us, so I quickly made my right arm long and stretchy and nabbed a cookie from the counter. "This is yummy," I said, my mouth full.

I wasn't kidding. It was melty and gooey and full of chocolate chips.

"I'm sure," Bruno said dryly. He knew all about my obsession with baked goods.

My eyes returned to the alley again. "Met Shocker in that alley last night. Had to teach him a lesson."

Bruno's brow crinkled. "What did he want?"

"He was talking about the museum, interestingly," I mused. "I didn't pay him much attention then, but now that I'm here, with all that . . ." I waved toward the exhibit hall beyond the kitchen doors.

"You think he's got some connection with the Mughal exhibit?" From his tone, Bruno obviously didn't think so.

I shrugged. "I dunno. He was here for something. I made him regret it, though."

"Good job, as always." Bruno's eyes shone with something I wasn't ready to acknowledge.

I quickly looked away and swiped a pita chip from Nakia's plate. It was close enough that I didn't need my stretchy arm.

"Hey!" Nakia shouted from the open doorway. "I saw that, you thief!"

"Eat fast or lose," I shouted back.

Bruno shook his head and picked up a cleaning wipe. "Let's clean up quickly so we can all get home."

Ms. Hibbert bustled into the kitchen, still looking fresh and bright-eyed. "That's the spirit!"

Too bad she was followed by the blond girl Friday. "Everyone, please stop dawdling and get to work," she snarked. Then she had the audacity to clap her hands like she was a kindergarten teacher. "Let's go, let's go!"

Nakia and I rolled our eyes at each other. I'd have included

Bruno in the exchange, but he was too busy grinning like a tool. "Sure, Miss . . . ?"

The girl flipped her hair back. "Brittany Myers. I'm an intern here."

"Cool," Bruno replied.

I didn't think a museum internship was that awesome, but what did I know? I was only a super hero fighting crime and saving the city. Bruno had never grinned at me so . . . bashfully.

Not that I wanted him to. No, sirree.

I turned away and began to wipe down a counter with vicious strokes. This kitchen better get cleaned up pronto so I could get out of here. I was a busy gal.

We'd almost finished when we heard the sound of breaking glass, and then a sharp alarm rose through the air, loud and screeching. Ms. Hibbert and Brittany looked up, their eyes round with horror. "That's the security alarm!" Ms. Hibbert hissed.

Brittany looked frozen. "What . . . what should we do?"

Ms. Hibbert was already running toward the kitchen doors. "You kids stay here. I'll check it out."

It was my turn to look horrified. What was she thinking, running out into possible danger? "Wait, you shouldn't go out there!" I yelled. "What if it's a burglar?"

Or what if the Shocker was back? This was a job for Ms. Marvel, not some romper-wearing curator lady, no matter how stylish and competent she was.

Brittany followed Ms. Hibbert, only pausing at the doors to throw me a frazzled look. "The police will be here in a few minutes. No need to be scared."

I huffed. Who was she calling scared?

Nakia and the other servers crowded around the window in the kitchen door, trying to see what was going on. Bruno hung back with me. "Who do you think it is?" he said quietly.

Before I could reply, there was a crash behind us. I took a deep breath and half turned toward the alley and the trash container. It seemed like the answers might be outside. "That's what I'm going to find out," I said in a hard tone,

Bruno nodded. "I'll hold down the fort here. You go do your thing."

I grabbed my backpack from the lockers and slipped into the staff bathrooms to change into my Ms. Marvel costume. By the time I got back, everyone except Bruno had left the kitchen.

He half turned when he saw me. "Seems like something from the exhibit has been stolen," he said urgently. "The police are on the way."

My heart thumped loudly in my chest. "Do you know what?"

He shook his head. "Ms. Hibbert and the others are taking inventory right now. Everyone's been called to help. I was waiting for you to get back, see if you needed anything before I headed out there."

I didn't really have time to ponder all the ways Bruno Carrelli was an amazing person. Dependable and supportive. Just what Ms. Marvel needed.

Kamala too, if I was being honest.

"No, I'm fine," I assured him. "You go get some intel. I'll check out the alley. The thief couldn't have gone far."

Without waiting for a reply, I slipped out of the back door and into the alley, closing the door behind me. I didn't need Nakia—or worse, Brittany—coming out here to investigate.

Then I blinked, because I'd almost stepped right into the middle of a fight. A blur of pink leotard and black boots and lots of grunting and clashing. Seemed like fun, but there was no way I was jumping in before getting all the deets.

I hid in the shadows against the wall, my heart thumping loudly. From the sounds of the fight and the shapes of the fighters, these were no regular humans.

The question was, who were they? And how were they connected to the museum?

"You think you're stronger than me?" a voice I knew well shrieked. "I can keep this up for hours."

Delilah. I'd tangled with her enough times to recognize

her. She was a super-strong assassin with advanced healing powers and an arrogant attitude I loved to knock down to smithereens.

What was she doing outside the museum this fine evening, right after the alarm rang inside? Was she the thief? And if so, did her villain supervisor Kingpin know she was stealing from the exhibit he had so publicly sponsored?

"Oh, yes, we've all heard about your superhuman strength, Delilah." Another voice. Smoother, rougher, definitely male. This didn't sound familiar to me at all. And the kicker: The accent was Desi.

What. The. Heck?

How? Who?

My head swam with the number of questions I now had in my mind. I was itching to join the fight, but I didn't want to show myself yet. Delilah was definitely a baddie, but that didn't automatically make Desi Dude a good guy. I knew most of the super heroes around here, and none of them had Desi accents.

I needed to know more about who he was, and why he was fighting Delilah, before joining the fray.

The duo moved closer to a streetlight, and I could see them clearly now. Delilah was her usual smug self, her long ponytail flicking side to side.

I focused on the other fighter. The Desi.

Tall, wiry black hair, a dark brown mask covering his face. The suit he wore was black and brown, with some sort of geometric design embossed on it.

He clenched his fists, and a green-and-white light erupted from them. It crackled and hissed like it was a tiny, furious being.

Whoa. Was that electricity? Magic? Some otherworldly power?

"Let's see if you're strong enough for this!" he told Delilah, and threw the light straight at her.

Delilah sidestepped just in time, and the shot landed on the fence behind her. I was close enough to feel the heat of the energy. It almost singed my eyebrows off.

"Oh, you'll need something much stronger than a party trick!" Delilah laughed mockingly, then ran at full speed toward him. At the last minute she half turned and aimed an outstretched leg at his stomach. He doubled over with a grunt.

"Hope you liked that, Mystery Man."

Hmm, interesting. Delilah didn't know who he was either. Yet they were fighting so bitterly, the shrubs around them were on green-and-white fire.

I chewed my lip, wondering if this was my fight. Your enemy's enemy was your friend, and all that. Something made me wait, though. I didn't know the masked man's name or what his motives were. I needed more information before I came to his aid.

As if in response, the man stood up and bowed. He wasn't even breathing loudly, despite the kick to his stomach. "Asaar, at your service."

I drew in a quick breath. Asaar. Definitely didn't sound English. What language was that? Urdu? Arabic? Something else?

"I don't care who you are." Delilah's face grew cold. She made a circle and kicked him again, this time in his back. Then she shoved him with her strong arms so that he fell to his knees with a grunt. "Just give me the magic spectacles and I'll let you leave here alive."

"Oh, just hand them to you, should I?" Asaar cupped both his hands around a ball of green fire, which grew larger and larger. Then, with a little yell, he turned and hurled it at her.

Delilah yelled back even louder as she absorbed the blast into her chest.

Ow. That had to hurt!

I watched as the two continued to grapple. They were pretty evenly matched, so they hit and got hit, then recovered for another round. Delilah pulled out a small knife and began stabbing the air with it.

Asaar knocked it out of her hand with his light energy.

I closed my eyes in frustration. Standing in the shadows while a fight raged on was so not me. Still, I needed a minute to figure out what the heck was happening. Delilah wanted some sort of magical spectacles? What were the chances that's what had been stolen from the museum tonight? The elderly uncle had been talking about a pair of spectacles too, trembling, calling them life-changing.

Turned out he might have been right. If Delilah and this Asaar guy were battling for them, the spectacles had to be really special.

Which meant neither of these tools should be keeping them.

Asaar's back was turned toward me, and I saw a glint of emerald in his pocket. The stones were so brilliant, this couldn't be anything other than the spectacles I'd seen inside.

Bingo!

That was the push I needed to jump in. No matter whose side Asaar was on, I couldn't let him steal something from right under my nose. I clenched my hands into iron fists and prepared to step out of the shadows.

Just then, the wail of police sirens split the air.

I froze.

Delilah threw a knife at Asaar, and he rolled to the ground.

Yikes! The spectacles! I cringed as he came close to crushing them. At the last second, the spectacles fell out of his pocket and lay half hidden in the gravel.

What was this dude thinking? I almost screamed, because oh my God, what if something happened to the spectacles? Magical or not, they were a historical artifact worth more than just money. They shouldn't be lying on the ground behind a building, five feet from a trash container.

The sirens were so close now, my ears ached. The sound of voices and running feet came from the front of the building. "Police!" someone shouted. "Over here!"

I stared at the spectacles, my brain working overtime to figure out how to grab them without showing myself to the authorities. Delilah strode over and grabbed Asaar with both hands, pulled him up to half standing, then slammed him back with tremendous force right into a brick wall.

Ouch.

He slid to the ground, unconscious.

Delilah strode over to Asaar, grumbling, "Not so strong now, eh, sleepy boy?"

I took a deep, steadying breath. This was my chance. There was no way I was letting Delilah have anything from this museum. I stepped out of the shadows and made my hand into a giant fist, as large as a house and probably just as heavy.

Then I sent the fist soaring through the air and right into her kisser.

Booyah! She went down like a sack of bricks and stayed down, her eyes closed, breathing shallow.

I stepped over both bodies and picked up the spectacles carefully. My hands noticed how pointy and delicate the frames were, and my eyes couldn't get enough of the emerald gleam. But I told myself to calm down. This was a job. Ms. Marvel had to protect this artifact until she could decide on a plan.

Not ogle them like all the snobs in the museum earlier.

Elongating my legs, I hopped over the fence and away from the alley with its unconscious bozos. I needed a minute to hide and think before I took the spectacles back to the museum, where they belonged.

Maybe.

On the other side of the fence, on the edge of the main street, the glare from the police cars' flashing lights was brighter. I stood deep in the bushes and stared at the spectacles in my hand. They sparkled so much my eyes blurred.

Round diamond frames. Deep green lenses, each one a complete emerald with no joints, no cracks.

Utter perfection.

I rubbed a gentle finger over a diamond. Were these

spectacles truly magical? Would they turn me into a fairy princess if I muttered a spell? Ha.

Being a super hero was way better than a fairy princess, hands down.

I looked up at the museum entrance in the distance, surrounded by police cars. A few cops stood at the end of the street, close to where I was hidden. If I walked out of the bushes and strode into the museum to return a stolen artifact, how would they react?

They'd probably arrest me. Try to pin this entire crime on me or something.

I looked down at the spectacles again. They were gorgeous. Otherworldly, really, in their brilliance and beauty. If I were a poet, I'd write an ode to this artifact in my hands.

The longer I stood there, staring at the spectacles, the more my brain screamed at me to keep them and run.

I mean, not forever. I wasn't a thief.

More like for safekeeping. Just until I understood why everyone and their mother wanted them so badly.

The next morning was a nightmare. My parents sat at the breakfast table, looking worried and stressed out.

Let's face it: This was normal.

The Khans were always stressed out about something. If it wasn't the state of quote-unquote "lawlessness" around here, it was the way American teens were dressed nowadays. Or the news. Or American teens on the news.

I slid into my chair and grabbed a mug of coffee. After last night, I needed it. "Salaam alaikum," I grunted.

"Why were you out so late again, huh?" Ammi demanded, slapping some butter on toast. "Just because you're in high school doesn't mean you can stay out late like those American girls. It's not safe."

Ah, so both lawlessness and teenagers were making an appearance in this morning's stressfest. Perfect.

"News flash, Ammi," I muttered. "I'm an American girl."

Abu opened his newspaper with a little crackle. "No, you're Pakistani," he corrected. "We may live in America, but make no mistake, we are Pakistani."

I gulped down some coffee. This was an ongoing debate in our house. Were we American? Were we Pakistani? Could we really be called the latter when our elders had relinquished their Pakistani passports and taken the U.S. citizenship oath? When two members of this family (me and my annoying older brother Aamir) were born in the U.S.?

"There was a burglary near the art museum last night," Ammi said. "Did you hear about it?"

I perked up. "How . . . how do you know?"

She shrugged. "My WhatsApp group. Someone shared a video at midnight."

I wondered who that someone was. I hadn't seen any news crews around, so it had to be one of the people in the museum kitchen with me. A server maybe? Stupid Brittany?

Ammi continued. "I can't believe what the world is coming to. In my day, it was always banks or jewelry stores that got looted, not museums."

"Ah, yes, remember that jewelry heist some years ago?" Abu mused. "It was front-page news for days."

A flash of the heavy jewelry on display last night—both in

the exhibit and on women's bodies—made me smirk behind my mug. My parents had no clue. As usual.

That flash was followed by another. The emerald spectacles, which were currently in the bottom of my backpack along with the Ms. Marvel costume. Gorgeous. Brilliant. Shining like the sun, but green.

My smirk disappeared. There was several million dollars' worth of an ancient artifact in my backpack right this minute. The same backpack that I dropped on the floors of dirty high school restrooms on a daily basis.

I gulped down some more coffee. What was I even doing with that thing? It had seemed a great idea in the darkness of the night, after knocking out Delilah.

Now, in the light of day, my eyes bleary with sleep, I was rethinking all my life choices.

Being stuck with a stolen item would *so* not be a good look for Ms. Marvel. The Avengers would have my hide if this became a public scandal.

"Salaam alaikum, family!" Aamir, my annoying brother, entered the kitchen with a wide grin. He stopped to ruffle my hair. "Where were you last night, Kamala?"

"It's not your business," I said angrily. "Do I ask you where you disappear to all the time?"

He sat down next to me and grabbed the plate of toast.

"Well, I'm much older than you. I don't have to report my comings and goings to anyone, Alhamdulillah." He smirked. "Unlike you, who's still a child."

I gritted my teeth. I could feel my face getting hot. Maybe steam would come out of my eyes like those cartoon villains. "I. Am. Not. A. Child."

Ammi patted my hand like she wasn't the one who started this whole thing. "No, you're a big girl, beta," she said soothingly. Then she spoiled the act by adding, "You should know better than to stay out late and put yourself in danger."

"Ugh," I groaned. "I wasn't in danger. I was working at the museum, remember? They had that Mughal exhibit, and I went with Nakia and Bruno to work. I told you about it."

Ammi gasped. "The same place that was robbed?"

Abu didn't gasp, thankfully, but he glared at me over his newspaper.

I waved away their concerns. "There were cops everywhere. Safest place to be, really, with Jersey City's finest surrounding the building."

Too bad the cops didn't catch everything. Never even noticed two super-strong villains fighting it out yards away.

Abu put down the newspaper and leaned forward. "The Mughal exhibit. Did you see it?"

"Yeah." I shrugged. "It was . . . good."

"Good?" He frowned. "That's all you have to say? You saw your heritage, and you thought it was good?"

"My heritage?" I blinked at the grandness of the phrase. I hadn't thought of it that way, but he was right. The Mughals were my people, I guess. Indian, which encompassed the entire subcontinent at that time in history. There was no Pakistan then. No political boundaries created by the British after World War II. And for a while, the Mughal Empire stretched across South Asia like the gorgeous jewels in a necklace.

Ammi took a bite of her toast. "This is what happens when you live outside your own country. You lose your heritage. Your identity. You don't know who you really are."

More blinking. I hated when I agreed with my mother about something. And most of the time, I ignored what my parents said to me. It was the only way to keep sane. But the exhibit I saw last night had brought up way too many questions. Why was Kingpin there? Who was the masked man in the alley? Why were there so many disgruntled guests at the event?

Did the emerald spectacles really have magical powers?

I couldn't ask my parents about the villains last night, but I could ask them something else. "So what's the deal with the Mughals?" I asked. "Why are they so important?"

Abu shoved a forkful of eggs into his mouth and chewed. "Hmph! Shameful."

I waited. Surely he'd have more to say than a grunted opinion?

"What he means is," Aamir began, "the Mughals were a powerful dynasty that ruled India in the sixteenth to nineteenth centuries with all their glory. After that, the British arrived and their power diminished, until finally they lost the empire to the British army."

The colonizers that Nakia was talking about.

"Look, here it is," Abu said. He opened the newspaper and pointed to a small headline. *Local Museum Holds Mughal Display.*

"Wow, that was fast!" I exclaimed. The news reporters from last night's events already had a piece published. I leaned closer and read it quickly. There wasn't much about the exhibit itself, more about the quotes from Kingpin and the curator. How happy they were to display such gorgeous artifacts, blah, blah.

"This right here is a travesty!" Abu said angrily, jabbing a finger at the center of the article. "They steal our wealth and display it like it's nothing."

"Not like nothing," I protested weakly. "They called it stunning. And they displayed it in these beautiful cases lined with velvet. . . ."

"The point is, they shouldn't be displayed here at all. They should be where they belong, with the people of South Asia."

This was exactly what Nakia had said too. I stared at my family. It was a rare day when they all agreed on something. "Okay, then," I whispered. "Good to know."

Then Aamir reached over and flicked me in the forehead. "So what did you do at the exhibit last night? Pick up the trash? Clean the floors?"

I took another sip of coffee to avoid the truth. By the time the event had ended, I'd had to do both things. You wouldn't believe the amount of trash left behind by a bunch of rich people.

Ammi gasped. "Hai Allah! My daughter cleaning floors? Why, Kamala? Why would you do that? Don't we see to your every need? Do we leave you hungry or without clothes? Why do you need to go out and do these menial jobs?"

I growled at Aamir. "Thanks, dude!"

He shrugged. "What? I didn't say anything false."

"You . . . you . . . !"

"Enough!" Abu let his fork fall on his plate with a loud rattle. "Stop your fighting, both of you! Aamir, I've been telling you for months you need to find a job. You're old enough to support yourself."

Aamir sputtered.

I lost some of my anger and gave him a sweet, mocking smile. How the tables had turned!

"And you, Kamala," Abu continued sternly, "you're not old enough to work yet. You need to stay home and study hard. No going out at night, with God knows who."

"I went with Bruno and Nakia!"

"It doesn't matter. They should stay home too. High school is important. You need to focus on your studies."

"Yes, exactly!" Ammi added, folding her hands across her chest. "And stay away from burglars."

I gritted my teeth but said nothing. This was nothing new. They wanted me to be the model Desi daughter, getting good grades and looking perfect, never doing anything weird or strange or, God forbid, dangerous. If they only knew my secret job faced me off against the worst villains the planet had ever seen. And that I defeated them all with a grin on my face.

Serving drinks to art lovers in a museum was nothing compared to my usual activities.

"Are you listening, Kamala?" Abu asks. "No more gallivanting about at night until they catch the museum thief."

That would never happen, I knew. I was basically sneaking out every night now, doing my duties as Ms. Marvel. "Sure," I said quickly.

Aamir scoffed.

I kicked my annoying brother under the table.

"Ow!" he hissed. "What does the Quran say about hurting innocent people?"

I didn't want to get into an argument about how he wasn't all that innocent. I quickly gobbled up some eggs under Ammi's watchful eye, then ran upstairs to get dressed for school.

"Leaving so early?" Aamir asked disbelievingly when I came back down ten minutes later.

I know, I know. I was always late. Kamala Late Khan, that's what he called me sometimes. Along with other names I didn't appreciate. But today I was on time because I needed to make a pit stop on the way. The museum.

It would be closed this early, but I was sure I could sneak in. It was the only place that could give me some answers.

Aamir, Abu, and Ammi were all staring at me now.

I gave them a bright smile, completely fake but they didn't seem to notice. "Have to meet up with my study group to discuss our project," I mumbled as I headed to the front door.

"That's good," Abu replied. "Make sure you get an A."

I paused at the little console table in the hallway. There was a pile of mail, and right on top was a yellow envelope. What caught my attention first was the stamp: a big green-and-white flag of Pakistan.

I checked the sender's name on the left corner, even

though only one person from Pakistan still sent letters the old-fashioned way. "It's from Fahad Uncle," I told Abu, smiling.

"I almost forgot," Abu replied. "I'll get to it after breakfast."

Fahad Uncle was seriously awesome. He was Abu's best friend for decades, and he loved us like his own family. He always brought lots of gifts for us when he visited and even sent cool things from Pakistan. Once, when I was in elementary school, he'd sent me red leather slippers with silver thread running through them, so pretty I insisted on wearing them everywhere until my feet grew too big. Ammi told me they were called khussa and were traditional shoes made in the Sindh and Punjab areas of Pakistan and India.

"Tell me what he wrote," I instructed Abu. "Maybe he sent me another gift."

"You wish!" Aamir grunted.

"Khuda hafiz!" I rolled my eyes and pulled open the front door with more force than necessary.

"Stay away from the museum district!" Ammi half yelled. Okay, she wasn't really mad-yelling, just raising her voice because I was now almost out the door. Still, I didn't appreciate it.

I didn't appreciate any of the drama. I didn't need it. My family didn't trust me and thought I was a kid, even though I was going around saving lives and fighting bad guys all the time.

They just never saw that side, obviously. All they saw was silly little Kamala. The younger sister. The not-so-great high school student.

"Fee AmanAllah," Aamir called out, like he was telling me farewell before a long trip.

Just before I shut the door with a bang, I heard Ammi mutter, "Unbelievable."

I rode the bus in a fog.

My heart was thumping. My forehead was all sweaty. My foot tapped like there was some sort of emergency situation going on.

Which, of course, there was. A pair of spectacles worth millions, from my heritage, for crying out loud, was hidden like stolen contraband inside my backpack.

Never mind that I hadn't stolen them in the first place. I'd picked them up, and now they were in my possession. If I was caught with them, I'd be hauled into the police station and Ammi and Abu would have to pick me up, post my bail, or whatever else one did for criminals.

I could imagine my brother giving me his classic superior look, acting all pious and perfect. *Really, Kamala? This is what you've resorted to?*

Ugh. What did he know? He'd never encountered Kingpin or his henchwoman Delilah. Never had to fight off shady masked people in the dark alleys of Jersey City.

My leg bounced up and down. Up and down. Maybe I could just return them to the museum and be done with it. Maybe I could call in other super heroes like Kate Bishop, A.K.A. Hawkeye, or Spider-Man. They did say two heads are better than one or something.

Nope. Not asking for help just yet. I didn't want to be the new kid on the block, always needing someone to bail me out. It's how my family saw me. I couldn't bear the same treatment from my fellow super heroes.

I could do this myself, no problem. All I needed to know was why three different villains were after a pair of very old spectacles. Oh, and whether said spectacles had magical powers. And if yes, then what exactly those powers were.

Argh! The list of things I did not know was growing every second. I hated that. Hated it.

The quicker I solved this entire mystery of the spectacles, the sooner I could return them to the museum for safekeeping.

A middle-aged woman turned to stare at me. "Are you okay?"

I dug my nails into my leg to stop it from bouncing. "Uh, yes, thanks, I'm fine."

She obviously didn't believe me. "If you need help, I know a good therapist."

"No thanks!" I said.

Thankfully, the bus came to a stop, and I jumped up.

I jogged the entire way, which wasn't the greatest idea because I was sweaty and breathless by the time I reached the museum. You'd think all my activities as Ms. Marvel would put me in better shape, but oh, no. Kamala Khan was her usual huffy-puffy self.

I slowed down as I rounded the corner into the alley where the staff entrance opened up. There was no sign of Delilah or Asaar, though I did see a few fence posts cracked where a body (or two) had landed the night before.

I banged both fists on the door, hoping someone was inside. "Hello!" I yelled. "Can you please open the door?"

After a few minutes, the door opened, and Brittany Myers peered out. Just my luck! She was wearing a smart business suit, and her hair was in a neat blond bob. She was cool and collected, with not a thread out of place.

You know, the complete opposite of me.

"What's the emergency?" she asked, looking at me like I was a disgusting mess.

She wasn't wrong. My T-shirt was crumpled, and I was panting like a dog on a summer day. I racked my brains to give her a good enough reason to let me in. "Uh, I left some things in the locker last night."

"Last night?"

Did she really not remember me, or was she pretending, as some sort of petty power play? I leaned closer so she could see my face better. "I was here serving drinks, remember?"

She smirked. "Oh, Drinks Girl!"

"Yup."

She narrowed her eyes. "What did you leave in your locker?"

"Uh . . . my spare keys. To my house." I let out a little laugh. "My parents are mad about it. You know parents, right? They can be so unreasonable. . . ."

Brittany sighed like she knew all about unreasonable parents. She held the door open wide. "All right, be quick about it."

I gave her a salute and slid inside. "You need my ID?" I joked. "Fingerprints or something?"

"Actually, it might be a good idea to take down your information," she replied haughtily. "You know, in case a muffin goes missing."

"Ha!" I chuckled. "I'm more a bagel kind of gal."

She took out her phone from her pants pocket. "Your name?"

I was already moving toward the locker room. "Kamala Khan."

"I'm Brittany Myers," she said, matching me step for step.

I moved a little to the right. In order to snoop, I needed to get rid of Miss High-and-Mighty, pronto. "I know. You told us last night."

"Us?"

I walked faster. "Me and my friend Bruno."

Brittany smiled a little. "Oh, yes, the cutie."

I sent her a death glare. Him she remembered.

Brittany's watch beeped, startling us both. She looked at it, then back at me. "Look, I need to make a call. Can you get your keys really quickly and then leave?"

I nodded casually. "Of course. You can trust me."

Brittany looked at me like she'd do no such thing. Her watch beeped again, and with a deep sigh, she hurried toward the exhibits.

Perfect.

I waited for a minute to make sure she wasn't coming back, then made a left turn from the lockers to the administration area. I'd seen it the night before when I'd put my clothes in the locker.

The hallway was quiet, lit only by the window at the far end. Most of the rooms were dark, but the last one was open. There were people inside, talking in quiet, angry tones. I crept closer to listen in.

"I demand to know what was stolen last night," a harsh male voice said.

"And who did it?" Another voice, just as harsh, but female. "Have you caught the thief yet? Has he been punished?"

Slowly, I leaned until I could see inside. Ms. Hibbert stood in the middle of the room with a couple I recognized from the exhibit. Monocle Man and Beehive Lady. What were they doing here?

"Mr. and Mrs. Barrington, please understand that we're trying our very best." Ms. Hibbert sighed. "The matter is being taken care of by the police. I really have no control over it."

Mrs. Barrington scoffed. "You mean you don't even know what was stolen from your own exhibit?"

"I do know, but I am not at liberty to say." Ms. Hibbert held out her hands in apology. "I've been asked by the police to keep the information private for now."

"But we're a big sponsor of the exhibit!" Mr. Barrington practically howled. "Surely *you* can tell us if anything we donated to *your* museum was stolen."

The argument continued, but I backed away a little to give myself time to think. So this Mr. and Mrs. Barrington had donated at least some of the items in the exhibits to the museum. They must be loaded.

The question was, how did they even get their hands on any of the artifacts? They were so not Desi.

Nakia's passionate speech about stolen artifacts echoed in my mind. So the exhibit pieces just a few feet away from me had first been stolen by colonial powers, and now one—or more—of them had been pilfered all over again.

Ironic, I'd say.

Just then, someone rushed into the alley. I could see the shadow through the window at the end of the hallway. Tall, wearing a suit of some kind.

Who wore suits while lurking in alleyways? Nobody normal, that was for sure. My pulse quickened. Someone villainous was out there.

Maybe the thief, back to steal more priceless items?

I lunged into the locker room. Ms. Hibbert could take care of the Barringtons. This bad-guy-in-the-alley situation was my forte, anyway.

In a flash, I changed into my Ms. Marvel costume and ran swiftly down the hallway, through the kitchen, and out onto the steps.

Everything was different from the night before. Bright sunlight streamed through the surrounding trees on the other side of the fence. Birds were trilling overhead, which usually I loved, but today I just needed them to shush so I could concentrate on the shadow.

I needed to get to the back of the alley, so I walked quietly, slowly in that direction. I didn't want to startle whoever it was.

Maybe Shocker or Delilah again? I wouldn't mind another chance to beat their asses.

There was a rush of air behind me, and I whirled around.

It was the man from last night. The one who fought Delilah and lost. "You!" he hissed, his voice low and raspy. And most definitely Desi. Yup, I hadn't imagined that.

He sounded just like Abu, only in better shape.

I smiled sweetly. Maybe I could sweet-talk him. "Ms. Marvel, at your service," I said nicely.

"I don't care," he bit out. "Give me back my spectacles before I roast you alive."

Whoa. That went south fast. "*Your* spectacles?" I asked. "Pretty sure they belong to the museum."

"Pretty sure they don't."

Since this was a debate I was currently also wondering about, I decided to change tactics. "I told you my name. Now you tell me yours."

He clenched his fists. "You can call me Asaar."

"What's that mean?" I crept closer. "Is it Arabic?"

"Urdu," he replied shortly.

"Wow, so cool!" I tried to keep up the sweet-talking, even though it was getting very tiring. "I know some Urdu. My family is from Pakistan."

Asaar held up his fists, which were now glowing with the same green-and-white light I'd seen last night. "I. Don't. Care." He threw a bolt toward me. "Where are the spectacles?"

I jerked myself to the left to avoid the light. It looked

freakishly hot, and I didn't want it touching me. "I have no clue," I replied, panting a little.

"You're lying!" he growled, sending another bolt at me.

I swerved to the right and then shrugged. He wasn't wrong, but I wasn't about to admit that. Yes, I had the spectacles, and no, I wasn't giving them back. Those bad boys were staying with me until I figured out what to do with them.

Asaar became angrier. He began to throw energy bolts faster and more directly in my face.

Since he was being rude, I was going to be rude back. I jumped backward to avoid the energy shower, then grew my arm long and heavy. With a yell, I swung the arm in a giant arc and knocked Asaar to the ground. "Why did you steal the spectacles?" I demanded. "Are you going to sell them to the highest bidder?"

Asaar struggled to his feet. "I'm not a robber, Ms. Marvel. I wasn't the one who stole that precious artifact from the museum."

"Then who did?" I said, ready to send him to his knees again.

He held up his hands to show they were light-free. For now. "Delilah, obviously."

"Yeah, right," I muttered. That made no sense. Delilah was on Kingpin's payroll, and he was sponsoring the whole dang exhibit, proudly standing by it like an evil stepfather.

Asaar continued harshly. "I'm the one who takes back what was robbed. Returns things to their rightful place."

He didn't wait for me to comment. He made a fist, and voilà! The green-and-white light was back.

I'd been waiting for that. I curled my lip and narrowed my eyes. He might have fancy light, but I had elastic limbs and a lot of muscles behind them, thanks to the gym Bruno and I trained at near the Circle Q.

This time, I didn't yell or swerve. I made a fist with my right hand and threw my arm out. Like a snake on a mission, my arm grew longer and longer, and then my fist punched Asaar right on the jaw. *Kapow!*

He swayed with the force of my blow, but he didn't fall. I'd never say it out loud, but I was impressed at his strength. He righted himself, then sent another bolt of light straight at my stomach.

Oomph. I staggered and fell against the side of the shed. It was hard and rough, and the impact shoved all the breath out of my body.

Asaar watched me as I straightened myself. No sooner had I shaken my fists out than he sent another shock of light right at me.

It sizzled and zipped and crackled as it threw me back into the shed wall.

Ow. This time, my head snapped against the rough wooden

slats of the shed. I had a moment of pure panic. Not only did my head hurt from the impact, but Asaar's green-and-white light came with its own evil brand of torture. Sharp, painful, corroding. What the heck was this thing?

I took my time getting up, and shockingly, Asaar didn't hit me with more light while I was down. "Tired already?" he called out. "Get up, princess. I've got more for you."

My head swam. Okay, so he was some sort of gentlemanly villain? This would be the perfect time to incinerate me with that blasted light, but he was waiting for me to rise.

Weird and sort of stupid, if you were a villain.

For me, it was perfect. I wiped the sweat off my forehead—ew, gross—and clenched my fists as I crouched low, face turned away.

I was so ready for this guy, and he didn't even know it.

I embiggened my fist, and my elongated right arm flew toward Asaar. I could hear the slight *swoosh* as it reached my target—his stomach.

He fell backward with a grunt.

"Yes!" I yelled. "Finally!"

Was that immature? Probably. I didn't really care. Now that the tables were turned, I was going to take full advantage.

He lay crumpled on the ground, panting loudly. From a few feet away, I curled an arm around his body to make sure he stayed in place. I didn't want any more surprise attacks.

I glanced at his hands. One of his gloves had come off, and there was a crown-shaped tattoo on the back of his left wrist. I stared at it, committing it to memory so I could ask Bruno to search for the image.

"Who are you?" I murmured.

Asaar's eyes swept open. "None of your business!" he snarled, curving his hands into claws again. Before I could jump out of the way a second time, he zapped me with his green-and-white light. Again.

It hit me right in the chest, and it was hella painful. I let go of him and fell backward into a stack of empty pallets, scattering them everywhere.

Oh. My. God.

I bit my lip to stop from whimpering. No way was I letting this dude get the best of me. Quickly, ignoring my aching bones and thundering heart and the sweat on my forehead, I scrambled up. With a yell, I made my fist into a huge hammer and threw it at him.

This time, Asaar flew back with the force of my fist.

"Ugh." With a groan, he landed in a pile of empty boxes waiting for the recycler.

I stayed where I was. "I'd ask if you're okay, but I don't care."

He let out a frustrated yell, throwing more zaps my way. I jumped away from them easily.

"I'm not a villain, you know," he said through gritted teeth.

"Oh, no?" I mocked. "You're a perfect hero, stealing from nonprofit organizations like the museum!"

"Nonprofit?" He scoffed. "Everything they do is for profit. I may not be a hero, but I'm a repatriation warrior."

I stopped. "A what?"

He threw more green-and-white light my way. It collided with my upper arm and sent me spinning to the ground.

Asaar continued like he didn't just send me to my knees. "The artifacts in that exhibit don't belong to Americans. They were stolen from us, and I'm just taking them back."

I blinked rapidly, trying to get my head to stop spinning. "Us? Who's us?"

He came closer, throwing little zaps to my left and right. "Never mind who." *Zap.* "They've done it to so many places. Everywhere that was colonized." *Zap.* "All the countries that were enslaved." *Zap.*

I gulped as he stood right at my feet, his face twisted and angry behind his mask. "The colonial powers looted all their riches," he snarled. "Left them empty and impoverished."

"Uh," I stuttered. It wasn't because I was scared of him. His lightning or whatever it was hurt, but I was holding my own. The truth of what he was saying hit me like the mightiest bolt. It was what Nakia had told me the night before. It was what some of the guests at the exhibit were grumbling about.

"Cat got your tongue?" he asked, this time looking furious.

"Even if you're right," I began, "this isn't the way to get justice. Breaking into a museum, stealing things. Fighting me."

"I didn't break in," he shouted. "Delilah did."

"That's still not the right way," I insisted.

"Sometimes you have to fight dirty to get justice," Asaar uttered with conviction. "You'll learn that when you get older, little girl."

Ugh! I hated when people called me that. I pushed myself up and made a humongous fist.

Before I could really teach him a lesson, a garbage truck came rumbling up to the mouth of the alley. I looked away, startled.

When I looked back, Asaar had leapt across the fence and disappeared from sight.

"We're in the news, people!" Bruno slammed his phone on the cafeteria table.

I peered at the *Jersey City News* app on the screen. *Priceless Artifact Stolen from New Exhibit.*

Shaking my head, I went back to my mac and cheese. I was starving after the morning I'd had. "That's not about us."

Bruno sat down next to Nakia. "We were there," he protested. "They could have quoted us or something."

I raised an eyebrow. "Did they?"

"That would be a no," Nakia said wryly. She picked up the phone and scrolled down. "It says a pair of emerald spectacles reputed to be worth several million was stolen by an unknown party."

I kept eating, but I knew that unknown party was actually Delilah.

Or Asaar, depending on who you actually believed.

That reminded me. "Hey, what's a repatriation warrior, exactly?" I asked.

Nakia and Bruno stared at me. "Where did that come from?" Bruno asked.

I shrugged. "Just something I heard at the museum."

Nakia sat up eagerly. "That's an intriguing term, actually. *Repatriation* is returning things to where they were from originally. You know, righteous return, or something like that."

"Okay, so repatriation warrior is someone who fights to return things to their rightful place?" I guessed.

Nakia nodded. "Someone trying to even the scales or whatever."

"Even the scales?" Bruno frowned. "The scales to what?"

I bit my lip. "The . . . person who used that term was going on and on about colonial powers stealing riches."

"Yes!" Nakia half shouted. "I know this! I agree with it!"

"What colonial powers?" Bruno asked. "The British, right? They ruled India for a while, back when it was Hindustan."

Nakia nodded. "There were several colonial empires in the sixteenth century and onward. The British Empire was probably the biggest, but there were also the Dutch, the French, the Spanish, the Portuguese, and a few more. Combined, their colonies stretched across Asia, Africa, Australia . . ."

"The Americas . . ." Bruno added.

"Yup," said Nakia. "Every American knows. We were a colony too, before we fought and gained independence from the British."

"For South Asia, it was the Partition," I reminded them. "The British finally left in 1947 after dividing the subcontinent into Pakistan and India."

"Didn't that lead to a lot of violence?" Bruno asked.

I nodded slowly. "Yes, there were riots on the streets, people were killed or displaced. Millions of refugees migrating from one side to the other. It was horrible."

Even though Partition happened long before my time, I'd often heard the stories from my grandparents, both sets of them. Stories of violence, grief, sadness. Stories of pain and suffering. It had been terrible. And very personal.

Nakia and Bruno made identical sad faces. Pouting lips. Scrunched-up noses. I knew what it meant: They didn't really understand how real and personal those stories were.

"Listen," I said, "my grandfather's sister disappeared during their forced migration, never to be seen again."

"Oh my God!" Nakia gasped. "What happened to her?"

I shrugged. "They said someone kidnapped her and a bunch of other girls from a train."

"Whoa." Bruno's sad face had morphed into horrified face. Nakia's too. Now they were getting it.

"My other grandfather's cousin's entire family was killed,"

I continued. "Not a person left alive! Abu talks about it all the time, even though he wasn't even born then."

Nakia and Bruno shuddered. "I'm sorry, dude," Nakia whispered. "Your family's been through a lot."

"So true." I jabbed a fork into my mac and cheese. "But it's important to remember, you know?"

Nakia leaned over and gave me a sideways hug.

Bruno cleared his throat. "Okay, so what did the colonial powers have to do with the Mughal exhibit?" he asked. "Connect the dots for me. From hundreds of years ago in India to Jersey City today."

Nakia sighed. "The empires took over foreign lands in so many different ways. In some places, like India, they usurped the throne, killed the last Mughal, and became the rulers. In others, they enslaved the people. Wherever there were riches, like jewels or state coffers, they took those too. Some by signing treaties that favored them, and others by subterfuge."

"That's . . . that's stealing!" I gasped.

"Not if they were the rulers, though," Nakia replied. "Everyone did it. The Mughals came from Central Asia and settled in the subcontinent first, taking over all the riches. It's war, right? It's the idea of might is right, blah, blah."

"Yeah, but they didn't take the riches away to someplace else," I said.

Nakia snapped her fingers. "Exactly! The colonial powers

took everything back with them: art, vases, daggers, crowns, jewelry, coins . . . all the things we see in museums around the world were just snatched and brought back to Europe. And now that the colonies have been dissolved, and those lands have their own governments, nobody's given the items back."

"Wait." Bruno held up a hand. "Why do they have to give them back now? It's been hundreds of years. Who cares anymore?"

Nakia shot him a disgusted look. "The previously colonized people care! Don't you remember that documentary last year about the Rosetta Stone and how the Egyptians have been demanding its return from the British Museum?"

Bruno and I both frowned. We'd studied the Rosetta Stone in history last year, and our teacher had put on a documentary about its history in the last class. Needless to say, nobody had paid attention.

Well, except Nakia, apparently. Her eyes sparkled as she continued. "Or—or the Benin Bronzes, which were taken by the British from Benin, which, by the way, is also demanding that they be returned!"

Bruno shook his head. "I dunno. It hardly matters which museum an artifact is in, as long as it's taken care of, right?"

I winced. Even I could tell this was absolutely the wrong thing to say. The mutterings at the Mughal exhibit made it very clear to me that it did, indeed, matter. A lot.

"Why do you think museums are so quick to display priceless items? It's a source of revenue for them. It brings tourism to the city, even to the country!" Nakia hissed.

"I get it," I interrupted. "It's not only about heritage but also about money. About power."

"Power?" Bruno asked.

"Many of those lands became poor as a result of colonization," Nakia explained, calming down a little. "Imagine how getting those artifacts back could make a difference to the local people and their governments. They could have so much of their economic power back."

"Even the scales," I whispered, my lunch forgotten. Asaar had said the same thing, about impoverished lands.

Nakia smiles sadly. "Yup."

I had physics homework, plus a history test to study for. But all I could think about when I reached home was Asaar.

Questions and half-baked theories tossed in my mind and made it seem like a wild ocean in the middle of a hurricane.

In other words, chaotic.

"Salaam alaikum," Ammi said as I flopped down on the couch beside her and closed my eyes.

"Walaikum salaam," I mumbled.

There was a pause. I could feel Ammi looking me up and down. "What's bothering you, Kamala?"

I opened my eyes and peeked at her. An Urdu novel was lying open on her lap. Seeing the script on the cover made me sit up. "Ammi, what does *asaar* mean?"

She went back to her book. "It's the plural of *asar*."

Was she being unhelpful on purpose? "Okay, but what does it mean?"

"It can mean lots of things," Ammi said, looking up again. "Signs, symbols, indications. Sometimes, when we combine it with a longer term, *asaar-e-qadimah*, it means relics or ruins."

I flopped back, smiling in a surprised sort of way. Now we were talking! It made perfect sense that a Desi villain—sorry, repatriation warrior—was named *ruins*. I couldn't wait to tell Bruno.

That reminded me, I needed to go to his place and figure out some things. The emerald spectacles had been burning a hole in my backpack all day, and I was so worried I'd lose them. Bruno could inspect them and maybe help me come up with some theories on their so-called magical powers.

Ammi was looking at me with narrowed eyes. "Is everything okay?" she asked. "You've never asked for an Urdu lesson before."

I shrugged. "I was just curious." I decided this wasn't the right time to bring up visiting Bruno's house. She always got weird about my hanging out with him alone. Something about girls and boys not being alone together in her day.

"Muneeba! Come listen to this!" Abu rushed into the room with his tablet, looking excited. He sat down next to Ammi and showed her the screen.

"Uh, what's going on?" I asked.

My parents' gazes were fixed on the screen. "The news has more details about the museum theft," Abu said. "Apparently it was one of the Mughal pieces!"

My eyes widened. "And you're happy about that?"

He looked up. "Not really. Perhaps."

"What do you mean?"

Abu shook his head and went back to the screen. "Haven't you heard that song by Alanis, what's her name, Morissette? 'Isn't it ironic?'"

"Not if it's a song from the nineteen hundreds, no."

He waved his hand like I was a pesky fly he wanted away from his face. "Never mind. It's ironic that something originally stolen from the Mughals was stolen again from the thieves. How do I explain this to you? *Ironic* means . . ."

I groaned. "I know what *ironic* means, Abu. I'm a senior in high school. I know the English language."

"Are you sure?" Ammi asked with a little smile. "The other day I asked you to clean up your room and you acted like you had no idea what I was talking about."

The sounds from the tablet continued. A female reporter was talking, and then another one. And then a male voice that made my teeth grind against each other.

I sat up. "Why's he on the news?"

"Who? Fisk?" Abu raised the volume of the tablet. "He's talking about the robbery."

I leaned forward and glared at the screen. First, Kingpin was being interviewed at the exhibit. Now he was being interviewed about the robbery of—you guessed it—the same exhibit. And they were standing right where I'd been a few hours ago: in front of the Jersey City Art Museum. I could recognize the gray stone building and the arch windows anywhere.

For an NYC guy, Kingpin sure visited Jersey City a lot.

"It's disheartening to see that something so precious has been stolen," he said in his pompous voice. "I will see to it personally that the culprit is found."

I was thinking, *Why? The culprit is most probably your own henchwoman Delilah!*

The reporter cut in to explain that Wilson Fisk, businessman extraordinaire, was a major sponsor of the Mughal exhibit.

Now I was thinking, *Why the heck?*

"Since when did this annoying individual become interested in Mughal history?" Abu grumbled, putting aside his tablet.

My head swiveled toward him. Abu and I almost never saw eye to eye, so it was a little weird to have such a similar thought at the same time. "Did aliens come down and cross-wire our brains?" I asked.

"Eh?"

Before I could explain, Aamir walked in from the kitchen, holding a mug of chai in his hand. "Aliens aren't Islamic, Kamala," he intoned.

It was like a switch went off in my head. Forget Kingpin and his arrogant voice. Forget Mughal artifacts. All I could think about was my irritatingly stupid brother with a religious streak that made the pope look like a gangster. "Aliens aren't Islamic?" I repeated. "What does that even mean?"

He shrugged as he settled into the armchair opposite me. "Just that. Aliens don't exist. Otherwise, God would've mentioned them in the Quran."

Abu rolled his eyes. "Here we go again. It's like you have a direct line to God or something, my delusional son."

I let out a small, surprised laugh. Again, Abu had repeated my thoughts. "Yeah, that," I said.

"I'm not delusional." Aamir scoffed. He took a careful sip of his chai and then winced at its heat.

"So tell me, O wise one," I said. "If something isn't in the Quran, it just doesn't exist?"

"Yup."

"So the internet isn't real?" I mocked. "It's just a fantasy? The movies? Electric toothbrushes?"

"Those are modern inventions," he replied. "We're not talking about those."

I was on a roll. "Ancient people? Historical events? Dinosaurs? None of those happened?"

He took another sip, slurping so loud I felt like smacking him. "Dinosaurs aren't real," he said calmly.

"Oh my God!" I yelled.

Abu raised his hand. "Kamala, no need to yell like an animal in my house. We're all right here."

I gasped. "Me? I'm not an animal!"

"Are you sure about that?" Aamir smirked.

"Children, stop arguing. You're giving me a headache." Ammi put her book on the table with a little thump and stood up. "I'm going to lie down for half an hour. Try not to bring the roof down with your shouting."

"But . . ."

"Sorry . . ."

We watched Ammi go upstairs. Abu sighed and turned to Aamir. "Oh, my son. Try reading a science journal once in a while. The Quran repeatedly tells us to ponder the signs of the heavens and the earth, and all the creatures that live there."

"Aha!" I point a finger at my brother. "The heavens! They could have aliens. If God created human beings, why couldn't he have created other . . . peoples . . . on other planets?"

"Yeah, right," he mumbled.

I didn't tell him I'd met plenty of aliens. Plenty of people who looked different from us and lived on other earths and other universes. His small mind and rigid views would never accept it.

But me, I knew better. Did it make me a feel just a tiny bit superior? Maybe.

I turned to Abu. Today, he was the voice of reason I never thought he'd be. "Tell me more about the Mughals," I said.

"The Mughals?" Abu's eyebrows rose. "Why?"

I shrugged. "I want to know what's the deal with this exhibit. Why it's so important to Fisk."

"Oh," he said, his face falling. "I thought you wanted to know more about your history. Your heritage."

My history? *My* heritage? Why did he keep saying that?

Also, was he right? Was the history of a country I wasn't even born in, or didn't have any attachment to, mine? Could I share heritage with a group of people I wasn't really connected to?

I glanced at Abu's face again. He looked disappointed. Sad, almost.

"Uh, sure. I want to know more about my heritage too," I told him, nudging him with my elbow.

Abu brightened. "Now you're talking. What do you want to know?"

"Everything," I replied.

"Well, the first Mughal king was Babur," Abu began, settling his body into the couch. "He was descended from Changez Khan. . . ."

"Who?"

"You Americans call him Genghis Khan. Now don't interrupt."

"Sorry."

"Anyway, Babur was from Central Asia, descended from the great Changez Khan. He conquered Delhi in the early fifteen hundreds. After him, his son Humayun came to the throne, and then his grandson Akbar."

"I've heard of Akbar the Great!" Aamir exclaimed.

"Are you sure?" Abu asked. "He's not in the Quran."

I giggled. Aamir scowled.

"Anyway, you're right, Aamir," said Abu. "Akbar was perhaps the greatest of the Mughals. He had a long reign, and he accomplished a lot. The Mughal Empire expanded considerably, all the way to north and central India, even as far away as Bengal. And he made a huge effort to unite the Hindu and Muslim populations. You see, Akbar was a Muslim—all the Mughals were—but the people they ruled over were mostly Hindu. He realized that he had to work together with them, make them happy, include them in government."

"So, what, he built a tolerant multi-faith society?" Aamir said sarcastically.

"Yes." Abu nodded. "The empire really grew and flourished under him, not only in a military sense, but also in social issues, art, architecture, things like that."

"The Mughal artifacts!" I exclaimed.

"Yes, Akbar was a big patron of the arts, unlike his father and grandfather, who never had time for anything other than fighting wars. He commissioned writers, poets, artists, painters, even designers for new palaces. He brought in the best of the best from all over India, even beyond. All religions, all cultures, they wanted to be a part of this renaissance, so to speak. It was the beginning of the Mughal style of art."

"Whoa," Aamir and I whispered together. I didn't know about my brother, but I was blown away by this story. There was a warmth inside my chest, this sense of belonging that I didn't feel often, and especially not when talking to my father. Is this what he meant by my heritage?

It was weird. Not in a bad way, but still strange. "Who came after Akbar?" I asked.

"After Akbar was his son Jahangir, and then *his* son, Shah Jahan. The one who built the Taj Mahal in Agra."

I sighed because the Taj Mahal was gorgeous. "I like that dude the best."

Abu chuckled. "Some say the Mughal Empire was at its peak artistically and culturally during Shah Jahan's reign. But soon, his sons started fighting, and finally the younger one, Aurangzeb, became king after defeating the older brother and his father."

"Tough guy," Aamir muttered.

"Yes, he was. And he was also more like you." Abu pointed at Aamir. "More religious, stricter, harsher. The previous Mughals had a reputation of partying and spending money, living lavish lifestyles, whereas Aurangzeb was the opposite. He fought more wars, went on—how do you say?—rampages that expanded the Mughal Empire more, to the point that it was the biggest and baddest. But that also meant that people got dissatisfied with him. His policies were very harsh compared to his predecessors, and he didn't provide equal opportunities in his court to Hindus. So there was a lot of unrest and backlash as well."

"What happened?" I asked. I realized I was leaning forward, hanging on Abu's every word. This hadn't happened in a very long time. Abu and I hadn't hung out and talked like this for years.

It took me back to when I was little and he'd tell me stories at bedtime. Stories that I'd buried in my memory bank because I didn't get along with Abu so much anymore.

Now here he was, telling me another story while I listened with bated breath. It felt nice. Oddly peaceful.

"Nothing happened immediately," Abu replied. "But the Mughal Empire started getting weaker because of rebellions and a Hindu population that was seriously unhappy. By the time he died and the next king came into power, the empire was diminishing. And so it continued. The later Mughal kings and courtiers were more interested in the lavish lifestyles and riches they commanded and less about ruling and protecting the empire. By the mid-eighteenth century, it was weak enough for the British to take over."

The British. The colonial power Nakia was talking about. "The Mughals were defeated in a war, right?" Aamir asked.

Abu's eyes narrowed. "Not immediately. In the beginning, there was a puppet king whom the British controlled while they remained behind the scenes. They came to India as traders through a corporation called the East India Company and slowly infiltrated the court."

"I don't get it," I interrupted. "How did a company become rulers?"

Abu laughed, but it was dark and ugly. "The East India Company wasn't an entity like you've ever seen. It had its own army, soldiers, and ships. It fought a series of battles called the Anglo-Indian wars, where it fought against different states in the Indian subcontinent. It had a flag, and a treasury. It was very powerful. And it had the political backing of the king of England, so it could do a lot with impunity."

I gulp. "Like looting the riches and taking them away to museums in England?"

"Not just museums." Abu scowled ferociously. "Private homes too, in the beginning. Rich military types, lords and governors, would bring home things they'd taken on their journeys and decorate their manors. They'd have parties to show off their riches."

"Like hunters putting the heads of the animals they hunted on the walls," Aamir whispered.

"Whoa," I said again. I was no longer leaning forward in excitement at a cool story. I was flopped back, feeling a little sick. I had a feeling that the Barringtons had been part of that legacy.

Abu sighed, his scowl fading. "It's a sad story all around. And it's not unique to India. The British did this in so many other places."

"Other countries were colonial powers too," I add, remembering what Nakia had told me. "Like, the Dutch and French, and . . . the Spanish, maybe?"

Aamir raised his eyebrows. "Look at you, being all knowledgeable!"

I scoffed. "I know stuff!"

Abu patted my knee. "I'm sure you do, Kamala. Now be a good girl and make me a cup of chai."

My mouth dropped open. Here I was, thinking warm, fuzzy feelings for my father, and he had to go back to his exasperating ways. "Why do I have to do it?" I demanded. "Because I'm a girl?"

"No, because Aamir makes terrible chai." Abu picked up his tablet and dismissed me with a shake of his head. "Now, hurry. And fry up some samosas or something too. Your ammi will be down soon from her nap."

An hour later, Ammi had come back downstairs, and we were still in the living room.

Chai and samosas were now on the coffee table, thanks to me. Aamir hadn't lifted a finger to help, but he had informed me that my frying technique was crap and I shouldn't have the flame so high if I wanted an even brown color on my samosas.

I'm not ashamed to admit I called him some pretty bad words in my head. I'd never say them out loud, not because of respect or anything, but because my parents would be totally, completely destroyed.

Well, not literally, but there'd be lots of yelling and dramatic praying to God about how I'd wandered from the right path, just like the heathen Americans I was surrounded with. Insert eye roll here.

Aamir leaned toward the coffee table. "That little dish looks like the one in the museum exhibit."

I frowned at him. "I didn't know you went to see it."

He threw me an arrogant look. "I took the guided tour this afternoon, when you were in school."

I scoffed. "What do you need tour guides for? It's a bunch of jewelry and coins and paintings. Not much to explain."

"For your information, our tour guide had lots of interesting tidbits to share," Aamir said with a scowl.

"Like . . . ?"

"Hmm, let's see. Did you know that the emperor Jahangir put zodiac signs on his coins?"

"What, like Capricorn and Aries?"

"Yes." He nodded. "Only, the emperor after him, Shah Jahan, ordered them to be destroyed in order to please the orthodox clergy. That's why the ones that still survive are so priceless."

Abu grunted again. "So there were people like you even in those days."

Aamir's scowl grew. "People like me? You mean Muslims who think zodiac signs are nonsensical superstitions meant to fool the masses? Yes!"

"Ya Allah, I'm so sick of all this arguing," Ammi muttered.

I giggled. Then I saw Ammi's face and decided I needed

to calm the men in my household down. "What else did you learn in this educational tour?"

Aamir relaxed a little. "Did you know some of those items have myths attached to them? Like legends of magical powers and such?"

I blink. "Um, what?"

Ammi leaned over to take a samosa. "Oh, yes, I've heard stories about those. My mother used to tell them to me when I was a little girl."

"Bah!" Abu grunted. "All useless fantasies."

"What?" I said, louder this time. I'd learned to be loud and insistent when I was being ignored—which happened a lot in my family.

"Tell us more about the legends, Ammi," Aamir prompted.

"No need!" Abu said.

"Shush," Ammi told him. "They may be fantasy, but they're still very interesting."

Abu grumbled under his breath but then settled down when Ammi started talking. Even he knew who the real ruler of the house was.

"Many of the Mughal-era—what do you call them?—artifacts had myths about magic and such. They were tall tales, I'm sure, and over time most people forgot the stories. But my mother—your naani—was into those types of things. She'd read a lot about the Mughals in college and knew some of the lesser-known history."

"That's so cool," I said. "Did she tell you any examples?"

"Well, let's see." Ammi chewed slowly. "Lots of talismans and ancient manuscripts. Paintings with words hidden under the art, thought to have been magic spells that only special people could reveal."

"Oooh!" Aamir said mockingly.

I slapped his leg. "Shut up," I told him. "You're the one who started this."

He closed his mouth. Secretly, I think he also wanted to hear the story.

Ammi continued. "One of my favorites was a pair of glasses, very beautiful, with big emeralds in place of the lenses. They say that Emperor Shah Jahan used the gemstone to soothe his eyes after weeping for days at the death of his beloved wife Mumtaz Mahal."

"He built the Taj Mahal for her, you know," Abu added helpfully.

I straightened up. "Wait, I saw those! They were in the exhibit, or . . . something very similar."

Ammi sighed. "I doubt it was the same pair, Kamala. Shah Jahan's glasses? What are the odds?"

I couldn't tell her I'd seen more outlandish things happen

in my short stint as a super hero. "Well, you never know," I finally said quietly, leaning back against the couch. If Delilah and Asaar both wanted to get their hands on something, that meant it was special.

Maybe even magical.

"That would be something," Ammi agreed. "They were supposed to have healing powers, you know. Because of the emeralds."

"I wonder how that worked," I mused. "Like, if you wore them, you were automatically protected? Or did you have to say an incantation?"

Aamir rolled his eyes. "They're just stories, genius. Those items don't really have magical powers."

I wasn't too sure about that. I wasn't the kind of person who denied the existence of something just because I couldn't see it or feel it.

"Stories can have power, Aamir," Ammi said.

I looked at her surprised. She wasn't usually so imaginative. She saw me looking and gave a little smile. "Thank you for the samosas, Kamala. They're fried perfectly."

I stuck my tongue out at my brother. "See?"

He shook his head but stayed silent. What could he say? He'd polished off half the plate all by himself.

I stood up. "Well, I'm off to do some homework."

Abu beamed. "Yes, good. Study hard, don't waste your time anywhere else."

I went up to my room, still thinking about the stories Ammi had told me. I lay in my bed for a while, trying to read my physics textbook, but my mind refused to focus. I kept wondering what Kingpin wanted with the Mughal exhibit, and my mind was scrambling for answers I didn't have.

Frustrated, I reached into my backpack, pushed aside my notebooks, and touched the spectacles, just to make sure they were still there. I didn't want to take them out, in case someone from my family burst into the room without knocking. They had a habit of doing that.

The idea that some of the artifacts could have magical properties made my spine tingle.

I sprang from my bed. I knew what—who—could help me. Bruno Carrelli. The genius who made research look easy. The guy who always had my back, no matter what. He'd help me figure everything out; I was sure of it.

"I'm going to Bruno's," I called out to Ammi as I passed the kitchen on the way out.

Ammi was stirring something on the stove. It smelled divine, like chicken and mint. And ginger. Lots of it.

Yum. For a second, I debated staying for dinner.

Ms. Marvel has a duty to others, I reminded myself, sighing. *I guess work comes before dinner, no matter how delicious.*

"Kamala," Ammi began. "You can't just go to a boy's apartment alone at night!"

"It's not night," I said, groaning. "It's not even six o'clock. Plenty of light outside."

"That's not important," she said. "Bruno's grandparents have gone out for their anniversary, remember? He's going to be alone there. You shouldn't go."

"Ammi!" I almost stomped my foot, then remembered I was supposed to be a mature young adult. "Bruno's been my friend since we were little kids. I've been hanging out with him forever. Don't you trust him?"

"Oh, one can never trust teenage boys, Kamala," Ammi told me darkly. She gave a vicious little stir with her spoon. "When two people are alone together, the third is the devil."

"You sound like Aamir."

"Kamala!"

I sighed and walked over to give her a little hug, because she was looking tense. "Look, Ammi, you may be right. Teenage boys are weird. But you know *me*, don't you? And you trust me? I'm your daughter."

She nodded. She was already looking more relaxed. I gave good hugs. That was just a fact.

"So trust me when I say I'll behave. I really need Bruno's help. You don't want me to fail physics, do you? Mr. Harper is so strict in grading!"

She chuckled. "Your father will burst a vein."

"Exactly." I gave her another squeeze and then hustled away before she changed her mind. No need for her to know that physics was the least of my problems right now.

I had bigger fish to fry.

"I can't believe your parents let you come here at night" was the first thing Bruno said when he opened his apartment door.

"It's not night!"

"It will be soon." He stepped aside to let me in.

I paused. "Dude, do you *not* want me to be here?"

He grinned and shoved me a little so I was all the way inside. "Don't be silly. You're welcome in my house no matter what time."

I put down my backpack and sank down on the couch. Weirdly, I felt awkward, like my hands were too big and my throat was dry. "Um, so your grandparents are celebrating their anniversary somewhere romantic, huh?" I wagged my eyebrows, then immediately regretted it when Bruno turned to look at me sharply.

Ugh, this was all Ammi's fault. Making me think the devil was here in the room with us or whatever.

"Not really," he said slowly. "They're gonna watch an off-Broadway play and walk around Times Square until they're exhausted."

"Cool."

"Yup."

Like I said, weird. "And your brother?" I asked.

"He's gone to a friend's house. He'll be home late."

"Oh, okay."

Finally, Bruno cleared his throat and pointed to my backpack. "Homework?"

I snapped out of whatever that was and reached over for my textbook. "Yes, please!"

My fingers brushed over the spectacles, but I decided to leave them for later. We studied for about an hour. Bruno found physics easy, but he didn't talk down to me. He explained concepts in a way that our teacher never did. Slowly, like I was seven years old and had the concentration span of a butterfly.

That's how I felt about school, honestly. It wasn't like I didn't want to be educated. I just found it incredibly hard to balance studies with my Ms. Marvel duties. Not to mention, patrolling and solving crime was way more fun. I wanted to live in a world where I defeated villains and saved countless humans, over and over again.

Not only humans. Animals too. Just the other day, I'd reached up a long arm to bring a cat down from a tree.

I'd never get bored with that stuff. Never.

Too bad I also had to be a regular Desi girl trying (and failing) to make my parents happy and struggling with stupid physics.

"You're doing really good," Bruno said, smiling a little when I got an answer right.

The way my pulse quickened at his words alarmed me. I didn't want Ammi to be correct in this situation. There was no devil here between us.

By the time we finished, it really *was* night. "Dinner?" Bruno asked, stretching. "I got pasta primavera leftovers."

We ate at the Carrellis' little dining table. Bruno was a pretty good cook, because his grandparents were usually busy with their convenience store and he wanted to help out as much as possible.

Husband material, as Nakia would say. Jokingly, of course, but still. It was something to think about.

No, Kamala! No thinking about Bruno that way! He's your friend. And he's not Muslim. Nothing can ever happen.

"You okay?" Bruno asked. "You look a little red."

"This pasta is spicy!" I muttered, taking a gulp of water.

"Sorry. I was experimenting with red pepper flakes." He laughed. "I'm getting inspired by your mother's cooking, I guess."

"Please!" I said, relaxing. "If I wanted to eat Ammi's spicy nihari, I'd have stayed home."

"Ooh, nihari! I love that one!"

I laughed too now. The first time Bruno had tried nihari at my house, he'd turned a bright shade of pink and sweat had dripped down his face. He'd drunk so much water, he'd spent half the night in the bathroom peeing.

"So what else do you need help with?" Bruno asked when we'd finished dinner.

I looked up. "What do you mean?"

He shrugged, then looked away and began to pick up our empty plates. "I mean, you usually come to me for help with something."

I froze. "I don't . . . I mean, I'm not . . ."

"It's okay, Kamala, I'm happy to help you. I like our dynamic, you know. I help you study and do research for your super hero activities; you grace me with your company and your friendship. It's a win-win."

I stared, not sure if he was joking. "Bruno!"

"What?" He put the dishes in the sink and turned to give me a little smile.

"You . . . you're being really passive-aggressive right now!" I couldn't believe it. Why had everything with my best friend become so strange and awkward recently?

His smile grew wider, more mischievous. "Sorry to disappoint you, but I don't have a passive-aggressive bone in my body." He picked up a steak knife from the counter and twirled it around his fingers. "Just aggressive!"

I rolled my eyes, because that was absolutely false. "Stop playing with that knife!" I said mildly. "Who'll do my research if you cut your hand?"

He laughed and placed it back on the counter. "Well, what's next?"

"Wait here." I went to my backpack and brought out the spectacles gingerly. "Ta-da!"

Bruno's jaw dropped open. "Whoa! Is that . . . ?"

I nodded smugly. "Yup, it's what Delilah and the new guy were fighting over."

"Kamala! The entire JCPD is searching for this item right now!"

I raised my eyebrow. "Are you gonna turn me in?"

"Of course not." Bruno sighed. "How did you get them, anyway?"

I quickly explained everything. How I took the spectacles from Asaar on the night of the exhibit opening and how he'd tried stealing them back the next evening. The crown tattoo on his wrist. The discussion—if you could call it that—of repatriation.

Bruno listened carefully. I could practically see the gears turning in his head as I spoke.

"I don't know what to do with these spectacles," I confessed.

He reached out a hand. "Let me see."

I handed the spectacles over and watched as he inspected them carefully, turning them around in his hand and bringing them closer to his face. I could see his eyes glaze over at the brilliance they emitted. "Whoa, stunning," he croaked.

"Yup." I knew what he was going through. These babies were dazzling, and more than a little hypnotic.

I could just imagine an elegant queen hundreds of years ago wearing these with a matching green silk or brocade gharara. Or maybe a king, a velvet-covered crown on his head, dripping with jewels, eyes covered with the brilliance of the green lenses.

"I wonder if they're truly magical," Bruno mused.

"I wouldn't be too surprised," I replied. "There's a reason that so many villains are after it. Delilah, Asaar . . . even Kingpin has a stake in it since he's sponsored the exhibit for some reason."

"We definitely need to do some research." Bruno leaned

back, one hand braced against the counter and the other holding the spectacles. "Why don't we— Ow!"

"Are you okay?" I took the spectacles back and led him away from the counter gently. He'd braced his right hand against the knife, the clumsy goofball, and it was actually bleeding.

Bruno made a face and dabbed his palm with a kitchen towel. "I'll be fine. It's a tiny cut."

"Still, go get a bandage or something. Then we'll get down to research." I pushed him toward the first aid kit on the top shelf and picked up the rest of the dishes myself. I'd been at his house plenty of times, and I knew where everything went.

Nonna would be proud of me.

The cut on Bruno's hand turned out not to be so tiny, after all.

It bled through the first bandage, so I had to use a larger one to fully cover the wound. "I'm fine," Bruno kept insisting, but I could tell he didn't mind all the attention.

Finally, we sat down to do some research on his laptop.

First, we got the latest updates on the robbery itself.

The good news was that the internet was flooded with video clips and news reports by now. Everyone was interested in the exhibit because of the sheer costliness of it. Not to mention the lavish opening party, with its minor celebrities from all over the world.

Bruno clicked on a news report. I took out a pen and notepad and got ready to jot down notes.

"I'm Tom Herrera of *Channel Six News.* Yesterday, early in the morning, the Jersey City Art Museum was broken into by unknown parties, who got away with an item from the famed Mughal artifacts exhibit the museum had put on. We're here today with the curator, Ms. Natalia Hibbert."

Ms. Hibbert looked nothing like she had the day of the party. Her shiny romper and black heels were gone, as was her brilliant smile. She wore a sensible white jacket with striped pants, and her face looked haggard. I suddenly wondered if her job was at risk. Surely the museum heads wouldn't blame her for what had happened?

"Ms. Hibbert, can you tell us how the perpetrator got in?"

"I don't know." She sighed. "We have the best security system money can buy, but somehow it was disarmed. We have no surveillance feeds starting from ten o'clock that night."

"So it had to be one of the guests," I said slowly, my heart sinking. There was no way we could investigate all those people. There were too many!

"Not to mention the servers and catering staff," Bruno added. "It could be any of those."

"Great." I picked up the notepad and jotted down *Who had access?*

We listened to the rest of the interview. Ms. Hibbert had nothing else to report, except how upset the museum staff was and how the public should come forward if they knew anything.

I pursed my lips. "So Delilah had an accomplice who attended the party as a guest and scoped the place out, maybe tinkered with the video feed?"

"Maybe," Bruno replied. "And what if the thief was the other guy. What was his name? Ass . . . ?"

I snorted. "Asaar. But I don't think it was him."

"Why not?"

I shrugged. "I dunno. When I was fighting it out with him this morning, he seemed very honest and adamant about his part."

"Ah, yes, the repatriation warrior role." Bruno rolled his eyes like he thought it was a stupid idea.

I ignored him and went on. "With Delilah, though, there's a stronger connection."

Bruno sat up. "Kingpin!"

"Exactly."

"Wait, he sponsored the exhibit, at least partly. Why would Delilah want to steal from him? Doesn't she work for him?"

"She does," I replied, writing *Delilah* in the notepad. "I'm curious about Kingpin's role too. What's his interest in Mughal art? It's not a subject he cares about, I can guarantee it."

"You're right." Bruno nodded. "His investments are very carefully thought out, so this seems out of character."

I wrote *What is Kingpin's interest in the Mughals?* I stared at it for a minute, then underlined it twice. I had a feeling this was a key question.

"What are you thinking?" Bruno asked.

I chewed my nail. "Kingpin probably sponsors plenty of things, right?"

"Sure. He's got a corporate empire, after all. That's what millionaires like him do, sponsor events for tax write-offs and to show they're good companies, not evil empires or anything."

"Ha!" I tapped my pen on the notepad. "Yet he doesn't go around making speeches at other charity or arts events. Like, ever."

"Maybe he does," Bruno protested weakly.

But we both knew I was right. Kingpin was big news, even in Jersey City. And especially with me being Ms. Marvel, Bruno always kept himself updated about the whereabouts of all villain activities. That was one of the best parts of his friendship, really. How he went above and beyond his role and did things to take care of me.

It was my number one reason for not messing with our

relationship. Well, that and my religion and culture and total fear of disappointing my parents.

"Kingpin does donate huge amounts to charity," Bruno stated. "But you're right, it's not the in-your-face, rah-rah sort of support."

"No showing up for opening-day festivities?" I asked.

"Probably not."

"No pledging to catch a thief using his own resources?"

"Absolutely not."

Yet he'd made speeches for the museum not once but twice. And all this for an exhibit about people of color living on the other side of the world hundreds of years ago.

Something was not right.

"What about other sponsors?" Bruno asked. "Do we know who they are?"

I frowned. "There was a list on a sign near the lectern," I said thoughtfully. "But all I remember is Fisk Industries."

Bruno typed for a minute, then turned the screen toward me. It was a list from the museum website. Fisk was on it, of course. A few local companies like ABC Gas and Tri-State Chemicals. Toward the end were individual names like Mr. and Mrs. Barrington—ugh, that couple again—and a few others, including the Bollywood movie director. Everyone was either American or famous, or both.

Except the last name. I used my fingers to enlarge the screen. *Shareef Deen, Lahore, Pakistan.* "Who's that?"

"No idea," Bruno replied. "Maybe a rando. Maybe not."

"I saw a Desi guy in a suit at the press conference," I said. "Right next to Kingpin."

"Oh, yeah? Maybe that's Deen."

"Maybe." I wrote down *Who is Shareef Deen?* in my notepad, even though my heart was telling me to focus on the big baddie in the ill-fitting suit. I flipped the page. *What is Kingpin's interest in the Mughals?* "The million-dollar question," I said, tapping my pen on the words.

Bruno chuckled as he went back to the laptop and typed something. "Talk about millions of dollars . . ."

I leaned closer to see the article he'd pulled up. It featured a stunning necklace with big red stones. I was pretty sure I'd seen it before. "Are those rubies?" I whispered.

"From the estate of some prince in India, circa 1750. Sold at auction for one point two million dollars a few years ago," Bruno replied. "Now part of the Mughal exhibit in Jersey City Art Museum."

"Whoa! Nakia would pair that with the perfect red heels and black leather pants."

Bruno didn't reply. He was staring at the necklace with a frown on his face. "How did this end up at the museum? They can't afford something this valuable."

I took the laptop and scanned the article. "The owner, Mr. Barrington, donated it to the museum last year. He also had a diamond-encrusted brooch in the form of a jasmine flower, which he donated to the Met in New York City."

"Generous."

"I wouldn't call it that," I muttered, thinking of Monocle Man and Beehive Lady badgering Ms. Hibbert this morning. "I've met those two, and they're not very nice."

I opened a new tab and started a deep dive into the Barringtons. The first few results were lifestyle pieces about their ultra-rich way of life: their charities, their jets, their galas where they were asked "What are you wearing?" by the paparazzi. Mr. Barrington was apparently a collector and had inherited his English maternal great-aunt's impressive collection. In addition to the pieces that were inherited, more were bought in auctions.

Bruno read over my shoulder. "'His extensive collection includes so many items from various parts of the world, they have to be stored in a warehouse. After Mr. Barrington II died, his son, Barrington III, began to dispose of his collection via private auctions or donations. Last year he donated his prized artifact, emerald spectacles belonging to the Emperor Shah Jahan, rumored to have magical powers.'"

"What?" I tried to grab the laptop.

Bruno pushed me back. "Let me read. . . . Um . . . Let's

see . . . blah, blah . . . Oh! You'll get a kick out of this, Kamala!"

"What?" I cried, louder. Bruno was being super annoying right now.

"The previous Mr. Barrington was a hundred and ten when he died," Bruno informed me.

"A hundred and ten?" I gasp. "How is that possible? Was he a vampire or something?"

Bruno grinned. "To his final days, Barrington insisted that the emerald spectacles were responsible for keeping him youthful."

"So they are magical!" I leapt up from the couch. "No wonder everyone is after them!"

"There's no proof, Kamala!" Bruno protested. "It could easily be the ramblings of a senile old man."

"An incredibly wealthy old man," I said hollowly, and sank down again. The pasta was sitting in my stomach like lead, and I wished I hadn't eaten so much.

"You okay, Kamala?" Bruno asked, looking sideways at me. "You look like the Barringtons murdered your puppy."

I groaned. "The Barringtons weren't the real owners of all this . . . stuff." I picked up the emerald spectacles from the coffee table and waved them around. "All this was taken from India. It's not fair!"

Bruno scoffed lightly. "You've been listening to Nakia, obviously."

I shook my head. It wasn't only Nakia. It was my parents too, and many people at the museum that night, all grumbling about the same thing. "You don't believe it?" I asked, oddly disappointed.

"No, I believe it." Bruno shrugged. "I just think it's wild that people are still complaining about this kind of thing hundreds of years after the fact. It's not like there's an easy solution to these complex issues, you know?"

"So what else can they do?" I demanded, even though I knew there wasn't really a good answer. Bruno was right in a way. What could anyone do, so long after the last Mughal king had died and the British Empire had dissolved into nothing?

I'm the one who takes back what was robbed, Asaar had boasted. *Returns things to their rightful place.*

Bruno shrugged again. "Return those spectacles to the museum, for one."

I glared at him and slid the spectacles onto my nose, turning everything in my vision a hazy green. "No way! They'll just get stolen again. I need to figure out what's going on so I can protect them from falling into the wrong hands."

Bruno shook his head and went back to his laptop. I noticed that the bandage on his hand had specks of blood on it. Tiny cut indeed! I explored the spectacle frame with my fingertips, wondering how a magical spell or formula would work. Theoretically, of course. I touched the whole thing softly, feeling for ridges or buttons or . . . something.

Anything.

I ran my fingers over the bridge that lay right over my nose and felt a buzzing pass through the frame. "What was that?" I whispered.

"I didn't hear . . ." Bruno looked up. "Whoa!"

"What?"

"Nothing. The spectacles glowed for a second, but they're back to normal now."

We stared at each other. Had something magical happened? Was it just our imagination? Were we both going to turn into hundred-year-old vampires?

Then Bruno smiled sheepishly. "I think we're both tired."

He was right. The buzzing had been so light, I'd probably imagined it. I nodded, took the spectacles off gingerly, and tucked them into my backpack. "I should head home. Ammi will be waiting."

As he walked me to the door and waved good-bye, the bandage on his hand looked good as new. No blood, not even a dot.

I blinked. I must be more tired than I'd realized.

It was ten o'clock by the time I got back home.

Ammi and Abu were in the living room, watching TV. I stood quietly in the entryway, debating. Should I sneak upstairs without telling them I was there? The sofa they were sitting on was angled away from the living room doorway, and they were focused on the TV screen.

But sneaking in would mean I had something to hide. Which I didn't.

On the other hand, walking in and saying salaam would mean facing disapproval at my "late-night activities" and answering a hundred questions about what I'd done at Bruno's.

It was insulting, really, the way my parents treated me.

I decided I didn't need any questions right then and quietly headed up the stairs to my room.

"Kamala, is that you?"

Aargh! Ammi had the ears of a predator. I wouldn't be surprised if she had the nose of one too. "Uh, yeah, it's me."

I went back downstairs to the living room. Abu and Ammi both turned sideways to stare at me.

"Why did you come home so late?" Abu demanded.

Okay, good. Abu was easier to deal with in some ways.

"Abu," I began. "It's not even that late. It's, like, nine fifty-eight."

Abu's stare became harder. "It's ten."

"Well, that's not too bad. Ten o'clock was my curfew last year. I'm older now."

"But not any wiser," Ammi inserted.

I kept looking straight at Abu. "I was studying. I had a really tough physics assignment and Bruno helped me with it, because you know he's a genius. And every time he helps me, I get a really good grade, so that's why I asked him for help. Wasn't that smart of me?"

None of this was a lie, by the way. Bruno did help me with my homework.

Abu's stare became softer. It was fascinating how he could communicate so much with just those eyes of his. "You think you'll get an A in physics this semester?"

"Unbelievable!" Ammi scoffed. "This is what you're

focusing on? Not the fact that she's creeping in at almost midnight from whatever she was doing?"

"Almost midnight?" I gasped. "It's not even ten!"

"It's ten," Abu said firmly to both of us. "So, about that A?"

I shrugged. "I'm trying."

He turned back to the TV. "Okay, go up to your room."

Ammi sighed dramatically. "Good Muslim girls don't come home so late at night."

Given that this Muslim girl was also a super hero who often had to sneak in and out of the house for her super hero duties, I didn't have much to say to this. "Sorry, Ammi," I finally muttered. "I'll try to be home earlier next time."

"Tell Bruno to come here next time," Ammi replied. "That way I can keep an eye on you."

"And feed him nihari?" I joked.

Her lips twitched. "Hai Allah, no way. That boy can't eat spicy food to save his life."

"You made it extra spicy that day, just to mess with him!" I shook my head as I walked back out.

"Maybe," Ammi called out after me, her voice lighter than before.

First things first, I needed a safe place to store the spectacles. I took them carefully out of my backpack and hid them in a lockbox in the back of my closet. The black box was old and battered, and nobody would guess there was anything of value inside.

Second, I flipped through my notepad again, reviewing the notes I'd made with Bruno. Ideas raced through my head like tiny busy bees trying to find nectar and not succeeding.

Kingpin. Asaar. Delilah. Shocker. Ms. Hibbert. The Barringtons. Brittany something. The silent dude in the corner near the lectern who was maybe this mysterious Shareef Deen or maybe not.

There were too many characters and not enough plot. It was like a B-grade movie that you stopped watching because it was too confusing.

My phone pinged. It was Bruno.

I know you're stressing about everything, Kamala. Go to sleep. We'll discuss everything in the morning.

How did this boy know me so well? *Thanks, buddy,* I texted back.

He didn't reply. One minute passed, then five. Then twenty. I kept looking at my phone, waiting, my heart thumping.

Was he mad at me for calling him *buddy*?

Or was he researching Shareef Deen like the awesome friend he was?

Suddenly, I felt a little icky. I shouldn't even be thinking things like this about Bruno. Definitely shouldn't be leading him on when nothing would ever happen between us. Maybe having dinner with him tonight was a mistake.

And now I was stuck on whether *buddy* was the right thing to text him in the middle of the night.

Kamala, get a grip. You've got more important things to worry about than boys.

You know who didn't care about boys or homework or even parents? Ms. Marvel, that's who. I needed some fresh air, and the streets of Jersey City needed a patrolperson. I put away my phone and scrambled up from my bed to change into my costume. Then I opened my bedroom window and jumped down into the backyard like I'd done a thousand times before.

Ten minutes later, I was near the museum, thanks to my long, stretchy legs. I didn't always patrol in this area, but today I was feeling antsy and protective. If the thief came back to steal other artifacts, Ms. Marvel would be ready.

I walked around, sometimes stretching my body higher than the lampposts to look ahead. A couple of times I sat on the closed top of the trash container, just to mix it up. When things got boring, I checked my phone. Nothing from Bruno, but Kate Bishop had sent me a meme with the caption *long time no see.*

I smiled to myself. Kate was cool, and we'd hung out a few months ago when we'd been patrolling the docks together. I sent her a thumbs-up so she'd know I was down for a meetup, if the villains ever left us alone.

I didn't know Kate too well, but suddenly I wanted to. I could send her a hundred *buddy* texts without feeling embarrassed or stressed out.

"Well, well, if it isn't Ms. Marvel, the teenage wonder," came a sarcastic voice that grated on my nerves big-time.

I tucked my phone away and jumped down. "Well, well, if it isn't Delilah, the pain in my neck!"

"Funny," she mocked.

"Thank you," I mocked back.

Delilah grimaced. "I'm not in the mood for games," she said roughly. "I want the spectacles back!"

"What spectacles?" I asked innocently.

"The ones I stole from the museum, and *you* stole from *me*!"

I blinked rapidly. I'd suspected that Delilah was the thief, and Asaar had said as much. But to have her confirm it . . . that was something else.

"Did I finally shock you into silence, Ms. Marvel?" Delilah asked with a mean little smile. She came closer, and I stepped back, making my hands into big fists.

I didn't want to fight before I got some answers, though. "What does Kingpin think about you stealing from his exhibit?" I asked.

Delilah's smile vanished. The next second, she leaned forward and punched me in the jaw. *POW!*

I was launched into the air and landed on my back several feet away.

If I wasn't Muslim, I'd be spewing some nasty curse words right now. Instead, I made my right arm long and picked her up, then threw her with all my might into a nearby building. "Does Kingpin know you've gone rogue?" I demanded. "Does he know you're stealing from *his* exhibit?"

Delilah got up and wiped her nose. "I haven't gone rogue, you stupid girl," Delilah sneered. "Kingpin knows exactly what's going on!"

Whoa. I didn't expect that.

Delilah cackled at my surprise. She took hold of a car and, oh Lord, lifted it up. With a roar, she threw the car. In. My. Face.

I ducked and put out a stretchy hand to grab the car and place it gently on the ground. I tried to keep destruction of property to a minimum on my watch.

Delilah cackled again, louder, meaner. "You're such a wimp!" she cried, then picked up another car and threw it at me.

I growled under my breath and reached a long arm to catch the car. I missed, and it crashed to the ground near my feet. A car alarm started blaring.

I growled louder. "You're acting like a toddler, throwing her toys around."

She made a mock-crying face. "Boo-hoo! Do you know any toddlers who can do this?" She picked up a dump truck with both hands, her arm and leg muscles bulging, and flung it straight at me.

I ducked, and it hit the road sideways, asphalt showering around me.

"Enough!" I cried. I made a fist and sent the arm careening toward Delilah, ready to beat her to a pulp.

She jumped backward, but I grabbed her foot at the last minute and swung her upside down.

Delilah made a furious sound, and kicked and kicked and kicked. "Let go, you silly girl! You don't want to make Kingpin angry, do you?"

I had to let go, not because I was scared of Kingpin, no way, but because her kicks were pure granite and steel.

She laughed loudly and ran away.

It took me another minute to get my breath back to normal. My only consolation was that Delilah was super strong, and even the biggest super heroes had a hard time with her.

My brain cleared as I trudged home. That's when I realized that the encounter with Delilah hadn't been a complete bust. I'd confirmed that she was indeed the burglar of the emerald spectacles.

Also, more importantly, that Kingpin knew about the theft.

A theft from the exhibit *he* sponsored. An artifact he was going on camera publicly to vow to find.

It was mind-boggling. Why was he pretending?

Wearily, I climbed into my room through the open window, changed into my pajamas, and lay down. I was almost asleep when my phone beeped.

You're welcome, buddy, Bruno had texted back.

The next day, I was groggy in school, which was to be expected.

I yawned so many times, our English teacher told me to go to the bathroom and wash my face.

Half the class giggled at me. The other half shot me sympathetic looks, because hey, who hadn't stayed up on a weeknight?

The only difference was, I stayed up past my bedtime to patrol the streets, keeping the citizens of Jersey City safe.

"What was up with you all day?" Bruno asked as the three of us walked home, Bruno and I in the front, Nakia trailing behind reading something on her phone.

"Nothing," I mumbled. I should update him on what I'd figured out about Kingpin the night before, but I kept my lips zipped. I'd never admit to feeling beaten by Delilah. Not in a million years.

Besides, Nakia was just a few steps away. We needed to keep this convo light.

Bruno gave me a sideways glance. "Did you watch the video I sent you?" he asked, smirking.

I scowled at him. It better not be a video of me in Ms. Marvel mode. He knew I hated watching replays of myself. There was so much I didn't want to see, like how ungraceful I was, blah, blah. I didn't even like watching home videos Ammi sometimes pulled out, from when Aamir and I were younger. There was one where I was three, dancing to a Bollywood tune, stumbling about like a drunk.

Seriously embarrassing.

"Don't tell me it's another one of those cat videos?" Nakia called out, giggling.

"I wish," I muttered.

"No, no," Bruno added, rushing to explain. "It's a video of Ms. Marvel fighting with, uh, an unknown villain outside the museum."

"The Jersey City Art Museum?" Nakia said loudly. "You mean, it was a super villain who stole the artifact?"

I groaned and sent another deadly scowl Bruno's way. Why had he told her? We both knew how smart she was. It took her literally two seconds to figure things out.

"Uh, yeah," Bruno said, shrugging lightly and sending a sheepish look my way. "Looks like it."

"Well, let's make sure." Nakia jogged up to squeeze between us and searched for the video on her phone. I shook my head, but my two best friends watched the entire thing, oohing and aahing at intervals.

"Wow," Nakia said when the video ended. "I wonder what a villain wants with a Mughal-era item."

Bruno and I exchanged looks, and he mouthed, "Sorry."

I shrugged. I guess I didn't really blame him for telling Nakia about the video. It was online. By now, every kid in Jersey City had probably watched it ten times.

Nakia's phone rang. "Oh, I need to get that," she said, her face lighting up. "It's an Indian blogger who'll hopefully give me a quote for my article."

She waved good-bye to us and sat down on a bench, already focused on her phone call.

Bruno and I walked on, and we turned the corner in silence. I daydreamed about finding Delilah and beating her up. Maybe I could bring in Kate Bishop and make it a group project.

Bruno cleared his throat. "I was thinking we should try to find out who the sponsors of the Mughal exhibit are."

I stopped. "What?"

"What?" he asked, puzzled. "Why are you looking at me like that? It's a good suggestion."

"I know!" I threw up my hands. "That's why we already did that last night, when I came over to your place."

His puzzlement grew. "No, we didn't. You came over for physics. And pasta."

"And to show you the spectacles!"

He nodded slowly. "Yeah, you showed them to me, and then you put them away and went home."

"No, we researched the artifacts, and the Barringtons, and . . . and . . ." I started to feel a little faint. What was happening? How could he forget all the research we did?

Maybe he was tired, like me. I forgot everything I learned in school some days. Bruno just needed his memory jogged.

I swung my backpack around and opened it quickly. Reaching in to take out my notepad, I flipped to the last page and showed him our notes. "See?"

Bruno grabbed the notepad and stared at my handwriting. "I . . . don't remember this. When did you . . . ?" His voice was not only confused now. It was also a little fearful.

My eyes fell to his right hand, clenched around the notepad. "Wait, where's your bandage?"

"What bandage?"

I took the notepad from him and held his hand in both of mine. Carefully, disbelievingly, I inspected his palm. It was smooth and unmarred.

"What're you looking at?" Bruno asked.

I realized with a start that I was rubbing my finger over his palm like a weirdo. I dropped his hand. "You, uh, hurt your hand with a knife yesterday, after dinner."

"No, I didn't," Bruno whispered, but he was also staring at his hand now. "Really?"

"Really. I put a bandage on it and everything."

"Why wouldn't I remember that?"

I had no answer, so I just shrugged. "Then we did all our research and talked, and laughed, and . . ." I stopped, and my eyes widened.

"What?" Bruno said, alarmed. "Kamala, tell me what happened then?"

"Oh my God!" I gasped. "We were talking about the spectacles and I put them on and rubbed the frame, and then I felt it buzz, and then you said IT GLOWED!"

"It glowed? Like a firefly?"

"No, not like a firefly! Like a magical object! It glowed because we somehow figured out how to use the spectacles' power!"

Bruno's face became less panicked. "So, basically, the spectacles healed my cut?"

I nodded solemnly. "Yup. Maybe that's why the elder Mr. Barrington was a hundred and ten years old! Not a vampire."

"What?"

I sighed. "Never mind."

"Why are you looking so sad?" Bruno asked.

I put away my notepad and swung my backpack onto my shoulder again. I should be thrilled that the rumors were true. Shah Jahan's spectacles did indeed have healing powers.

But something else was horrifying me now. "You forgot everything, Bruno," I whispered. "From the time you got hurt to the time the spectacles healed you. You lost all that time from your memory."

Bruno nudged me with his shoulder. "Yeah, but it's not a big deal," he assured me. "It was just—what?—an hour, tops? And you kept notes, so it's not like we lost any research."

I exhaled sharply. He was right. Losing an hour of memory wasn't a big deal.

Magical spectacles having the power to heal cuts so not even a faint scar remained? That was a huge deal.

"You're right," I said, smiling. "We didn't lose any research."

That night, after dinner, I pulled out my notepad again and made some updates about the spectacles' powers. I noted the approximate timing of Bruno's injury with the knife and then when the spectacles had buzzed and glowed.

I chewed my lip as I wrote *Memory loss related to time?*

The previous day's notes were also bugging me, especially Bruno's list of exhibit sponsors. Everyone was accounted for except for one person.

I opened my laptop and typed *Shareef Deen* into the search bar.

Nothing.

I mean, there were a few random people named Shareef on Facebook and Instagram, but most of the search results were only partial hits. Most were for a past prime minister of Pakistan named Nawaz Sharif or for various religious shrines in Pakistan with *shareef* in their titles.

I started a new search and typed again. *Shareef Deen Lahore Pakistan.*

Bingo. There weren't a lot of results, but they existed. Mr. Deen was a Pakistani businessman who owned a number of companies making a variety of things like pipes, kitchen and bathroom fixtures, carpets, tile, and such. The umbrella name of his group was PakPro.

"How patriotic," I whispered. "And boring."

I clicked on a recent news article that referenced Deen. *Lahore Police Caution Against Illegal Smuggling of Antique Tiles.*

My back straightened at the word *antique*. Same as artifacts, right? I read the article quickly. It was from five years ago, a pretty basic account describing the smuggling of three-hundred-year-old tiles outside Pakistan and how the police were trying to solve the crime. What caught my interest was this:

Respected businessman Shareef Deen, CEO of PakPro Inc., said he was horrified at this blatant disregard for our country's history. "These tiles are part of our heritage. They should stay here in museums or other collections, and be a source of pride and inspiration to everyone. Smuggling them into other nations for a profit is the worst kind of theft."

There was a link under Deen's name that I clicked next. It took me to a basic bio page on PakPro's website, with things like when he was born (same year as Abu) and where he'd studied (a Pakistani university followed by an American business school) and how much his company was worth (several billion rupees).

What the bio page didn't have? A picture.

"What sort of About page doesn't have pictures?" I growled. It was like getting little tastes of what I wanted instead of the full meal.

I'd even take a half meal at this point.

Just a snack of samosa and chai. Anything, really.

The tiles article made me think, though. Maybe the newspaper had other articles about him. I went back to the newspaper site and typed his name into its search bar. Two articles came up, both written by Shareef Deen. Both opinion pieces.

I leaned forward.

Article one: *Western Countries Should Admit to Colonial Theft.*

Article two: *The East India Company: Nothing More Than Corporate Looters.*

I sent the article links to Bruno via text, then kept reading. Honestly, I was impressed. Deen sounded like a smart, articulate, knowledgeable Desi uncle. He was passionate about keeping old artifacts in their countries of origin. He blamed the colonial powers for draining resources from their colonies, becoming rich in the process. He called the East India Company a bunch of looting hacks, for crying out loud!

Abu would be his best friend, no doubt.

So why was he sponsoring the Jersey City exhibit?

What's the deal with Shareef Deen? I wrote in my notebook. Then I underlined it twice, like that would make it clearer.

Unfortunately, my eyes were drooping by now. I looked at the clock and saw it was after midnight. Ammi would freak.

Another small article caught my eye just as I was closing my laptop. It was old, a news piece from almost a decade ago, describing power fluctuations in a factory in Lahore. Workers complained for months, after which they staged a series of protests.

> *Owner Shareef Deen, who arrived at the scene this week to satisfy workers and investigate the fluctuations, was involved in a minor accident on site. He will speak with the press as soon as he has recovered.*

There were two photographs along with the article. One showed a group of people standing in front of a factory. The other was a close-up.

By this time, my eyes were bleary and my brain exhausted. I blinked a few times to inspect the images carefully, but my face split into a humongous yawn. Then another one, even bigger.

Okay, time to go to sleep.

I put away my laptop and snuggled into the bedcovers. Maybe things would make more sense in the light of day.

"What are you doing today?" Ammi asked as she cooked me my favorite weekend breakfast of poori and chole.

"It's Saturday," I replied, setting a big pitcher of mango juice on the table. "You know what that means."

"Masjid lecture?" Aamir jumped in. "I'm going too."

I glared at him and his stupid ideas, but it was too late. Ammi clapped her hands once, like a queen with a command. "Good idea. We'll all go. It's been a long time since we listened to one of the sheikh's incredible lectures."

"I wouldn't call them incredible," I muttered.

"Extraordinary?" Aamir suggested. "Mind-blowing?"

"You're ridiculous."

He smirked. "We're not talking about me right now."

Ammi put a steaming poori on my plate. "Sit and eat," she told me. "You can argue with your brother later."

"Ammi," I protested. I was going to give her some long speech about the injustice of spending my Saturday at the mosque listening to something I had zero interest in. I tore a piece of my crispy, fluffy poori and dipped it in the chole. The chickpeas were soft, the potatoes melted in my mouth, and the spice level was just right: high. "Oh my God, this is so good!"

"Aamir, go call your abu," Ammi said, putting the rest of the food on the table.

We all ate our breakfast in silence. For a long time, there were only the sounds of chomping and the occasional "Pass the chole, please." At one point, Abu asked why the kids got more pooris than he did.

"They are growing," Ammi replied. "You're not."

He grunted his displeasure, then opened his mouth to say something.

Nope, not happening. I wanted to eat my delicious breakfast in peace. "So, I did some research on the Mughal artifacts in the museum," I stated.

Abu took the bait. "Oh, yes?" he asked, forehead easing. "Did they find who stole the pieces?"

"Not yet," I replied. "But I checked out the sponsors list,

and there's a dude your age from Lahore on it. Name's Shareef Deen or something."

"Oh, isn't that where you're from, Abu?" Aamir asked.

Abu grunted again, but it was a happier sound now. "Yes, I was born there. You kids have visited Karachi because your mother's family is from there, but Lahore is a very amazing city. Full of culture and history."

Ammi shook her head. "Karachi is very amazing too."

Yikes, now they'd argue over whose hometown was better? Please. "So do you know this Shareef Deen?" I asked quickly.

Abu stared at me. "Do you know how many people live in Lahore, child? You think I know all of them?"

Aamir smacked his hand on the table, making me jump. "Exactly, Father dear! It's like when someone finds out I'm Muslim, they ask if I know some guy called Mohammad in California."

"You know my cousin Abid Mohammad in San Diego," Ammi said dryly.

It was my turn to stare. Did she just make a joke?

"Good one, Muneeba." Abu went back to his chole. "No, Kamala, I don't know Shareef Deen. But I can ask my friends who live in Lahore. Maybe they've heard of him."

"Are you serious?" I almost dropped my poori. "That would be awesome!"

He munched loudly, then swallowed. "Why not? In return,

you'll make sure you get an A on your next physics test, eh?"

Aamir chuckled.

I flushed. "That's . . . that's not how it works, Abu! I can't just magically get an A because I need something from you!"

Abu shrugged. "Give and take, that's what life is all about."

Ugh, how I hated his stupid little sayings. They never made any sense. Ever.

Ammi patted my hand. "Accha, beta, forget all this. Finish your breakfast."

I grabbed another poori and put all my energy into eating. There was really no point in talking to my family. They made everything into a whole drama.

I finished and began to debate if I could get away with licking my plate. My phone pinged. It was Nakia. *Going to masjid today?*

I groaned, but not too hard. If Nakia was going, it would be fine. We could just go do our regular Saturday thing afterward. *Yup,* I replied. *Shopping later.*

"Shopping?" Aamir said, leaning over to read my screen. "You don't need anything; your closet is already full."

I scoffed. "And you know this how? Sneaking into my room, are you?"

He shrugged and drank some mango juice. "I'm assuming, since you go shopping with Nakia every single Saturday."

"It's called thrifting, for your information."

He sits up, face serious. "You shouldn't care so much about material things, Kamala," he began. "Our beloved Prophet, peace be upon him, warned us against the dangers of this worldly life."

"Then why were you waiting for the latest Air Jordans to be released this summer, huh?" I asked, crossing my arms over my chest. "And that watch you have, the one with the gold face? How much did it cost?"

"That watch was a birthday present to myself!" he sputtered.

"But our beloved Prophet, peace be upon him, didn't celebrate his birthday with material gifts, did he?"

"Uh . . ."

Abu held up his hand, brows knitted together. "Be quiet, please. You two are giving me indigestion."

That was probably the four pooris he'd inhaled, but I wasn't going to say it out loud. "Sorry," I said sweetly, getting up from my chair. "I'm going to go get ready."

"Wait," Ammi called. "I need you to clean up."

I didn't turn around. "I helped you already. Tell Aamir to clean up."

Back in my bedroom, I felt guilty. I shouldn't have refused Ammi like that. She'd cooked all that delicious breakfast, and I'd gobbled it up without even a thank-you. "You're a bad daughter, Kamala," I told myself in the mirror.

The next second, I shook my head. Nope, it wasn't my fault. I'd helped her a lot in the morning, draining the chickpeas for the chole and kneading the dough for the pooris. Aamir didn't even show up until the food was ready. He was the one who needed to clean up.

Instead, he'd probably sit at the table drinking his mango juice, acting like he was king of the castle.

Ugh, he made me so mad! What wouldn't I give to be an only child!

My phone pinged again. Nakia had sent a picture of the outfit she was wearing. Blue tunic with black jeans, and a patterned blue-and-red hijab. And golden hoop earrings, of course.

Looking good, I texted back. We usually coordinated at least one thing in our outfits for our weekly trips. I rummaged through my drawers until I found a blue-and-white-striped shirt. It wasn't the height of fashion, but it would do. No dangly earrings for me, though. I preferred tiny studs in my ears.

When I went back downstairs, the kitchen was silent. The table had been cleared, but dirty dishes were stacked on the counter.

"AAARGH!" I pushed up my sleeves and began to load the dishwasher, thinking of creative punishments for my awful brother.

"You didn't have to wash the dishes, you know." Abu stood in the doorway, looking surprised. "Aamir said he'd take care of them after we came back."

"Yeah, right."

"You don't believe him?" Abu asked. "He may be a lot of things, but your brother isn't a liar."

I sighed, because that was true. He might annoy us all with his over-the-top religious pronouncements and rigid beliefs, but he was an honest person. Sometimes too honest, like when he told me I looked awful after a disastrous haircut in middle school.

"Never mind, it's almost done now," I said.

Abu came closer and patted my head. "You're a good daughter, Kamala."

My eyes blurred at hearing the very thing I hadn't been sure about less than an hour ago. That too from my father, who was usually pointing out my mistakes. Had I gone to sleep after breakfast? Was this all a dream?

"Kamala?" Abu growled. "I give you a compliment and you say nothing? Have you forgotten all the manners your mother and I taught you?"

Okay, so not a dream.

Still, he was right. He'd given me a rare compliment. I cleared my throat. "Um, thanks."

"Hurry up, we don't want to miss the sheikh's lecture. You need all the guidance and advice he can give you, otherwise you're gonna mess up your future."

Yup, I was definitely awake, and this was definitely still my stupid life. I couldn't wait to see Nakia and get some retail—thrifting—therapy.

Sheikh Abdullah wasn't too bad.

He was old, but not too old. Approachable but not overly friendly. Truthful, never hiding anything from us "youth," as he called us.

"It's wonderful to see so many youth here today," he began when everyone had settled in.

Nakia, Ammi, and I sat on the carpeted floor of the women's section, separated from the men by a wooden half wall with a cutout pattern. We could see through the pattern into the other side, but only by squinting.

"Kamala!" Ammi slapped me on the head lightly. "Stop ogling the men."

I gasped. "I am not! Ogling the men!"

Nakia clapped a palm over her mouth, but her dancing eyes gave her away. She was laughing.

I jabbed my elbow into her side. "There's nobody good enough to ogle here, anyway," I muttered.

Ammi shook her head and sat back. She was covered head to toe in black, which was the look she always wore for her visits to the mosque. She said it made her focused and prayerful.

I thought it made her look pale, but whatever. Nakia always said fashion was an expression of your thoughts, so I guess Ammi's thoughts were a little unyielding. It's not like I didn't know that already.

"Today's topic is avarice," Sheikh Abdullah continued. "Now, I know all the youth are well-versed in the English language, but the rest of us are mostly immigrants and may need a little explanation. Avarice means greed. Not just greed for a little more food, or a slightly better job, oh, no. Those are good things, wanting to improve yourself, increase your reach and all that. There's nothing wrong with wanting to get that promotion or a bigger house because you have children now, or wanting to go on a nice vacation to relax. We're human, and we all want nice things, don't we?"

The crowd agreed by murmuring "Yes" and "For sure."

"That's not what I'm talking about here," the sheikh said. "Avarice, my friends, is not a normal desire to do better. It's an immense greed fueled by a need for material wealth. It's the kind of greed that doesn't care what you do to achieve something. It doesn't care who you hurt or what you sacrifice. Avarice changes you. It makes you inhuman."

The hall was quiet. I took a deep, deep breath. I couldn't imagine that type of greed. It didn't sound normal. Why was the sheikh talking about it? It wasn't like we kids—or grown-ups—were amassing billions of dollars or something.

"Now, you may be thinking," the sheikh said, "why am I talking to you about avarice?"

Ha! Great minds thought alike. I leaned forward, wanting to know more.

"You may be sure that none of you have avarice in your hearts, eh? Well, maybe. Maybe not. But the Allah subhana wataalah in the Holy Quran warns us about avarice several times, and He knows better than anyone what is in our hearts, doesn't He?"

More murmurs from the crowd. They definitely agreed. I nodded too.

"In Surah Al-Nisa, Allah describes the disbelievers as people who 'hoard their wealth and enjoin avarice on others.' And then in Surah Al-Baqarah, He says, 'And do not consume one another's wealth unjustly.' Those are strong words, but there are also many verses about how to rid ourselves of greed and avarice, from the love of wealth and material things."

Sheikh Abdullah kept talking, but I was stuck on his words, the ones where he quoted from the Quran. Hoarding riches. Amassing fortunes. Consuming other people's wealth.

Wasn't that what the colonial powers had done in India and Africa and so many other places?

Wasn't this exactly what Allah was warning about? How the avarice in our hearts could lead to horrible consequences for not just individuals but nations?

My eyes wide, I stared through the cutout patterns in the wall in front of me. Sheikh Abdullah was talking about how to rid our hearts of avarice by spending our wealth in the cause of Allah, by giving to charity, by helping others who had less.

All that was awesome. I was totally on board.

But what about the wealth that had already been stolen?

Quickly, I pulled out my phone and clicked on the link for one of Shareef Deen's articles. The ideas were hitting me more deeply this morning. I could practically feel the ache in his words. The pain of losing heritage.

Suddenly, I remembered the exhibit on opening night. The lights, the food and drinks, the opulence. The riches, not just in the glass cases, but also dripping from the necks and arms of the guests. The fancy cars parked outside. Everything.

I felt sick.

That was avarice, I guess.

Ammi slapped my head again. "Put that phone down!" she hissed.

"Ow!"

Sheikh Abdullah paused and squinted in the wall's direction. "Is everything all right back there?"

We all stayed quiet. Ammi tightened her lips, her universal *I'm not happy with you* sign.

"Uh, yes, Sheikh," I finally replied. "We're enjoying your lecture."

And guess what? I wasn't lying even a little bit. It was the best lecture he'd given in a long time.

"What was that?" Nakia asked later as we browsed through the racks in our favorite thrift store.

"What was what?"

She looked at me sideways. "In the masjid. You looked like you'd been hit by a lightning bolt."

I grabbed a pair of white jeans from the rack. "I guess I was," I admitted. "The whole topic about avarice, it really spoke to me."

"Why?" Nakia frowned. "You're the most socially conscious person I know, apart from me. You borrow stuff from me so you don't have to buy. And you shop at a thrift store."

"That's me being stingy, Nakia," I said, laughing a little. "I'm Desi, after all. It's a whole stereotype."

"No." She took the jeans from me and put them back.

"You're not stingy, or miserly, or whatever. You're the most generous person I know. You give your time and help others without any regard for yourself."

I felt my cheeks flush. That was only because I was Ms. Marvel, but she didn't know that. "Whatever," I finally replied. "Give me back those jeans. I'm buying them."

"White jeans? So 1980s." Nakia grinned and handed them back. "How about those jelly bracelets to match the era?"

"How about no."

"Just once, Kamala Khan, I'd like to see you wear some flashy jewelry!" She grinned wider, then headed to the counter.

I followed her, grumbling. "You wear enough for the both of us."

"I heard that!"

We paid for our purchases—sixteen dollars for the jeans and ten for a cute vintage band T-shirt. Nakia bought a purse, all cracked brown leather that looked seriously cool, even though it probably only got that way because of its age.

Our next stop was a gyro truck two streets over. It wasn't my favorite, Gyro King, owned by Najaf, but it was a close second. "Mmm, how does this get more yummy every week?" Nakia mumbled with her first bite.

I chuckled. "I think it's the secret sauce. Makes us addicted."

"Not a bad thing to be addicted to."

I took a bite and sighed. She was right; it was seriously delicious. We chatted while we ate, then Nakia pushed her empty plate away and took out her phone. "I wanted to show you the pics I took."

"What pics?" I asked, peering at her screen.

They were from the Mughal exhibit's opening night. How she'd taken pictures while also serving food was a mystery to me, but they'd come out great. The artifacts gleamed under whatever filters she'd used.

"Nice, huh?" Nakia smiled. "I'm going to use them for the article I'm writing."

"The one where you'll expose the colonial powers for stealing wealth from other nations?"

"Yup, that one," she replied happily.

I didn't reply right away. Deen's articles and Sheikh Abdullah's words were all tangled up in my brain, making my thoughts heavy and uncertain. I was a super hero. I should have clear ideas about right and wrong, good versus evil. If you stole things from a museum, you were a bad guy. If you helped old ladies cross the street, you were a good person.

But what happened if you stole back something that was already stolen?

"I hate gray areas," I groaned, dropping my head into my hands.

"What?" Nakia laughed in surprise.

"Nothing," I mumbled. "Carry on."

Nakia went back to her pictures, explaining which one she'd use to illustrate which point in her article. I picked my head up and listened with growing admiration.

Who was I kidding—she always impressed me. Always.

"This is gonna be great, Nakia," I told her when she stopped to take a breath. She looked excited and also a little bit frazzled.

"Thank you," she replied. "There's lots of work still to be done, though. Not sure how much I can handle with all the assignments this week. Can you believe I have to write a ten-page essay in English about my dream vacation? What are we, ten?"

I chuckled. My dream vacation was to crawl into bed and sleep for a week, no parents or annoying brother around. "Well, at least we got some really cute pieces from the thrift store today," I offered with a grin.

Nakia put away her phone and side-eyed me. "You know what's cute? The way Bruno looks at you."

"Ugh, Nakia!"

"What?" She shrugged innocently. "I'm just saying. That boy likes you for real."

"I doubt it," I said as I grabbed some leftover pita bread,

because this was the perfect time to eat my feelings. "Anyway, we're Muslim. Plus, my parents are . . . you know. My parents. Nothing can come of it."

Nakia took my other hand. "That's a whole different story. What I'm really interested to know is whether you feel the same way."

I blinked at her. "Why does that matter?"

"I'm your best friend. I want to know what's in your heart."

I blinked some more. Now my eyelashes felt wet. She had such a way with words; they pierced you in the best way. "I don't know. He's great-looking, and a wonderful person. . . ."

"The best person."

I nodded vigorously. "Yes! But . . ."

"But you don't feel the same way," Nakia finished, letting go of my hand.

My stomach clenched. "I don't think so. I'm not sure that I feel those butterflies in my tummy when I see him, ya know?"

She giggled a little. "Oh, those butterflies can get you in trouble!"

I smiled, but then my face fell. "Honestly, it's not something I've let myself think about, or explore. You know that dating is forbidden in our religion. What's the point of really falling for someone and then not being able to do anything about it? I don't want to sneak around, disappoint Ammi and Abu. They already get disappointed enough because of me."

Nakia leaned over and gave me a hug over the table. It was awkward and messy, but it was what I needed. "I get it," she whispered. "You don't want to go down a road that you know you shouldn't."

"Exactly."

On Monday, I headed to the museum after school with Bruno.

"What do you hope this will achieve, Kamala?" Bruno asked as we stepped off the train.

"Chill. I just want to know what's going on with the investigation."

"And you think they'll just tell you?" He rolled his eyes. "Yes, girl who served drinks on the night of the opening, let us share all our secrets with you for no reason."

I rolled my eyes right back at him. These were the times when I did not get a single butterfly in Bruno's presence. He could be so . . . irritating. "I'm not stupid, Bruno."

He groaned. "I know that! I didn't mean . . . Look, can you just stop for a second?"

I stopped and turned around. "What?"

He stopped too. "I know you're smart. I didn't mean to imply otherwise. I'm sorry."

I sighed. "Thank you."

"But can we have a game plan before we get there? Please?"

I turned back and started walking again. "I have a game plan."

He jogs after me. "And that is . . . ?"

I shrugged. "Can you wait and see?"

In reality, I had no game plan. I just knew I had to do something. Kingpin had been talking to reporters again, holding a press conference early this morning somewhere inside the museum. He'd droned on and on about solving the robbery and finding the culprits, blah, blah.

It was his third appearance in Jersey City in a week. And the third time he'd supported the museum vocally in the past few days.

I needed to know why.

I also needed to find Asaar, but I had no clue how to go about that.

The Jersey City Art Museum was the only place both these men were connected to in some mysterious way. So that's where I'd go for answers. Bruno didn't have to hang around if he didn't like it. "You don't have to come with me, you know," I told him over my shoulder.

"Shut up," he replied.

I laughed a little. We reached the museum, and I went straight to the back door. It was locked, but there was a little keypad near the lock. I raised my eyebrow at Bruno.

"What, you think they gave me the code?" He was a mixture of shocked and amused. "I was just there for a one-time gig."

"You hack into things all the time!"

"Yeah, but I need the right tools for that," he replied. "My laptop, for one."

"Crap." I thought for a minute. I could try banging on the door and shouting like I had the last time I was here, but Bruno would probably die of mortification. Or he'd drag me away kicking and screaming. Either way, it probably wasn't the right action.

"Let's go to the front." I led him out of the alley and to the main entrance.

"Kamala, this isn't gonna work!" Bruno protested.

I ignored him. I knew the chances of anyone even giving me the time of day were low, but I had to try. I was determined to do something, anything.

Sitting around, waiting for things to happen, for Asaar to make a reappearance or for Kingpin to reveal his plans, was stupidity. Delilah showing up would be okay with me, even if she tried to bury me with her super-strong punches and kicks.

I'd take them, just to get some answers.

"You know, Bruno," I said as we trudged up the stairs to the front, "I was wrong. My dream vacation would never be sleeping for a week."

"What are you talking about? What dream vacation?" Poor Bruno sounded totally lost.

I reached the top and pulled open the heavy glass door. "The essay for English class? Never mind. I just meant I'm too determined and inquisitive to stay still doing nothing."

He held open the door for me as I passed through, like a proper gentleman. "That's true," he said in my ear. "You are all that."

And that's when I realized that I might have been wrong about one more thing. There were definitely butterflies in my stomach.

Not a lot, just one or two. But they were there, letting me know that I wasn't as indifferent to Bruno Carrelli as I wanted to be.

There was a long line of people buying tickets at the museum front desk. I stood to the side, in no hurry to reach the counter until I knew what I wanted to say.

Bruno kept silent for once, which was perfect. I didn't need his questions and comments right then.

From the corner of my eye, toward the left of the entry, I spied a sleek blond head of hair.

Then I heard a queenly voice say, "Ms. Hibbert wants these files right away, please!" and my plan of action fell into place like little bricks in some kids' video game. *Click-click-click*, a hundred points, woo-hoo!

I grabbed Bruno's arm and pulled him toward the side of the entryway. "Hi, Brittany. Remember me?"

Brittany looked up, her face blank. "No . . ."

I stepped closer, trying to smile like a normal person, even though desperation flowed through my veins. If she didn't remember me, it was game over. Or she could just pretend she didn't. She'd seemed pretty mean-girl-ish the first couple of times we'd met. "I came by the other day to get my spare keys?" I prompted. "You were, ahem, nice enough to let me in."

"I can be very nice if I want," Brittany said dryly.

Behind me, Bruno chuckled in his throat.

Brittany looked at him, and her lips curved into a smile. "Oh, hello! How can I help you?"

Seriously? That was all it took for this girl to turn helpful? Way to knock down a century's worth of feminism, lady. "Uh, we're here to ask about the robbery," I inserted quickly. "We were there when the alarm went off, remember?"

Brittany looked my way again, smile gone and eyebrows wrinkled. "Why do you need to know anything?"

Bruno jumped and gave me a nudge. "We feel really concerned about the theft," he told Brittany, smiling persuasively. "I'm Bruno, and this is my friend Kamala."

I gave a little wave.

She stared at me. "Okay . . . ?"

Bruno added quickly, "She's especially invested in the exhibit because it's her culture, you know."

Brittany narrowed her eyes at me. "You're Indian?"

"I'm American," I told her, trying to keep my tone even. "But my parents are from Pakistan."

"But the Mughal exhibit is from India."

I gritted my teeth. "India and Pakistan used to be one country. The Mughals ruled over that entire area centuries ago."

"Are you sure?" she asked, in the same tone one would use with a small child who insisted he'd seen a ghost.

"Yes, I'm sure!" I replied loudly. "It's basic world history."

Bruno nudged me harder this time, probably telling me to back off. I nudged him back.

Bruno stepped forward. "Listen, Brittany, could you please tell us everything is okay with the exhibit? Maybe answer a couple of quick questions? We're just concerned."

Brittany dismissed me with an eye roll and turned a bright smile at Bruno. "Of course, Bruno, I completely understand. What would you like to know?"

"Did the police catch the thief?"

I knew the answer was no, but it was a good question. That's the first thing a regular "concerned" teenager would ask.

"Unfortunately, no," Brittany said. "The surveillance cameras had been disabled, so we couldn't get anything from them."

We already knew this, but Bruno nodded like it was brand-new information.

I just kept still, listening.

"That's scary," Bruno said. "I hope everyone is fine?"

"Our curator has recommended crisis counseling for staff," Brittany replied, looking around like she was divulging state secrets. "I think it's a bit much, but whatever."

"Taking care of your mental health is so important," Bruno said, nodding wisely.

"There are videos of Ms. Marvel fighting with a masked man in the alley," I said, trying to keep them on subject. "Surely the police know about it?"

Brittany sent me a pitying look. "Videos can be doctored. Or it could be two kids dressed up in costumes. Who knows?"

I bristled. Who was she calling a kid? And Asaar was *old*.

"So basically, the police are regarding this as a regular robbery?" I bit out. "Not super hero related?"

"Definitely not," Brittany replied firmly. "They're not stupid."

"I'll show you—"

"What will happen to the exhibit?" Bruno interrupted, pushing me a little.

I pushed him back but stopped talking. There was no point. This Brittany person wasn't the one in charge. She was just a glorified lackey, relaying information to us.

A lackey with an attitude.

Brittany brightened. "It's still business as usual at the museum. We're not letting a small theft get the best of us. Those gorgeous items need to be displayed to the world."

"Something we can agree on," Bruno said, flashing his teeth.

I rolled my eyes hard. Why was he flirting with her, for God's sake? Couldn't he see how fake and empty-headed she was?

Brittany had gotten an internship at the museum, so she was probably very smart. They didn't just give out internships to anyone, I was sure.

But still. That didn't excuse her behavior.

"Wilson Fisk said he would leave no stone unturned to find the thief," I said loudly.

Brittany turned to me, frowning. "Yes, so? That's nice of him, right?"

I tried not to laugh in her face. If there was ever an adjective one couldn't use to describe Fisk, it would be *nice*. He was the complete, utter opposite of nice.

"Kamala was just wondering why he was so involved in the museum's work," said Bruno, saving me once again.

Not that I needed saving from this little mean-girl blondie.

The blondie in question smiled. "He's our biggest sponsor, as you know. That's why he feels invested, I suppose. He loves the artifacts. He really does."

I must have looked disbelieving, because she started talking faster. "No, really. He came to inspect all the pieces before we launched the exhibit, wanted to know all the details about each one, what time period it was from, who owned it before, and even what myths and legends were associated with it."

"Myths and legends?" I broke in. "Why would he want to know that?"

She shrugged. "He was really into it, that's all."

Bruno and I exchanged knowing looks. This was it. The Kingpin connection.

My brain was practically whirring with this new information, trying to make sense of it, trying to figure out the bigger picture.

The door behind us opened, and a man peeked through. "Brittany, Hibbert's looking for you."

Brittany flipped her hair and gave us—Bruno, really—a last smile. "Sorry, I have to go."

"Sure," he replied. "Thank you for your time."

Her eyes gleamed. "If you want, you can give me your contact info. I can try to get some answers for you later."

"Perfect."

Bruno and I fought all the way to my house.

"I can't believe you gave her your number!" I said for the tenth time.

"It's not my fault! She asked for it!"

My eyes widened. "So you just . . . just . . . hand out your number to girls who ask for it?"

He shrugged uncomfortably. "I mean, if they're pretty, yes."

My eyes widened further. I think my mouth dropped to the train floor. "Wow."

"No!" he said quickly. "Not only pretty. Smart too. She was really intelligent, and clever . . ."

"Bruno, she had no idea India and Pakistan used to be one country!" I interrupt.

He shrugged again. "Well, most people don't know that. Doesn't mean they're not smart."

I shook my head and looked away. "Whatever."

He was quiet for a minute. "Forget Brittany," he finally said. "I think our fact-finding mission was a success, don't you?"

I sighed deeply, trying to get rid of the weird, yucky feelings I'd had watching Bruno and Brittany chatting it up. "Yeah, we did learn quite a bit." Then my ire came flying back. "Oh my God, what a bad employee she is, gossiping about museum business with a couple of strangers!"

Bruno gave a little laugh. "Are you serious, Kamala?"

"Yes!" I replied indignantly. "They should fire her. I'm one hundred percent sure she's not supposed to do that!"

"But it helped us, right? We got some info we needed." He looked at me for a minute. "Why are you so upset about this? What do you care who I'm talking to?"

Talking to? Okay, maybe he hadn't meant it like that, but still. "It's nothing to do with you," I insist. "I just don't like her."

"Why? She let you into the kitchen the other day to find your supposed spare keys. And today we had no idea how to get our questions answered until she was there to spill the beans."

I looked out the window. We were almost at our stop, and then my house was just a few minutes' walk away. I needed to make sure we parted on talking terms. I needed to get my stupid emotions under control.

I wasn't even sure why I was having said emotions. I hadn't lied to Nakia. I didn't really like Bruno that way.

Maybe. Probably.

"You're right," I said, looking back at him. "It's none of my business who you give your number to."

He sighed like he'd been waiting for a different response. "Good," he said quietly.

The bus came to a whooshing stop, and we stepped out. I waited until we were out on the street before saying, "Ammi told me that some of the Mughal artifacts have myths around them."

"And Kingpin was interested in the myths too," Bruno said thoughtfully. "That's concerning."

"Exactly!" I snapped my fingers. "We already know about Shah Jahan's spectacles, thanks to your miraculously healed injury. . . ."

Bruno held up his left hand, palm upward. "Not a scratch! I half don't believe it even happened."

"It happened," I snapped. "Believe it."

Bruno's eyebrows flew up at my tone. "I trust you."

"Thank you." I took a deep breath. "So anyway, seems like Kingpin is sponsoring the Mughal exhibit to get close to the magical artifacts?"

"There's more than one?"

I shrugged. "I dunno. Maybe? We don't know what myths

and legends are circling about the others. We only know about the spectacles."

Bruno hummed in response. "So what do you think his motive is? To steal them?"

"Makes sense," I replied. "That's what Delilah meant when she told me he's aware of the theft."

"Okay, we need to find out as much as we can about the myths, then!"

"I'll ask Ammi, and . . ." I snapped my fingers again. "Oh! We could take that guided tour of the exhibit tomorrow after school. Aamir said they talk about some of the legends."

"Genius!" Bruno grinned. "Let's ask Nakia to come with us. She can take a closer look for her article."

"It's a date!" I flushed. "I mean, it's a great idea."

He burst out laughing as if he knew what a blunder I'd made. "Thank you. See you tomorrow, Kamala."

When I got home, I went straight into the kitchen to wash my hands and eat some food.

Walking and thinking—and dealing with bratty interns—made a girl hungry.

"Salaam alaikum, Ammi!" I called. There was no time like the present to ask about the myths.

"Upstairs, beta!" she called back.

There was a plate of biryani covered with foil in the fridge. I took out half and heated it in the microwave. I guessed story time could wait.

I was halfway through my plate when Abu came downstairs with a paper in his hand. His face was drawn into heavy lines, and his shoulders were slumped. "What happened?" I asked, slightly alarmed.

He sank down on the chair next to me. "I was reading my friend Fahad's letter just now."

"What did he write?" I asked, putting my spoon down. Fahad Uncle had been sick on and off for several years. Sometimes he was in the hospital, but other times, he was doing well and traveling the world.

He sent Abu letters from every country he visited. I'd assumed this letter was the same, but it didn't explain why Abu looked so sad and worried.

"He's very sick," Abu replied heavily. "His cancer is back, worse than ever."

The biryani turned to stone in my stomach. "Oh no! Will he be okay?"

"I don't know, beta." Abu stared at the letter with a faraway look on his face, as if he were miles away. "Fahad is my best friend, the one who's always been there for me, even when we lived so far away from each other. He's the first person I called when both you and Aamir were born, you know that?"

I hadn't known that. "I get it," I said softly. "He's your ride or die."

"Hmm." Abu nodded. "The point is, Fahad is very important to me, and I don't know when—if—I'll see him again."

"I'm so sorry, Abu," I whispered. Poor Fahad Uncle and his family! His wife must be so worried.

How would I feel if Abu or Ammi were badly sick, the kind of sick one might not recover from?

A sudden wave of nausea shot through me. I pushed away my plate and ran to the stairs. For the first time in a while, I wasn't thinking about school or my super hero duties, or anything else. My mind was an echoing blank. My eyes felt wet and gritty, like I hadn't slept in a while and was really sad about it.

"Kamala?" Abu called out.

I turned with one hand on the banister. "Yes, Abu?"

"I'm thinking of going to Lahore, to see my friend one last time."

I nodded shakily. "Yeah, that's probably a good idea."

I collapsed on my bed, my eyes going straight to a little painting on the wall above my desk. It was a picture of Minar-e-Pakistan, an iconic structure that looked a little like the Eiffel Tower. Fahad Uncle had sent it to me a year ago, on my last birthday. He'd included a little bit of the history of the building in a note he'd written by hand, and that's how I'd known that it was a symbol of freedom and national identity for Pakistanis.

I bowed my head and began to recite the prayer Sheikh Abdullah had taught me when I was in Sunday school. *Ashfi wa antash-shaafi. Ashfi wa antash-shaafi.* There was more, but I couldn't remember it. I could look it up online, but I didn't want to get sidetracked.

God knew what was in my heart. I frantically hoped Fahad Uncle would get well soon.

My phone rang, and I picked it up. "Hey, Bruno."

"Uh, hey. Why are you sounding so . . . low?"

"Abu just got some bad news about a friend," I replied, looking at the Minar painting again. Staring, more like.

"I'm sorry," Bruno said. "Wanna talk about it?"

I sighed. "This old friend of his, Fahad Uncle, has cancer. They've been treating it for a while, and it was manageable, but now it's worse."

"Worse how?"

"Worse like he probably won't survive," I admitted in a choked voice.

"That's horrible. I'm so sorry. I'll tell Nonna, I'm sure she'll want to send over some food to your family."

"No need. Abu is going to Lahore to visit his friend."

"That's good." Bruno fell silent, but not in an awkward

way. It was comforting, like he was giving me time to rest with my sadness.

Finally, I cleared my throat. "Um, why did you call?"

"Oh! I was wondering if you've had a chance to ask your mom about the myths about Mughal artifacts. Did she have any stories to share?"

I perked up a little. This was just the distraction I needed. "Not yet, but I'll see if Ammi has time. She may be helping Abu pack and stuff. He's not great at that sort of thing."

Bruno chuckled. "Didn't he forget all his shirts on one trip?"

I chortled. "Oh my God, yes! It was some trip when we were kids. He brought a bunch of pants and no shirts. Ammi was so annoyed!"

"Your parents are a hoot."

"Well, let's not get carried away." I realized I was grinning.

There was another brief silence, and then Bruno said, "So are you going with your dad? To Lahore, I mean."

"What? No. Why would I do that?"

"To pay your respects to your Fahad Uncle. Seems like you love him a lot."

My grin faded. It was true. Fahad Uncle had been a part of my life since forever. But going to Pakistan seemed a stretch. Didn't it? "It's the middle of school. I can't just . . ."

Bruno continued like he didn't care he'd made me sad

again. "You have the spectacles," he insisted. "He's sick. You could heal him, like you healed me!"

My heart skipped a beat, then started to race. "We have no proof it can actually do that, Bruno! A little cut is very different from freaking cancer!"

"I know that," Bruno said soothingly. "But don't you want to find out if it's possible?"

I took a deep breath to try to calm my heartbeat down to manageable levels. "You're actually suggesting that I smuggle a priceless, ancient, possibly magical artifact out of the country onto a rickety plane and then parade around Lahore with it . . . ?"

"Well, *smuggle* is a strong word. More like *sneak*."

"Bruno, be serious."

"I'm perfectly serious, Kamala. Tell your dad to take you with him. See your Fahad Uncle. Spend some time with him. See if the spectacles work on him. If not, no harm done, right?"

I sighed. "Right."

"Also . . ." Bruno paused. "Isn't Lahore where Shareef Deen is from?"

I blinked rapidly. "Well," I replied slowly, "PakPro's website says its headquarters are in Lahore, and that Deen grew up there."

"Great! While you're there, you can do some fact-finding on this Deen character."

"Fact-finding?" I cried. "No! I can't go knocking on every door to find a guy who wrote some incredibly articulate and persuasive articles and ask him why he's sponsoring an exhibit in America."

"Why not?"

"Because . . . because . . ." I looked around my room wildly. "It sounds insane, that's why! Who does that?"

I heard beeping on the line. "Hold on a sec," Bruno said. "I'm going to put Nakia on the line."

"Aargh! Bruno!"

The phone rang twice, and Nakia picked up. "What's up, babes?"

"Nakia, you're a journalist, right?" Bruno asked.

"Trying to be," she replied.

"Well, in your expert opinion," Bruno continued, "if a journalist wants to find out something important, they'll travel a long distance, won't they? Say, if they need to interview someone in another city or country? Maybe take pictures and investigate a place?"

"Sure," Nakia replied. "If her expenses were covered, then she'd go anywhere for the story."

"Bingo!" Bruno sounded very pleased with himself.

I mock-gasped. "Nakia, et tu?"

"What?" She laughed. "It's true. Journalists go anywhere and everywhere for the story."

"Well, I'm not a journalist," I retorted.

"Doesn't matter," Bruno said firmly. "You want to find out more about Shareef Deen, who lives in Lahore. You have the opportunity to go to Lahore. Take it. Find out all his secrets. See if you can meet with him. The newspapers say he's very reclusive and doesn't give interviews, but maybe he'll be willing to talk to a girl who's visiting family instead."

I groaned. "I hate it when you make sense, Bruno!"

"What's going on?" Nakia interrupted. "You're going to Lahore?"

Another groan. "Ugh, yes, apparently."

Abu was in his bedroom, sitting in the armchair with his tablet. "What are you doing?" I asked as I came closer.

He looked up. "Checking airline tickets."

"Must be expensive since you're buying last minute."

He made a humming sound and went back to the tablet.

"You didn't come down for dinner," I accused.

"Wasn't hungry."

I bit my lip, not sure what to say next. Talking to Abu on ordinary days could be difficult. Right now, with the whole sadness of Fahad Uncle's cancer news, it seemed like torture.

Finally, Abu looked back up. "What do you want, Kamala?"

"Um, if it's not too late, I'd like to go to Lahore with you." I shrugged, trying to act like it was no big deal.

His eyebrows flew up. "You?"

"Uh, yeah, I wanna see Fahad Uncle, like you said . . . maybe for the last time."

"What about school? What about your grades?" Abu squinted. "Is this your way of playing—what do they call it? Hockey?"

"Hooky," I corrected with a little eye roll. Nothing major, because that would be seen as disrespectful.

"Doesn't even make sense," Abu grumbled. "What in the world is a hooky?"

"I have no idea." I sat down next to him. "Look, it's just for a few days, right? I don't have any tests or major assignments coming up. And I'll get notes from Bruno so I don't miss anything."

"I don't know, Kamala. . . ."

I leaned forward eagerly. "And I'll study for a couple of hours every day, even in Lahore. Promise!"

Abu looked at me silently, like he wasn't buying a thing I was selling.

I sighed. I couldn't tell him about Shareef Deen, or the spectacles and how they could maybe, possibly help his best friend, but at least I could tell him the partial truth. "Look, I spoke with Nakia and Bruno, and both of them thought it would be a good idea to . . . uh . . . to visit the land of my, you know, my paternal ancestors."

"That would be my family?"

"Yup." I nodded again. "I mean, it's a good opportunity. I've gone to Karachi before with Ammi, but never to Lahore."

Abu smiled faintly. "Hmm, Lahore is superior to Karachi, you know."

"Ha! Don't let Ammi hear that!" I smiled back. "And, uh, I want to see Minar-e-Pakistan."

"You do?" Abu's eyebrows jumped. "How do you know about that?"

"Fahad Uncle sent me a picture of it once, remember?"

Abu's smile disappeared, and he slumped back in his chair. "I didn't remember that."

"Yeah, I love how he's always sending us gifts and things. He's a great uncle, even if he's not related to us."

"That's very true." I worried for a second that Abu would burst into tears, his eyes looked so sad. But then he took a deep breath and went back to his tablet like nothing had happened. "Okay, you're going! That's good—think of it as an adventure!"

I wasn't sure *adventure* was the right word, but I smiled anyway and gave Abu a thumbs-up. "I'm going!" I repeated loudly. "Yay!"

The bathroom door opened, and Ammi came out. She was wearing a pink pajama set with white flowers. "What are you so happy about?" she asked.

"I'm going to Pakistan!" I almost yelled. Now that it was decided, I was starting to get excited. Seeing Minar-e-Pakistan with my own eyes would be epic. And hugging Fahad Uncle, telling him I appreciated all his love and attention over the years? Yeah, that would be pretty special too.

"Good for you," Ammi replied, walking over to the bed. "Now go to sleep, it's almost midnight."

I checked the clock on the wall. "Ammi, you do know that nine and twelve are two different numbers, right?" I joked. "You can't say it's midnight until it's actually twelve o'clock!"

"You think I'm stupid?" Ammi patted my head. "If I say it's almost nine, you'll think, oh, there's plenty of time, no need to settle down right now. But if you think it's closer to midnight, you'll hurry to go to bed. It's psychology."

I stared at her. "It's not psychology—it's lying!"

"No, no, not lying." Ammi pursed her lips. "Look at it as tricking your brain to do something it wouldn't normally do. Someone shared a clip in my WhatsApp group, you know. A scientist did research on rats—"

I stood up quickly. "I don't wanna know."

"But it's science!" Ammi protested.

"Good night!" I walked to the bedroom door and opened it.

"Kamala!" Abu called at the last minute. "Go tell your brother. Might as well take him along too."

My shoulders slumped. This was totally unexpected. The thought of Aamir being his irritating self on a twenty-hour plane ride was enough to give me a headache. Dang Bruno and his stupid ideas.

"Go on," Abu said, pointing to the door. "Go tell him right now."

"But . . ."

"No buts. It's a family trip to my birthplace. We'll go tomorrow evening."

I didn't tell Aamir immediately. I went to my room and paced a little bit.

Now that Abu had agreed to take me with him, I was rethinking the whole plan.

There was no way the spectacles could cure cancer, for crying out loud.

What if they can, Kamala?

I fell backward onto my bed with a groan. I didn't really doubt the spectacles, if I was being honest. The fact that three villains—and one repatriation warrior, ha!—were after them made it obvious that we were talking serious power.

The bigger problem was my role as Ms. Marvel. I couldn't just disappear from my patrol duties for a week, maybe more.

Who would take care of the citizens of Jersey City? The second Delilah or the Shocker—or any of the other riffraff that prowled the streets after dark—knew I was gone, there'd be chaos.

How could I shirk my responsibility to millions, just for the sake of one uncle?

I stared at my ceiling for a long time, trying to bury my guilt and worry. Trying not to imagine a scenario where Delilah went back to the museum and sent her energy blast right through the glass windows.

She'd feel nothing if someone got hurt.

As opposed to me, who would feel like crap. I already did, and it was all in my imagination.

With another groan, I picked up my phone and scrolled through the messages. Maybe Bruno could talk me down from the edge of madness.

My thumb paused at a meme. It was the one from Kate Bishop.

I sat up quickly. Of course! Kate could help! She always told me she was happy to help if I needed it.

Well, I needed it now.

Hey, I'm taking a trip to Pakistan with my dad. Can you keep an eye on things in Jersey City for a few days?

I followed up with a GIF of a guy dressed like a sunflower saying *THANK YOU SUNSHINE.*

Kate took less than a minute to reply. *Of course, don't worry about it. Have fun on your trip.*

This time, I sent a heartfelt *thank you so much* instead of a GIF.

Anytime. We gal pals have to stick together.

I leapt off the bed, feeling a hundred pounds lighter. With a grin, I headed to Aamir's room to tell him the good news.

Knowing my brother, he'd have a lot to say about this trip.

The door was open, so I peeked in. Aamir was standing over his bed, a pile of clothes in his hands.

"Hey, guess where we're going, big bro!"

Aamir gave me a brief look. "I already know."

"How . . . ?"

"Abu just came by. Said he was sure you didn't tell me, like you were supposed to." Aamir gave me another look. "Don't worry, I didn't snitch and say you never showed up."

I rolled my eyes. "Gee, thanks."

"You're welcome." I stepped inside and saw the small carry-on suitcase on his bed. "You're packing already?"

"I don't do things last minute like you."

I gritted my teeth. He didn't know that I was juggling way more than the average teenager. I usually didn't have time to do things like packing and studying in advance.

Lately, I felt like I was flying by the seat of my pants all the time.

Aamir shoved a pair of jeans into the carry-on. At least, he tried. They didn't really fit with everything else that was stuffed inside, all messy and haphazard.

My annoyance dimmed a little. "Calm down, dude, you can't just push clothes in. You'll ruin them."

"It's fine," he replied. "I can do it."

I snatched the jeans from him. "If you roll them up and place them side by side, there's more room." I rolled up a pair of pants and showed him.

"Wow, genius!" Aamir's voice was mocking.

"It is," I agreed nicely. My life had changed ever since I learned the rolling trick. He'd become a true believer in time too.

"So going to Pakistan with Abu was all your idea?" he asked. "That's major."

"Were you eavesdropping?"

He shook his head. "Abu told me, and I quote: 'Be nice to your sister. She really wants to go. I don't want any trouble.'"

"Ha!" I put another pants roll into the case. "By *trouble* he means arguing. And fighting. And name-calling."

"Yes, I figured that out." Aamir raised an eyebrow. "I don't do all that, you know. I'm a good Muslim. It's all part of my religion."

My mouth fell open at his arrogance. "Your religion? Dude, it's my religion too!"

He shrugged. "Is it really?"

I pushed the rest of the clothes I was holding into his chest. "Oh my God! You're so . . . so . . ."

"So what?"

I threw up my hands. "I dunno! Arrogant. Egotistical. Conceited. Take your pick!"

Aamir rolled up a long-sleeve T-shirt and held it up to his eyes. It was crooked, and one sleeve hung out. I grimaced and snatched it from him. "Give it!"

He looked at me. "I'm not arrogant, you know, Kamala."

"Yeah, sure." I rerolled the shirt and tucked it in. "You're just . . . you."

"I know my strengths," he insisted. "That's not being conceited. That's being factual."

"Knowing Quranic verses and quoting long hadith aren't the only things in life, Aamir," I said softly. "All that doesn't mean much if you can't be a good person."

He gasped. "I'm a great person!"

I bark out a laugh. "Like I said, arrogant."

He scowled at me. "Forget it. You don't understand. You're just a little girl who can't even do her physics homework without help from a guy who secretly likes you. You've never gone away from home by yourself or had a big adventure. It's hard for you to see me as who I am."

I just stood and blinked at him.

A scream rushed up my throat, but I caught it before the noise exploded out of my mouth. There were at least ten things wrong in his statement. There was so much he didn't know about me. How far I'd traveled as Ms. Marvel, not just around the world but to other dimensions. Other realities.

Truly, Aamir had no clue about the adventures I'd had. The danger I'd been in. The incredible times I'd experienced.

I kept my mouth shut and watched him roll clothes like an expert. Slowly, my heart rate went down to something close to normal.

Or as normal as it could be in my brother's presence.

My phone pinged. So did Aamir's. We both checked our messages together, without looking at each other.

Tickets have been bought. We leave tomorrow evening at 6 pm.

I took a deep, trembling breath. I wasn't sure what I was still doing in my brother's room. I had to pack and finish up some homework. Pray for patience. Something.

"Tomorrow at six, huh?" Aamir said, looking up.

His face was red, like he was ashamed of his outburst. I doubted it, though. He was never ashamed of acting like he knew everything, and I nothing. In fact, he was proud of it.

"I'm sure it will be fun," I muttered.

In the Khan family, patience was the key to sanity.

Ammi whispered this in my ear when she dropped us off at the airport the next evening. "Don't fight with your brother," she told me. "Or your father."

"What else is there in life?" I joked.

She gave me a *What's wrong with you?* look.

"Okay, fine," I said. "No fighting. But if they start it . . ."

"Kamala," Ammi sighed. "You know what I learned in the last twenty-some years of marriage with your father?"

"To cook in large quantities?"

Her lips twitched. "That too. But more importantly, I learned that arguing doesn't help. The Khan men are very stubborn. They don't know how to listen."

"And the Khan women?"

"Ah, the women!" Ammi hugged me. "We are the sacrificing ones. The strong ones."

"The sassy ones," I added.

"Yes, that too." Ammi shooed me out of the car. "Just remember, be patient with them."

I scrambled to the sidewalk, where Abu and Aamir were waiting with our luggage. At the last minute, I stuck my face into the window to stare at her. "Did someone share this nugget in your WhatsApp group?"

Ammi shook her head. "Those groups have lots of good advice, beta, it's true. But this is my own little piece of wisdom. Something I've learned over the years." She paused and tapped her chin. "Hmm, maybe I should share it in the group. Let the other ladies also benefit."

I narrowed my eyes and tried not to scream. "Yes, but how is that even possible? Showing patience is so passive! Like . . . like admitting defeat."

"It's really not," she said with a little smile. "Try it sometime."

Abu growled behind me. "Come on, Kamala. We'll miss the flight."

"Go, beta." Ammi patted my cheek. "And try to have fun. See a bit of Lahore. It's a lovely place."

I leaned down to kiss her cheek. "Khuda hafiz, Ammi."

"Khuda hafiz," she replied. "Remember what I told you!"

"Yup, Khan women are sassy badasses!"

"Kamala!" Aamir called harshly.

Ammi raised her eyebrow at me before driving off. I bit back my retort and turned away from Aamir.

He followed me. "Don't use bad language, okay? This is a public space. How you act reflects on all Muslims."

I didn't say anything. I just sighed patiently and walked away.

"Kamala! Wait! Didn't you hear me?"

I giggled under my breath. Maybe Ammi was right. Showing patience had its own reward.

The plane ride to Lahore was long. Very, very long.

I slept for a few hours, then woke up and fiddled with the in-flight entertainment. Aamir was sitting next to me, watching some sort of documentary on the screen set into the seat in front of him.

I found a gangster movie, with guns and bombs and action, and settled in to watch.

"Astaghfirullah," Aamir whispered in my ear.

I opened my mouth to tell him off, then closed it again. *Be patient,* Ammi had said. I fixed my eyes on the screen and listened to the explosions and music filling my ears through the headphones.

Aamir lectured a little more about watching age-appropriate content, but I hardly heard him. The movie was loud enough to scare the dead.

Finally, my brother went back to his boring documentary.

I tried to focus on my movie, but my concentration was lost. Plus, watching the hero and villain struggle in a bar fight was making my thoughts stray. I kept thinking of Asaar, and the way he'd fought with me. How quick he'd been on his feet. How vibrantly shocking his green-and-white energy had been.

I reached into the bag at my feet and took out my phone. I'd saved the video Bruno had sent me, and I clicked on it.

Watching myself fight with Asaar sent a chill down my back. Or maybe it was the air inside the plane, set to almost freezing for some god-awful reason.

The video was grainy and shaky, but it didn't matter. My memories filled in a lot of the blanks. I already knew my own fighting style, how I jumped and punched and embiggened. What my face looked like just before I made a cool move. But the video was the only way I could analyze Asaar's moves. So that's what I did. Again and again, I watched the video from start to finish, taking mental notes of how Asaar jumped back nimbly whenever I approached, how he raised his hands almost up to his face and curled his fingers into claws before sending out his fiery energy blasts. He stepped farther away from me when I embiggened but closer when I tried to punch him. That was interesting.

I also noticed he favored his right leg just a tiny bit, like he had an old injury that still bothered him. Or maybe he was unconsciously protecting it.

Whatever the reason, I could use this against him in our next exchange.

At the end of the video, there was a close-up of his green-and-white energy. I leaned forward a little, wanting to figure out what it was made of.

My eyes landed on Asaar's left wrist, where the crown tattoo was clearly visible. I'd seen it before, when I was fighting him outside the museum. But somehow, seeing it again niggled the back of my mind, like a tiny itch. I had a hunch it was a connection, but to what? And why?

Aamir leaned toward me again. "Stop watching fights, Kamala. No wonder you're so aggressive all the time."

I set down my phone carefully and cracked my knuckles. I'd show him aggressive.

Then I remembered Ammi's words. Be patient. Be strong. The two are not mutually exclusive.

I smiled sweetly at my annoying brother and said, "Sure," like it was no big deal.

His eyes widened; then he shrugged and went back to his documentary.

Perfect. Crisis averted. Nobody wanted to see a pair of siblings fighting it out thirty thousand feet in the air.

Plus, my mind was still itching.

I picked my phone again and scrolled through the saved files until I found what I was looking for. The decade-old article about Shareef Deen's factory incident. With everything else going on, I'd forgotten all about the two pictures included in the article.

I peered at the first picture. A group of men dressed in shalwar kameez stood outside the factory. They looked like workers or laborers, with tired faces and hands holding tools. One man in the center stood out. He was dressed in a suit and very, very familiar.

It was the man beside Kingpin at the museum press conference the night of the exhibit opening.

The caption below the picture said *Mr. Shareef Deen meeting with factory workers to listen to their complaints.*

I enlarged the photo with my fingers, zooming in on Deen. It was the only picture of him I'd been able to find online, so it made sense to examine it carefully.

Yup. It was the same guy for sure. I'd sort of figured as much earlier, but it was nice to have the confirmation.

I smiled to myself. Now I had a face to go with the name of the person I was unofficially going to Lahore to find.

If all else failed, I could walk around the city, asking if anyone had seen this man. Ha!

My smile dropped as I switched to the second picture. It was a close-up of Deen with a factory worker, probably from the same event as the first one. Deen was shaking hands with the other man, with his left hand on the factory worker's shoulder.

I stared at the left hand, transfixed.

It had a crown tattoo.

My heart jumped in my chest. The tattoo looked very much like the one Asaar had on his wrist. Just to make sure, I switched back to the video I'd been watching earlier and checked.

Yup, the crowns were exactly the same.

Same image, on the same place on the left wrist. The thumb had a little scar near the nail. That was the same too.

Hold. The. Phone. This was epic! I had zero doubt now.

Asaar and Shareef Deen were the same person.

I spent the rest of the flight with one question swirling round in my brain. Why was Deen standing proudly by Kingpin at the Mughal exhibit while also dressing up as Asaar and talking smack about artifact theft?

The air outside the Lahore airport was hot and musty.

I was tired and sweaty, which was a tragedy. I tried to air my pits by flapping my arms in the air like a crazed hen.

A woman next to me hissed "Excuse me" in a Desi accent.

"Sorry," I replied. "Just . . . it's so hot, you know?"

She shook her head and moved away from me and my stink. I gripped my backpack with both hands. The precious emerald spectacles were hidden safely inside, and I was more than capable of fighting off any robbers who tested me.

If only I could also fight off this heat.

Aamir cleared his throat and smoothed out his forehead. "Look, Kamala, Lahore is not like Jersey City."

"No kidding," I snapped, completely forgetting my patience rule. "The temperature must be a good twenty degrees higher."

"That's not what I meant."

I was on a roll. "Can you believe it's not even summer yet? How hot must it get here in June or July?"

Aamir rolled his eyes. "I meant that Lahore can be quite dangerous, all right? There's no law and order here. In all of Pakistan, actually. There are gangs and killers and who knows what else."

Was he serious? I totally regretted breaking my silence.

How could he continue this superior act for so long? Didn't it get exhausting?

It was definitely exhausting listening to him.

"You're exaggerating," I bit out. "And stereotyping."

"No! I'm not!" he insisted. "They have a lot of crime here."

"So do American cities. We literally had a theft at the museum last week!"

"No, it's worse here, because . . . well, just because." He waved a finger in my face. "Stay close to me when we go into the city, okay? Don't go anywhere alone. They don't treat women well, especially if you're not with a man."

"Wow, dude. You're messed up." I narrowed my eyes. "We haven't even set foot inside the city and you're already insulting it left and right. Why did you even come here if you think it's so beneath you?"

Aamir frowned. "It's not an insult if it's true."

"Oh my—" I broke off and spun around to face away from him. "Forget it. I should've remembered, there's no way to be patient or kind to you. It's basically impossible."

"Kamala, I'm serious!"

"I'm serious too." I refused to look back at him. "Just stay away from me."

Fahad Uncle and his family lived at the edge of Lahore. I figured this out because it took us forever to reach from the airport.

It was fine, though. I watched the sights and sounds of Lahore in the early afternoon from the taxi window. Everything was bright and sunny. Wind rushed into my face and made me forget how hot it was outside.

There were cars around us, of course, but also motorcycles that went too fast, and colorful buses with musical horns and people hanging off the sides. "Whoa!" I whispered, tugging Aamir's sleeve, forgetting that I was mad at him.

"That looks dangerous," he whispered back.

I shook my head. Of course my careful, unable-to-take-a-risk brother would think that. "It looks like fun."

"No, it doesn't."

I leaned over to Abu, where he sat in the front passenger seat. "Abu, can I take a ride on the bus tomorrow?"

Abu chuckled. "We'll see. Maybe a rickshaw too."

I'd never seen one of those, but they sounded cool. Based on the choked sound from Aamir, it would be a blast. "Good idea," I told Abu, and settled back to look out of my window again.

"Do you even know how awful those rickshaws can be?"

I sighed noisily. I was honestly so sick of Aamir. "Sure," I said, not looking at him.

"You'll regret it when it's going full speed, and you fall out of it and get crushed under a car or something."

This time I did look at him. "Way to be gory, Aamir!"

He looked angry and scared at the same time. "I told you, stay close to me and don't do stupid things."

"People ride those things all the time," I reminded him. I'd rather not talk to him at all, but he seemed a little stressed out. I didn't want him to have a freak-out so far away from home and Ammi.

Aamir opened his mouth to say something dire, probably, but Abu interrupted with a "We're here, kids."

I quickly peered out the window to see where *here* was.

The taxi slowed down next to a guarded entry. Before it came to a complete stop, Abu had leapt out and was talking to the guard. The man wrote something down, then spoke on his walkie-talkie.

"See—safe!" I pointed to the guard.

Aamir scoffed. "It's just an illusion. The only safety is with Allah."

"Yeah, but we're supposed to try our best too, right?" I snapped my fingers. "What's the saying about the camel?"

"Trust in Allah, but tie your camel," Aamir said reluctantly.

"Exactly. That guard with his cute little walkie-talkie is the equivalent of tying up the camel."

Abu came back to the taxi, a satisfied look on his face. "Let's go," he told the driver.

A gate near the guard opened slowly, and we drove into Fahad Uncle's neighborhood. I felt my lips curve into a smile as I watched. We were surrounded by tall white walls and lush trees. One house had a fountain in the front yard; another had a birdhouse shaped like a castle.

And birds. There were lots of birds everywhere, small brown sparrows by the dozens, even an eagle here or there. Their sounds were loud and melodious, unlike anything I'd ever heard before.

A sense of calm flowed into my chest, relaxing me for the first time since I began this trip.

My father was obviously feeling the same. "This is fantastic," Abu breathed. "Alhamdulillah."

"Haven't you been here before?" I asked, puzzled.

"No, I haven't. When we were teens, Fahad lived with his parents in a very different part of the city. Lots of noise and traffic. A bunch of apartments. Now he's an adult with a family of his own, and he's moved to this nicer area."

"It's safer here," I commented. "Look at the guards."

I nodded toward the far wall, where a few armed security guards stood at ease, talking under the shade of the tree.

"Yes, there's a sense of security here, that's for sure."

The taxi stopped outside a three-story house with a wrap-around porch and a garden in the front. Again, Abu leapt out before the taxi even stopped.

"Your father is eager, eh?" the driver said, laughing a little.

Aamir and I both nodded. We'd never seen Abu like this. He was usually angry or stressed out. It was like entering his birthplace had wiped away his worries.

Fahad Uncle didn't look too sick, which was a good thing.

I mean, his eyes were sunken and he looked frail, but I'd imagined way worse. I heaved a sigh of relief when he hugged me like he used to do when I was little. "How's my beti?" he asked in that hoarse voice of his.

Only, it was hoarser than normal.

I swallowed. That was because of his cancer. It was in his

throat and lungs, Abu had told us on the plane. "I'm good," I replied shakily. "How are you?"

He winked at me. "Grateful to Allah for everything."

He let me go and shook hands with Abu and Aamir. We were in a formal sitting room, with white leather furniture and blue and gold accents. It was pretty. Fahad Uncle's wife, Sumera, patted the couch where she was sitting, so I went to sit next to her. "Salaam alaikum, Aunty."

"Walaikum salaam, Kamala dear," she said. "Did you have a good flight?"

I nodded as I placed my backpack on the floor next to my feet. "I slept most of the way."

She smiled, but it was a sad little smile that made my heart ache. "That's good," she said in a low voice.

I looked down at my hands. I had no idea what to say to her. Should I tell her I was sorry about her husband's illness? Should I act like nothing was wrong, and we were just here on a normal family trip?

Ugh, someone should have taught me the protocol.

"Uh, your house is very beautiful," I offered.

Another smile, a little brighter this time. "Thank you. I decorated this room myself."

I looked around. "It's gorgeous." My eyes fell on the wall adjacent to us, where a series of small miniature paintings were hung. "Is that Mughal?"

"Yes. How did you know?" Sumera Aunty's smile broadened. She was really pretty now that the sad look was gone.

"There's an exhibit in our museum these days," I told her. "It's got all sorts of stunning artifacts from the Mughal era."

Abu turned his head toward us. "Kamala has been learning a little about our Mughal history!"

"Oh, really?" Sumera Aunty said. "That's nice. I didn't know American kids cared about Pakistani history."

"Not all history," Aamir jumped in. "Just the Mughals."

I kept quiet because that was mostly true. It wasn't something I was proud of, but with the American history and world history we had to learn in high school, it was tough to find time for anything more specific.

"The Mughals were . . . great at . . . creating art . . . spending their wealth," Fahad Uncle said, wheezing between every word. "Not so good at . . . governing . . . in the latter years."

"Ha! Very true!" Abu turned back to his friend. "Remember that boy in tenth grade who insisted he was a direct descendant from a Mughal emperor? How much fun we'd make of him!"

The two laughed; then Fahad Uncle went into a coughing fit that alarmed me so much, I sat forward. Did he need help? Could he breathe?

"He's okay, Kamala," Sumera Aunty told me. "Don't worry." Still, she watched her husband with worried eyes.

I sat back and tried to distract myself with the art around me.

An end table next to my couch was crammed with photographs. Fahad Uncle and Sumera Aunty stood in front of a variety of cool backdrops: the Colosseum in Rome, Big Ben in London, the Lincoln Memorial in D.C. . . .

"Wow, is that the Great Wall of China?" I gasped.

Sumera Aunty nodded. "Yes, Fahad and I travel a lot. Ever since he got his cancer diagnosis, he's insisted he wants to see the world."

"Oh, yeah?" I gulp. "Is it because . . . ?"

"Think of it as a bucket list. Most people keep putting off travel plans because they can't get away from the daily grind of life. But Fahad and I . . . we decided we should do this while we are still together. While he's still healthy and . . ."

She stopped, but I knew what she was going to say. Healthy and alive.

I looked over at Fahad Uncle, who'd stopped coughing now but looked even weaker than before. He was alive, but he didn't look healthy at all.

I nudged my backpack closer with my leg. I couldn't wait for a moment alone with him, to see if the spectacles would heal his cancer.

It was a long shot, but I was willing to try.

"Hello!"

Someone sat down next to me, shaking me out of my thoughts. It was a girl with Sumera Aunty's cheekbones, her hair in a short, shaggy cut. She was wearing jeans like me and a long collared shirt that was almost a kameez. Every one of her fingers were adorned with rings, and her wrists with multiple bracelets. They made me think of Nakia.

"I'm Maleeha," the girl said, her lips curved into a little smile, as if she knew the secrets of the universe.

"Hey," I replied warmly. Right away, this girl's style blew me away. She was so effortlessly cool.

"This is my niece," Sumera Aunty told me. "She's about your age, I think, Kamala."

"Nice to meet you," I offered politely.

"Same."

"Ah, Maleeha," Abu said loudly. "I remember you as a little girl when I visited Lahore years ago! You had pigtails tied off with yellow ribbons."

Maleeha smiled, flashing her dimples. "Wasn't it Khalil Gibran who said yesterday is but today's memory, and tomorrow is today's dream?"

Abu's face split into a grin. "Wah, wah! What a quote! We used to read Gibran in our college days, do you remember, Fahad?"

Maleeha looked at me with a raised eyebrow. Uh, did she want me to be impressed with her knowledge? I might not be able to quote Gibran, whoever he was, but I could make a super villain cry for his mommy like a baby. Too bad that was a skill I couldn't brag about in people's sitting rooms.

I smiled sweetly at her, then relaxed on the couch. Everyone chattered around me, but I was tired after the long flight, and my eyes flickered closed from time to time.

Soon, a servant came in with chai and snacks. "This is how you fry samosas, Kamala," Aamir joked, holding up a perfectly browned piece.

I narrowed my eyes at him. "Shut up," I hissed, then looked around guiltily because if Abu heard me, he'd get mad.

I didn't want him mad this week. I wanted him to be exactly how he was now, talking with his best friend, laughing at old memories, sharing food and chai.

Maleeha took a samosa and put it on my plate. "Here, try one. It's good."

I took a bite. Flavorful beef and onions, mixed with the taste of cumin and cilantro, burst onto my tongue. "Oh my God, delicious," I mumbled. "We don't get samosas like this in the States, that's for sure."

"We have the best food here. Better than anywhere else in Pakistan! Karachi may boast about all their restaurants, but they're wrong. Lahore is *the* foodie city!" She flashed her dimples again. I was realizing that this smile of hers was only 70 percent nice. The rest was pure arrogance.

Okay, this superior attitude was getting old. "My ammi is from Karachi," I needled. "She's always arguing that her city is better."

Maleeha scoffed. "Huh, there's no contest. Lahore rules. I'll take you around to all the restaurants once you've rested a bit."

"Oh my God, really?" I decided to forgive her. "That would be awesome!"

This time, Maleeha's smile was 100 percent nice. "I agree!"

Aamir frowned. "What are you girls talking about?"

I ignored him, but Maleeha didn't know any better, so she turned to explain. "Kamala and I are planning on going out to some restaurants."

"It's too dangerous," Aamir scoffed.

Maleeha's grin faded. "What are you talking about? Lahore is a great city. . . ."

I grabbed Maleeha's hand. "Forget him, he's nuts. Can you show me to my room? I really need to get out of these travel-funky clothes."

"Of course," she replied, standing up. "Let's go."

My room was small but very comfortably furnished with a single bed, a tufted chair, and a desk-and-bookshelf combo.

Maleeha showed me around briskly. "The bathroom is in the hallway outside. But towels and linens are in the closet in here."

"Uh, thanks," I said with a frown. I hadn't known she lived in this house.

The dimples made another appearance. "I came by yesterday to help Sumera Khala get your rooms ready, so I know where everything is."

"Perfect," I replied, smiling tiredly, taking out my phone. I should tell Ammi that we had arrived.

I took a selfie and sent it to her with the message *reached Lahore safe and sound.* It would be late at night in the U.S., so I didn't expect her to respond right away. But at least she'd know.

My face split into a big yawn. I tossed away my phone and flopped down on the bed. It was so soft I wondered if I was already asleep and dreaming of clouds or something.

"No, no, don't go to sleep now!" Maleeha bent and pulled me back up. "You've got jet lag disorder. You have to stay awake until the evening so you can reset your circadian rhythms."

"What's that?" I groaned, my eyes still closed.

"Your body clock, silly." She clapped her hands sharply right next to my head. "Come on, open your eyes!"

God, she was bossy. "I don't want to stay up until the evening!" I whined.

"I'll keep you awake. You can tell me all the gossip from America, and I'll answer all your questions about Lahore."

I opened one eye. "How do you know I have questions about Lahore?"

She laughed. "You look like someone with a lot of questions."

I opened the other eye too. I couldn't decide if she was being funny or rude. I was too tired to figure it out. "Yeah," I finally said. "I do have a lot of curiosity in general."

"Don't worry." Maleeha settled on the chair and crossed her legs. "You'll find I have all the info you could possibly need."

I raised my eyebrows. "About . . . ?"

She shrugged. "Anything. Everything. Whatever you need. I'm a walking, talking encyclopedia."

"Uh, okay."

"Oh, wait." Maleeha pulled out her phone to text someone. "I'll ask the servants to make us some popcorn."

The whole idea of servants bewildered me. "You can text the servants?" I asked, a little horrified and a lot fascinated.

She let out a peal of laughter. "No, silly. I'm texting Sumera Khala, and she'll tell the kitchen staff."

"Oh." I relaxed against the headboard, yawning again. "And why do we need popcorn? Didn't you eat enough samosas?"

She grinned cheekily. "Isn't that what they do in American movies? Eat popcorn and gossip?"

I grinned back and threw a pillow at her. "I have literally seen zero movies in which that happens."

"Don't care. Now I have a craving." She finished texting and looked at me. "Okay, so tell me your life story. Any cute white boys you're crushing on?"

It was weird how I'd just met this know-it-all but we already clicked. I felt like I'd known her for years. She had this thing about her, open and honest, eyes glittering with joy, mouth always curled up in a smile. She and Nakia would be immediate besties.

Still, I wasn't sure I was ready to spill the beans about Bruno. Mostly because there were no beans to spill. Also, because I had no clue how to explain the *Kamala Khan + Bruno Carrelli* pairing.

Not that there was a pairing, in reality.

"Well?" Maleeha prodded.

"Well," I began with a great sigh. "It all began a long time ago when I met this cute guy in a Circle Q outside our school."

"Wait, what's a circle queue?"

I mock-gasped. "You mean you *don't* know everything? Ya Allah!"

"Shut up and keep talking."

20

Abu knocked on my door early the next morning.

"Get ready, Kamala. We're going sightseeing."

I scrambled out of bed and grabbed my clothes from the open suitcase lying on the floor. Thanks to Maleeha's gossip session the day before, I'd waited until the evening to fall asleep and avoided the horrible jet lag threatening to take over my brain and body. She'd been right. She knew a ton of stuff about everything.

I couldn't wait to pick her brain now that I felt more energized.

I got ready in the bathroom, my mind churning. Abu hadn't sounded grief-stricken, which was a good thing. But going sightseeing? Wasn't that a little extreme? And also, I wondered if this was a strictly father-daughter trip, or would Aamir tag along?

On one hand, ugh. Aamir coming with me on a sightseeing trip was a recipe for disaster.

On the other hand, having him there would act as a buffer between me and Abu. I didn't want our bickering to spoil the Lahore sights.

Turned out, Aamir was still sleeping. "He's feeling the jet lag," Sumera Aunty told us at the breakfast table when I went downstairs with my backpack. "I found him wandering into the kitchen at three in the morning, poor baby."

I smirked at Aamir being called a baby; then my face fell when I wondered what Sumera Aunty was doing up so late. Taking care of Fahad Uncle? Worrying? Praying?

Aamir always stayed up late to pray Tahajjud prayers whenever he was stressed out about something. Maybe Sumera Aunty did too. She definitely had a lot to pray about.

I bit my lip. I should have been praying more too, instead of arguing with my family and making new friends. *Ashfi wa antash-shaafi. Ashfi wa antash-shaafi.*

Sumera Aunty pushed a plate toward me. "Eat, child."

I took a paratha and some spicy omelet. "Yum, this is so good!"

"I'll be sure to tell the cook."

"So it's just the two of us today, eh?" Abu said, piling eggs onto his plate.

I shrugged. *Ashfi wa antash-shaafi. Ashfi wa antash-shaafi.*

"Are you listening, Kamala?" Abu tapped the table. "Why are you always lost in your own dreamworld, eh?"

"Yes, I'm listening." I sighed. We weren't even out of the house yet, and Abu was already mad at me.

Perfect, Kamala, perfect.

Abu's mood improved by the time we got in the taxi. It was the same driver from the day before, which meant Abu had called him specially.

"Do you need to take that thing with you everywhere, Kamala?" Abu asked, nodding to my backpack.

Um, yes. I wasn't leaving the precious spectacles alone for a single second. Plus, the backpack had my Ms. Marvel costume, which I hoped I didn't need, but you never knew. I smiled sweetly and said, "Feminine products, Abu! Just in case."

Abu's face turned red in embarrassment. He cleared his throat and looked out the window.

"Where to, bhai?" the driver said in Urdu.

"Show us the major sights," Abu said, relaxing a little.

I leaned forward. "Can we go to Minar-e-Pakistan first?"

"It's where all the tourists go, Kamala," Abu protested weakly. "There will be a mad rush!"

"I don't care!" I gave him my best smile. "Pleeeease?"

He chuckled. "Okay, fine. Minar-e-Pakistan first."

"Yay!" I clapped my hands.

"Don't be excited," Abu said. "It will be too hot and crowded."

"You're just grumpy," I told him.

"Respect your elders!" But Abu's voice was low and almost laughing. He had the window rolled down and the sleeves of his shirts flapping, and his face had a . . . smile? Wow. This was so unlike him. Usually, he hated going out anywhere, especially for fun.

"Ready for that adventure, Abu?" I asked him.

"Ready, beta."

We drove out of the neighborhood and down a bustling street. Then another, even bigger and busier. I took my phone out to take pictures and saw that Ammi had replied to my message. *Hope you have lots of fun. And patience!*

I hope so too, I wrote back.

We reached the Minar half an hour later, and I scrambled out of the taxi. "Finally!" A big park with lush green lawns surrounded the monument.

And what a monument it was! Tall, slender, with a base that looked like flower petals. I took pictures again, sending a few to Ammi so she wouldn't feel left out.

"Do you know the history of this minar?" Abu asked as he stood beside me, taking it all in.

"No," I replied. "Tell me."

"In 1940, the Muslims of India passed a resolution calling for the creation of Pakistan here. It became a historic site for Pakistanis, so in the 1960s, they built this monument to mark the occasion. It's very nice inside too. Lots of inscriptions, Quranic verses, plus the entire text of the resolution in Urdu and English."

"That's seriously cool," I said.

Abu took a deep breath. "I haven't been here since I was in middle school. We came with our school on a field trip."

Imagining Abu as a sixth grader was impossible. "Was Fahad Uncle with you?"

"Yes, he was." Abu smiled a little. "We ran around the base of the monument, shouting at each other, until the teachers caught us."

I let out a startled laugh. "Did you get in trouble?"

"No, no! Fahad was the teacher's pet. He never got into trouble for anything."

"Let me guess—you took full advantage of that!"

Abu's smile grew. "I would never! What are you talking about?"

We walked into the monument and read the inscriptions,

Abu translating the Urdu bits that I didn't understand and pointing out special parts, like one of his favorite poems by Pakistani poet Allama Iqbal. "This is fabulous," I whispered.

"Yes, it is," Abu replied softly.

"So, you admit, you're glad we came?" I teased.

He rolled his eyes in a way I didn't know he could. "Okay, I admit it—I'm glad we came here. It brought back some good memories."

"Okay, where to next?"

"Badshahi Mosque," he replied, heading back to the taxi.

I made a face. "A mosque? That's more Aamir's area of interest."

He waved his hand to tell me to hurry up. "This one is everyone's area of interest. You'll see."

He was right. The Badshahi Mosque was incredible. It was made of red stone, which made it glitter and shine in the heat of the afternoon. Abu told me it was built in the 1600s by the Mughal emperor Aurangzeb. "More than four thousand people can fit inside to pray," he added.

"Whoa. That's a lot of people." I looked around. "I can't wait to tell Aamir."

"Your brother can visit this place himself once he's feeling better," Abu replied. "There's another mosque here too, the Wazir Khan, which is pretty special."

"Khan!" My eyes widened. "Are we related to them?"

"Maybe—who knows? There are millions of Khans around. It's a very common last name here."

I digested this information while we walked back to our taxi. The driver was dozing under the shade of a tree and woke with a start when Abu called him.

"Where to next?" I asked Abu.

"How about we fill our stomachs?"

We ate lunch at a little café Abu called his "old haunt" like he was some cool dude once upon a time.

"I was very cool," he insisted when I mentioned what I was thinking.

"Oh, yeah?" I picked up some spicy fries and dipped them in mayo sauce. "Name one thing that made you cool back in the day."

He bit into his chicken burger and thought. "One, I had a motorbike. All the girls thought it was—what do you kids say now?—sick."

My mouth fell open. Abu on a motorbike? That sounded insane. "Do you have pictures?"

"Probably," he replied. "I'll ask Fahad when we get back."

"What else?" I asked, my mouth full. The spicy fries and mayo sauce were so good together, it wasn't even funny.

"Two, I had a longish hairstyle, just like this one Pakistani movie star, and whenever I'd go out, people would think I was him. One time, some girls even asked me for my autograph."

I choked on my fries. "Did you give it?"

He chuckled and ducked his head like he was embarrassed. "Of course. I was nineteen. It was the best day of my life at that time."

"And now?" I asked, looking at him carefully. "Is it still your best day?"

He ate another bite and then put his burger down. "Now? Oh, no. The best day of my life is now split into two. The day Aamir was born and the day you were born."

He went back to his food, but I kept staring at him. Heart-to-hearts with Abu were rare. It seemed like these days, he was always pointing out my mistakes. I knew he loved me, but sometimes the gap between us seemed pretty big.

My birthday being the best day of his life? That was incredible.

Incredible and slightly unbelievable.

"Really?" I finally whispered.

"Really." He wiped his mouth with a napkin. "Now hurry up and eat. I want to show you my college next."

The University of Punjab reminded me of the old universities in the U.S.

I'd seen plenty of pictures and videos of the Ivy League schools, thanks to Bruno's obsession to get admission into one of them. Abu's university in Lahore had a similar vibe. Old stone buildings with gorgeous details, lush gardens, big verandas. Some parts were newer, with modern architecture in white and blue.

"This is huge," I gasped.

We'd been walking around for a while, Abu pointing out where his classes had been and what was new to him. Now he led me to a little bench in the corner of a field. A bunch of guys were playing a game with flattened bats and a ball. "That's cricket," Abu told me. "It's Pakistan's favorite game."

"Kind of like football for us?"

Abu sat down on the bench with a grunt. "Yes, but way less violent."

We watched the game for a few minutes. The guy with the bat stood on one end of a pitch in the ground. A second guy would run up the pitch with a ball, then throw the ball at Bat Guy. If Bat Guy hit the ball, he would run to the end of the pitch and then back again.

"This is stupid," I finally pronounced. Bat Guy couldn't hit a ball to save his life. Why was he even playing?

Abu shrugged. "It takes a while to get used to. But it can get very exciting sometimes."

"Did you ever play?"

He shook his head. "Oh, no, I wasn't into sports."

"What were you into, then?" I suddenly realized that I knew nothing about Abu's interests. He went to the bank for work, came back home, then watched the news on TV or read the newspaper. "Wait, let me guess. Something with numbers, right?"

Abu gave a sad little laugh, his eyes focused on a building in the distance. I think he'd told me it was the library. "Actually, no. I hated numbers. Wasn't any good at them either."

I gaped at him. "Then how come you work at a bank? Isn't that all numbers, all the time?"

"It is," Abu replied. "My parents pushed me into this career. They wanted me to go into finance or accounting. Told me I'd get a better job, make more money."

Abu talking about his parents? That almost never happened. I'd never even met my dada and dadi. They'd both died when I was little. "Well, I guess that makes sense," I said awkwardly. "The job you have at the bank is pretty good, isn't it? We have money. I guess your parents were right about things."

Abu scoffed, still looking away. "They just didn't tell me I'd have to sell my soul to do it."

"I'm sorry, what?"

"Never mind." Abu sighed. "I'm just being, how do you say? Nostalgic. It's strange to be here after so long. Makes me relive some not-so-good memories."

A shout went up at the pitch. Bat Guy had hit the ball again, and it rolled afield. One of the other guys went running after it, and Bat Guy ran to the other end of the pitch, then back again like his pants were on fire.

"Hey, you were right! It got exciting!" My face broke into a grin, but when I turned to Abu, he was still serious and semi-sad.

"You're allowed to be nostalgic, Abu," I said softly.

He looked sideways at me. "Am I?"

"Sure." I patted his back. "Tell me, what were you into, if not numbers? Like, if you could have chosen any field, what would it be?"

"I loved art. I took a few art courses in university and completely fell in love."

"Like, drawing and stuff?" I couldn't believe this. Abu had zero artistic talent. We played Pictionary when I was younger and nobody could make out what he drew. Ever.

"No, no!" He shook his head. "I was into other people's art. Like, art history, studying the great creators of the time, learning about various art movements, finding meaning in them . . ."

I gaped at him like I'd never seen him before. "That's the complete opposite of working in a bank."

He nodded. "Yes, Kamala, it is. My parents never understood my passions. It was the reason we weren't close. There was a fundamental barrier between who they were and who I was. It was devastating to know I could never live up to their expectations."

"Wow," I whispered, my head spinning with these revelations.

How do you go from knowing zero about someone to knowing too much?

We sat there for a few minutes; then I grabbed his phone for some selfies. "For Ammi," I told him.

He hated selfies, but he relented this time. I took about a dozen, and only one in which Abu wasn't scowling or looking constipated. I sent that one to Ammi with the message *Hanging out with my favorite daughter.*

"You're my only daughter, Kamala," Abu protested.

I giggled. "I know."

He stood up. "Come on, time to go. I'm getting a headache from all this heat."

My phone beeped. It was Ammi, even though it was the middle of the night in Jersey City. *Glad you two are spending time together.*

Then she spoiled it by adding, *Too bad you had to go thousands of miles away to do that.*

"Look at this mess!"

Abu looked out of the taxi and shook his head. The road was crowded with cars and motorcycles, all honking.

"What's going on?" I asked. We'd traveled down this road a couple of hours ago, and it had been clear.

"I'll go see," the driver said, climbing out.

I watched him weave through cars and talk to people as he went. "People just . . . get out on the road here," I murmured, amazed.

"It's a traffic jam, Kamala," Abu said impatiently. "What else are they going to do? Many of these cars don't have AC, you know."

"No kidding," I groaned. The taxi we were in clearly didn't. The sun was near the horizon now, but it was still pretty hot. I leaned back and closed my eyes. Maybe I could imagine myself at the North Pole, surrounded by penguins and polar bears.

A beep sounded at my ear. I opened my eyes and saw Abu reading a text. "It's the driver," he reported. "Says there's a truck overturned up ahead."

I sat up. "You mean stalled? Broken down?"

"No, overturned. Flipped right over!" Abu showed me a picture the driver had sent.

The truck was an eighteen-wheeler, blocking the road completely. People stood around it, their faces frozen in shock. "Wow, this looks bad," I whispered. "Is this . . . normal?"

"I'm sure accidents happen, Kamala!" Abu grunted angrily, putting away his phone and massaging his forehead. "The driver said he found a friend up ahead, so he'll wait there to keep an eye on things. I'm going to try to nap a little. My headache is getting worse."

"Okay, sure." I closed my eyes again, but this time instead of the North Pole fantasy, I couldn't stop seeing the picture on Abu's phone in my mind's eye. The truck was humongous. There was a picture of a flame on the side, which meant it contained something flammable.

That part was really making me worry.

I didn't mind sitting here in the heat. Well, I didn't mind *much*.

What I did mind was not knowing if something dangerous was going to happen on this road. Why had a truck overturned in the middle of the street? If it was a normal occurrence, would the people in the picture look so shocked and stressed?

It was no use. I couldn't relax when innocent people were in potential danger. I was Ms. Marvel no matter which country I was in.

I opened my eyes and sat up. Abu was snoring lightly, his mouth open and his head lolling against the seat back.

Perfect.

I slowly opened the door and crept out, pulling my backpack after carefully. I'd just take a look at the truck and make my way back before Abu woke up. It was the least I could do.

I walked for a few minutes before I came to the truck. Yup, it was huge.

I turned to a woman wearing hijab and jeans. She was leaning against her car, recording on her phone. "Do you know how it happened?"

The woman lowered her phone. "I saw a zapping sort of light, and then the truck flipped over," she replied, and shook her head disbelievingly. "I'm sure it was my imagination. I'm just tired."

The hair on the back of my neck prickled. "What color was the light?"

She stared at me. "I don't know. I think . . . green? Or white? Maybe both. Like I said, it was probably my imagination."

An elderly man nodded from our left. "I saw it too. It was a mixture of green and white. Just for a second, but I saw it."

I inhaled sharply.

A green-and-white light.

A zap that flipped a heavy truck onto its side.

A blocked road.

"Asaar!" I gasped, whirling around to see if I could catch a glimpse. If my guess about Shareef Deen was correct, Asaar could very well be right here in Lahore, sowing mischief and mayhem.

Only, why would he do that? What was he here to steal? There weren't any artifacts here, as far as I could tell. It was a run-down area with shops and restaurants on one side and a gas station on the other.

"Are you okay, lady?" the man asked.

I didn't reply. I'd caught a movement in one of the storefronts lining the road. A figure dressed in black. Tall.

I heaved my backpack over my shoulders and went sprinting toward the nearest store. I picked a little coffee shop, empty except for a busboy watching the chaos on the street wide-eyed. There were no customers, thankfully.

My guess—it was way too hot for coffee of any kind.

Except iced coffee. That I'd drink in a snap.

Later, Kamala. Get the villain first.

With a thirsty look at the menu wall, I slipped into the restroom at the back and changed into my costume. A minute later, I snuck out through the back door with my backpack slung over my shoulder. I didn't have much time before Abu woke up and wondered where I'd gone. I needed some answers, and I had a feeling today was the day to get them.

The side street behind the coffee shop was empty and littered. A few broken pieces of furniture lay scattered about, and a big black trash container spewed filth everywhere.

God, why did I always end up near trash containers?

Holding my breath, I dropped my backpack behind the container. Nobody would want to stick their head back there, that was for sure.

Then I strode toward the back of the building to another side street. This one was lined with trees that gave the place a shady, slightly sinister vibe.

I hadn't gone more than a few steps before a movement caught my eye from the side, followed by fiery green sparks.

I whirled around, breathing hard in anticipation.

A man in a familiar brown mask and dark suit stood in front of me, a smirk on his face. "Caught you," he said in a low, menacing voice.

I refused to be scared of this dude. What did he think he was doing, blocking an entire road for no reason?

"Hello, Asaar, fancy meeting you here," I replied sweetly. "Or should I call you Shareef Deen?"

His smirk dropped. He stared at me for a few seconds, then shrugged. "So you figured it out. I always knew you were smart, Ms. Marvel."

It was my turn to smirk. "That's right."

"Then you must also know why I'm here." He didn't wait for me to respond. "I want the spectacles. Now."

"Ha! Good one!"

Asaar growled and curled his fists in front of his face. Green-and-white fires rose from each of his fingers. "Don't mess with me, little girl. I can turn over an entire truck full of petrol without breaking a sweat. I can make mincemeat of you."

"Whoa, that's graphic!" I stepped back a bit, just to show I wasn't here to fight.

Yet.

Sure, I was wary of his horrible green energy, but I also needed answers. Last I'd heard (or seen), Asaar was in Jersey City. How had he known I was in Pakistan? Had he followed me? Was he working in cahoots with someone else?

"Give me the spectacles, Ms. Marvel," Asaar commanded. "They belong here, with me."

"With you?" The way he'd said that was more than villain-y greed. It was almost like he was staking a claim or something. Ownership.

Asaar hurled some energy at me, and I ducked. It hit the wall behind me, and I was so close I could feel its heat and smell the electricity. Tendrils of hair on my head waved in the breeze it generated. Droplets of sweat sprang up on my forehead.

I waited breathlessly for the next hit, but it didn't come. He looked like he was debating whether to batter me with light energy or shake me with his bare hands.

Thankfully, he did neither. "I'm a direct descendent of Shah Jahan," he said. "Those spectacles were in my family for a hundred years before the British stole them. I want . . . need . . . them back."

My mouth fell open. "Wait, the Mughal emperor Shah Jahan?"

He gave me a pitying look. "Who else?"

Come on, that was a fair question, wasn't it? Asaar was claiming to be an actual descendant of Mughal royalty, like the kid in Abu's school who everyone made fun of. He wanted the spectacles back not only because he was a repatriation warrior, but also because he literally owned them? Nope, I wasn't believing this. Not yet.

"How do I know you're telling the truth?" I asked. "There are thousands of Mughal family members scattered around the globe."

Asaar gritted his teeth. I could tell from the way his jaw clenched behind his mask. "There aren't many of us left. The British killed entire families in the various battles along the way. Displayed their bodies for all to see. Those who survived were left destitute and fearing for their lives. Are there many of us? Probably. Do they know who they are? Have they kept their history and records after all this time? Maybe not, but I have."

"Wow." This time my comment was completely free from humor. The more I learned about the British history in India, the angrier I got.

Nakia was right. Colonization was the devil, and it wasn't even in disguise. It was evil and proud of it.

Asaar came closer. "You know what none of the other descendants have, wherever they may be?" he continued in a low, tense voice. "Super-powers."

"How do you know?" I asked weakly. "There could be others. . . ."

"Enough," he growled, throwing buzzing energy right at me. It hit my shoulder like a hot poker and shoved me back so that I stumbled into cool, stinky metal.

My first thought: *Freaking OW!*

My second thought: *The trash container!* That's where I'd hidden my backpack! I could see the blue fabric sticking out from behind the dumpster.

I pulled all my strength together and straightened up. Hands braced on hips, I stood in front of the container, hoping Asaar didn't figure out what I was protecting. "Tell me how you found me!" I said quickly, trying to distract him while I streeeeetched my foot to kick my backpack out of sight. "My travel plans aren't exactly advertised on social media."

He shook his head. "I don't need social media. All true descendants of the Mughals can track the location of certain artifacts."

"You mean magical artifacts?"

He shrugged. "That's for me to know and you to never find out." Then he held up his hands again. No way was I getting hit with that green-and-white fire again!

With a yell I grew my arms long and thick like serpents, then picked Asaar up into the air.

He looked like a doll, his limbs waving in the air. I almost laughed, but he threw more energy bolts my way, right, left, center. They showered over me like hot, heavy bullets of pain.

After almost getting hit with his lightning one too many times, I had no choice but to drop him.

Right in the trash.

This time, I did laugh. "Seems like the Mughals have really fallen on bad times," I mocked.

Was it mean? Yup.

Did I care? Not a bit. He'd basically called me stupid. It was the ultimate insult, as far as I was concerned.

Asaar stood knee-deep in filth, uncaring. "Give me the spectacles!" he roared so loudly, the entire trash container rattled.

I couldn't help it. My gaze slipped from him to the ground, where I'd hidden my backpack. One strong shake, and the container would collapse right on top of a priceless ancient artifact. Maybe Asaar was right. Maybe I was stupid for bringing the spectacles along with me wherever I went.

It was only a matter of time before they got lost or stolen.

Or, in this case, crushed by day-old garbage.

Asaar followed my eyes with his own. With another triumphant roar, he jumped down to the ground, zapping me with his green-and-white light to keep me away.

I looked on in horror as he reached behind the container and dragged out my backpack. Quickly, he dug around my clothes and books and pulled out the gleaming spectacles. "Found you," he whispered, almost lovingly.

"Nooooo!" I squeaked. I wasn't proud of it, but being hit by a constant barrage of energy blasts did something to a gal.

I struggled forward, putting my arms up to shield my face. I was exhausted, but I couldn't give up.

At the last minute, Asaar turned and shot a final energy bolt that sent me to my knees.

Again, freaking ow!

I watched as he disappeared into the twilight.

I looked around me, my heart racing in my chest, my knees aching. The street was silent once again.

And the spectacles were gone.

"So how's Pakistan?" Nakia asked on video chat.

I sat cross-legged on my bed, my laptop on my legs and a plate of delicious chaat next to me.

I brought a spoonful of chaat to my mouth. "This is the life, man!" I swallowed, then waved the spoon at the screen. "Servants to clean your room, and chefs to make yummy food for you . . . I may never come back!"

Okay, I was joking. I loved my independent American life too much to ever leave it. But right now, I really needed some humor. After watching Asaar walk away with the emerald spectacles, I was in a real funk. I'd hurried back into the shop and changed so I could return to the taxi before Abu woke up. It had been a close one.

"Sounds awesome," Bruno said dryly. "What about your uncle, the one who's sick?"

I put the spoon back and got serious. "He's really weak. Like, he gets out of breath and starts coughing every few minutes. His wife wants him to get an oxygen tank, but he refuses."

This had been the discussion at the mid-morning snack table today. I hadn't wanted to see the frown on Abu's face or hear the heartbreak in Sumera Aunty's voice, so I'd grabbed my plate and come upstairs to hide out.

"That's tough," Nakia said. "How's your dad taking it?"

"Surprisingly well," I replied. "He took me sightseeing yesterday, and—"

"And you didn't kill each other?" she interrupted mockingly.

I snapped my fingers at the screen. "No! Listen! We didn't kill each other, *and* I found out so much about him that I never knew before!"

"Like what?"

I told her about Abu's disagreements with his parents, how he'd wanted to do something so different from their wishes. How it had caused a rift between them that existed until the day they'd died. "Isn't that sad?"

Nakia nodded thoughtfully. "Yes, true, but it's also great for you."

"Ha!" Bruno snickered.

I frowned at them both. "How is this great for me?"

"You guys finally have something in common!" Nakia replied. "You can bond over how awful parents can be!"

"Nakia!" A shocked giggle burst out of me, and I spewed bits of cilantro all over the place.

"Ew, gross!" Nakia and Bruno started laughing at the mess I'd made. Soon, all three of us were full-belly laughing.

It felt good. It felt like I was back with my friends in Jersey City, while still enjoying the warm, comfy feeling of this Pakistani home that I'd come to love so quickly.

It also made me forget, for a little while, how I'd lost a priceless magical artifact that I was supposed to be protecting. I don't think Nakia and Bruno noticed that my laughter was hollow, and my face felt frozen with worry.

Nope, not at all. Nothing to see here.

"I miss ya, girlie," Nakia said, wiping a tear. "I don't have anyone to go shopping with, or bounce off ideas for my article!"

Drat. I'd forgotten all about her article. "How's it going?" I asked. "What help do you need?"

"I wanted to see what you thought of some of my word choices."

I made grabby hands at her. "Tell me. Tell me."

She reached over to the side to get some papers. "Okay, here's an excerpt. 'The Mughal era was one of magnificence, riches, and revelry. When the British appeared on the subcontinent in the form of the East India Company, their eyes must have widened and their mouths dropped open in shock to see such opulence in a supposedly inferior, heathen culture.'"

I gave her a thumbs-up. "That's great! Very impactful!"

"You don't think it's too harsh?" Bruno asked, frowning.

"But it's true, isn't it?" I demanded. "Harsh is what the British did, stealing things that didn't belong to them. Killing off the locals and hanging their bodies at city gates to be shown as examples of their wrath."

"Whoa, did that really happen?" Bruno's eyes widened.

"Yesss!" I nodded emphatically. After the traffic jam had cleared the evening before and we'd come back home, I'd kept thinking about Asaar's claims. How the British had killed off his royal ancestors and driven their families away to live in poverty and anonymity. I'd stayed up way too late researching the local history of the British in India, and yup, it was gory and heartless, just like Asaar had said.

I ignored the way Asaar now didn't feel like an enemy, despite having run off with the spectacles. Nobody needed to know that. Yet.

"Your writing is really good, Nakia," I assured her. "As always."

She looked at the papers in her hand. "It's the least I can do after all that's happened over the centuries, you know?"

I did know. The chaat suddenly sat too heavy in my stomach. I'd agreed to come to Lahore to find more about Shareef Deen. And here I was sightseeing with Abu and eating delicious food somebody else made.

In some ways, I was like the Mughals myself. Enjoying the rich lifestyle and ignoring the dangers that were coming.

Nakia signed off, saying she needed to work on her article. That left me and Bruno.

"So what's new?" I asked sadly. I needed a win. Something that would make me feel like less of a loser right now.

"Well, let's see. Kingpin and the Barringtons did a joint press conference yesterday."

"Wow, that's a weird combination." I chewed my lip. "What did they say?"

"Not much. They went on and on about the emerald spectacles, and how they were both going to use their combined resources to try to find them." Bruno laughed. "Too bad they're all the way across the world right now, in Lahore!"

I winced. Ugh, what was he going to think of me when he knew the truth?

Bruno leaned forward. "What's wrong, Kamala?"

"The spectacles are in Lahore, that's true," I began cautiously. "But . . . I don't exactly know where."

"What are you talking about?"

My shoulders slumped as I told Bruno about my fight with Asaar. How he struck me again and again with his horrible green-and-white light and totally overwhelmed me. How he took my backpack and ran away like he was stealing a piece of fruit from a tree, instead of an ancient artifact. "He overturned an oil tanker, Bruno! He's strong, and so . . . stealthy."

"Are you okay? Did you get hurt?"

My stress and worry mellowed a little. Trust Bruno to focus on my injuries instead of the bigger picture. Why was he so . . . ugh, caring? "I'm fine," I said, waving away his concern.

"Good. That's the most important thing."

"Is it, Bruno?" I snapped. "I thought the most important thing was to heal my uncle! Which, now I can't, because guess what? No spectacles!"

"Listen, you're Ms. Marvel. You'll get them back—I know it."

My eyes popped as my anger surged higher. "How?" I almost yelled. "I have no way to contact Deen! Don't know where he went or what he plans to do with them . . ."

"Wait, Deen?" Bruno frowned. "Do you mean . . . Asaar?"

I breathed in and out harshly. In and out. "Uh, I forgot to tell you. Asaar is Shareef Deen, the businessman who sponsored the museum exhibit in Jersey City. I'd figured it out on the plane, and yesterday when I confronted him, he basically admitted it."

"Wow, okay, that's interesting."

"Interesting? That's all you have to say?"

"Look, at least you know who has the spectacles. Deen's

got a presence in Lahore. He's got all these businesses. He's not going to disappear into thin air."

This was true. My breathing slowed down until it was almost normal. "You're right, I guess."

Bruno smiled comfortingly. "I'll try to find an email address for him. Sometimes these things are well hidden, but you know my tech skills!"

I smiled back softly, ashamed of my outburst. "Thanks, dude."

We looked at each other for a long time.

Actually, it was three or four seconds, but it felt really long and soulful.

What're you doing, Kamala? Keep it friendly. I cleared my throat. "Well, I should go."

"Yeah, sure," Bruno said. "Spend time with your family. See your parents' country. Try to have fun."

I nodded even though I wasn't sure how I was going to do all that. But one thing I knew, I trusted Bruno with everything I had.

"And, Kamala?" he added with a faint smile. "Don't worry. I'm here, always."

I gulped as I shut off the video chat and flopped on my back. Why was he always saying such lovely things to me?

And why did I like it so much?

The next morning, a text message from Maleeha was waiting for me.

Want to see the real Lahore?

I jumped up from my bed so quick my arm slammed against the headboard. "Ow!"

When I got on my feet, I texted back *heck yes* with lots of exclamation marks. I needed to get out of this funk I was stuck in, and a day full of exploring was just what the doctor ordered.

In this case, the doctor was Bruno.

"Where are you going?" Aamir asked when I got downstairs to the breakfast table. His plate was full, and he was munching away like it was his last meal.

I raised an eyebrow. "Hungry much?"

"Where are you going?" he repeated with a scowl. "I told you not to go anywhere alone—it's not safe."

I grabbed a piece of toast. "And I told you to stop acting like my caretaker. I already let Abu know that I'm going shopping, and he's okay with it."

"Have fun, Kamala," Sumera Aunty said, smiling.

"Thanks, Aunty," I replied cheerfully. "I lost my backpack, so I definitely need to get a new one."

"You lost your . . ." Aamir began.

I waved to Sumera Aunty and dashed outside before he could finish his lecture.

Maleeha was waiting with her car and driver outside. "We match!" she exclaimed when I climbed in.

I looked at her, then at myself. We were both wearing blue jeans and black T-shirts. Only hers was longer, kind of like a tunic or kameez. "Cool," I said, nodding. "Can't go wrong with a black top."

Maleeha took the last bite of toast from my hand and threw it in the little plastic trash bag behind the front seat. "You don't need this where we're going."

"Hey!"

She smiled with those dimples of hers. "Patience and perseverance have a magical effect, my dear. John Quincy Adams said that."

"Oh!" I snapped my fingers proudly. "The sixth American president!"

"Very good!"

The driver had just started the car when Aamir came running out. "Wait, Kamala!"

I rolled down my window. "What?"

Aamir panted. "At least . . . turn on your FindMe!"

Maleeha and I exchanged amused glances. With a dramatic sigh, I took out my phone and switched on the FindMe feature, which connected to all my family members, plus Bruno and Nakia. "There—happy?"

The driver moved forward with a little jerk, and Aamir scowled. "Take care. . . ."

I rolled up the window while he was still talking. Then I gave him a little grin and a wave.

Maleeha laughed. "You're so bad!"

Twenty minutes later, we were walking into a fancy-schmancy hotel restaurant with well-dressed waiters, sweet, low classical music, and a buffet-style breakfast. Five types of eggs, pastries, croissants, parathas, chole, halwa, and who knew what else. It was a mixture of cuisines, and it looked incredible.

I raised my eyebrow. "This is the real Lahore?"

Maleeha shrugged. "We need sustenance for the rest of the day."

"And what's the rest of the day?"

"Shopping, of course." She passed me a plate and took one for herself. "Start eating!"

I piled my plate high, because suddenly, I was starving. "Ah, the most important meal of the day!"

"In the Middle Ages, people thought eating breakfast was basically gluttony."

I scoffed. "They also didn't take baths in the Middle Ages."

Maleeha turned to give me an impressed look. "You definitely know your history!"

"Not all of it. Just what we learn in school." I shrugged and picked up a fork. "It's mostly European and American history."

"Well, eat up, you big glutton!" Maleeha winked. "We need all our strength for shopping later."

The shopping she mentioned was a humongous place called Emporium Mall. A tall gray building, a huge space inside with escalators and winding staircases. Shops lined with elegant mannequins. An indoor amusement park with an actual roller coaster.

My mouth dropped open. "This is . . . this is . . ."

Maleeha bumped shoulders with me. "Made you speechless, eh?"

"Seriously, dude, *this* is the real Lahore?" I pretended to be shocked. "I thought it was all old vibes, like tombs and forts and museums."

"Yes, this is the real Lahore of this century. This decade. You can go see the ancient monuments and buildings, which are great, but don't forget that there is also the real, authentic side of how people live here. We're not stuck in the past. We're modern and cool and . . ."

"And foodies," I added, grinning, thinking about delicious breakfast earlier.

Maleeha grinned too. "Yes, definitely foodies."

I looked around, trying to forget how different this place was from the typical thrift store Nakia and I visited every week.

But this was Lahore. An adventure, Abu had said. "Okay," I finally agreed, striding to the escalator. "Let's go shopping."

As we walked around, Maleeha recited some facts about the mall. "Eleven stories. Two point seven million square feet. More than two hundred stores," she said with a satisfied little smirk.

"Wow," I sighed. I was too enthralled to get irritated by Maleeha's facts.

Would two hundred–plus stores count as avarice?

"First stop, clothes!" Maleeha stated, grabbing my hand.

We shopped till we dropped, almost. We tried on outfits and shoes and bracelets. I wrapped myself with the softest silks and satins, just to send pictures to Ammi. Maleeha did a mean catwalk in the middle of a dressing room, putting a hand on her hip and flipping her shaggy hair like she was a runway model.

I laughed so hard my stomach ached.

We also talked. A lot. Mostly about high school and crushes, because Maleeha wanted to know everything about me and Bruno, who she now called Romeo.

"I am *so* not Juliet," I told her with a pretend scowl. "I'm way too smart to give up my life for a dude."

"Poor Romeo." Maleeha sighed. "Maybe he'll find another Juliet while you're here in Pakistan."

My mouth fell open at the thought. "Hey!"

She started laughing again, then walked into a makeup store like she hadn't just freaked me out.

Bruno can go after whoever he wants. What do I care?

Two hours later, we dragged our shopping bags to the car and collapsed inside. "Ah, bless this cold AC!" I sighed loudly.

"You got some nice things," Maleeha said, looking through my bags. "Ooh, this necklace is awesome. I didn't even see you buy it!"

My phone beeped with a message from Ammi. *Love the pictures, beta. I'm posting them on my WhatsApp group. The ladies will be so envious!!!!!*

I felt a pang of guilt course through me. Nakia would have a fit if she knew how much money I had spent, all on brand-new things. "I think I went overboard," I admitted. "I don't even know where I'll wear this necklace, and one of those outfits is way too formal for anything in my life."

Maleeha turned to me, eyes unsmiling for once. "Listen. Do these things make you happy?"

"Uh, yeah."

"Then they're worth it. You didn't even spend that much money. Everything was on sale."

"I guess."

"No guessing. Be sure. Be firm in grasping life—and happiness—by the horns!" She made a pulling gesture with both hands, and it looked vaguely obscene.

I giggled. "What's that supposed to be?"

"I don't know. It just felt right." She tapped the driver on the shoulder. "The art museum next, please."

"Art museum?" I asked, surprised.

"Yeah, I thought you might want to see some culture after that blatant materialism."

My giggles got louder. "Oh my God, the things you say with a straight face!"

"What?" She raised an eyebrow. "I'm not joking."

The museum wasn't big or fancy, but it was full of cool art. There was a modern art section, with trendy pieces by current artists, as well as art from what Maleeha called the bygone era.

I walked around slowly, feeling a little sad, and then annoyed at myself for feeling sad. It was confusing.

"What's wrong?" Maleeha asked. "I thought you'd like this."

"I do!" I paused, trying to put my feeling into words. "This place is fabulous. It's just strange because I feel like I should know this art, but I don't. Like, everything here is strange yet familiar, you know?"

"You don't have this kind of art in your museums in the States?"

"The styles are the same, but the pieces are different." I stopped in front of a piece that looked like the *Mona Lisa*, but it was a Pakistani woman in a full wedding dress and a huge circular nose ring. "Like this—it's so . . . traditional, but also something I know, right?"

Maleeha's eyes glittered. "Ah, I see. You're used to seeing Western art, so when it's in the Eastern style it makes your brain hitch."

I barked out a laugh. "I guess that's one way of putting it."

"How else would you put it?"

We started walking again. "Over there, I have to mostly go to a special museum or wait for a specific exhibit before I can see my own heritage showcased, you know? Like, there's a regular art museum, and then maybe once every few years they will put on an Islamic art exhibition or something."

"Ah. I see what you mean. The default is always the Western."

"Exactly." Suddenly, I didn't care that Maleeha acted so knowledgeable or superior. She got me, in a way that often Bruno and Nakia didn't.

We smiled warmly at each other and kept walking, spending a few minutes at each piece hanging on the wall, inspecting it, admiring it.

"You're into art?" I asked Maleeha after a while. She definitely seemed the creative, bohemian type, from her cool hairstyle to the bulky jewelry she wore.

Maleeha shrugged. "I dabble in painting, but not much. I'm not very good."

"Wait." I grinned. "You're admitting you don't know everything?"

She rolled her eyes. "Being artistic and having knowledge aren't the same thing, Kamala dear."

I grinned bigger. "They aren't?"

"No." She narrowed her eyes, obviously not sure if I was joking. "I'm not the next Van Gogh or anything."

"Only the fountain of knowledge," I teased.

She huffed and walked ahead of me. I laughed outright, then followed her, looking at the paintings around us with interest. "You know, my abu would've loved to come here."

"He likes art?" She sounded totally shocked. "He doesn't look the type."

"Yeah." I shook my head. "It was something he was into when he was younger, apparently. His parents didn't approve, so he never pursued it."

"They sound like my parents."

I frowned. This was the first time Maleeha had spoken about her family. "What do you mean? They don't think you should be an artist?"

"Who knows? They're too busy with their own lives to know what I'm into. All they want is for me to follow them into the business world, make tons of money, like they have."

"Well, money is important too," I said weakly. "How else would you go shopping in more than two hundred stores?"

Maleeha smiled a little. "You're so right, Kamala."

We reached the ancient art wing, and I opened the door quickly, wanting to be done with this sad conversation. That's when my jaw dropped, because this part of the museum was pure magic. Glass cabinets taller than me stood at regular intervals bathed in soft yellow light. Each cabinet held crumbly, faded items, like testaments to another time.

If I focused hard enough, I could almost see the rich history written in the molecules.

"Those are artifacts from Mohenjo-daro," Maleeha said, sounding happy again.

"What's that?" I asked, still focused on the beauty around me.

Her mouth dropped open. "You don't know about Mohenjo-daro?" she squeaked.

"Okay, stop!" I flushed. "No need to embarrass the uncultured American. Just tell me."

She closed her mouth and stared at me.

I gulped and waited. This was the perfect time to get back at me for the fountain-of-knowledge comment. Cue some know-it-all factoid in three, two, one . . .

"I'm sorry, I didn't mean to make you feel bad!" Maleeha said, squeezing my arm. "I forgot you didn't grow up here. I'd know nothing about American history if I visited a museum there."

My flush deepened. "It's not the same," I muttered. "I'm from here—I should know this stuff."

"Kamala, don't be silly." Maleeha pulled me gently toward a glass cabinet. "Mohenjo-daro is translated as 'mound of the dead.' It's the site for one of the most ancient civilizations known to humans."

I relaxed. "How ancient?"

She leaned forward to read an inscription. "It says here between 2500 and 1700 BC."

"BC? Yikes, that's old."

"Yeah, we Desis go way, way back."

I didn't reply, but inside, my heart was jumping something fierce. I loved what she said. I loved the fact that *we Desis go way, way back*, even though I'd never thought of myself as part of a *we Desi* grouping, ever.

Being part of a group that had incredible art and traditions and culture and history . . . yeah it felt amazing.

Kind of like Ammi and her WhatsApp groups, only less gossipy.

We looked our fill, then walked to the back to another exhibit. Something new stirred in my chest. "Wait, I know this stuff," I whispered. "It's from the time of the Mughals, right?"

"Right." Maleeha looked pleased, like a teacher happy with a student's response.

The exhibit was small but magnificent. I saw miniature paintings, jewelry, coins, and daggers. Some of it was similar to the Jersey City exhibit, some was different.

"Did you know some of the Mughal artifacts are rumored to be magical?" I murmured.

Maleeha laughed. "Sure, I've heard the stories." Then she saw my face and stopped laughing. "Wait, do you actually believe them?"

"Obviously not!" I looked away. "I'm just saying. There are lots of myths."

I wished I knew more about the Mughals and their art. Abu had told me a little, but it had only made me more curious.

Plus, I needed as much information as I could get if I wanted to get to the bottom of Asaar/Deen's motivations. Sure, he said the spectacles were part of his heritage, but what did he really want to do with them? Did he want to sell them for millions? Was he a collector? Or did he want to use their healing powers?

Then there was Kingpin too. His motivations for sponsoring the exhibit and Delilah's for stealing from it were even more hazy.

"It's not just Mughal artifacts," Maleeha continued. "Throughout history, ancient items are said to have magical powers. Relics from various Christian saints, for example. Swords of destiny or with other powers. Oh, and there's the Buddha's tooth in Sri Lanka that is supposed to be connected to military might or something."

"His actual tooth?"

She nodded. "That's what they say."

This was seriously cool. Maleeha didn't think these things were real, but I knew better. "Is there a gift shop around?" I asked.

"Sure, why?" She winked. "Want to spend some more money, eh?"

I shrugged. "I wanted a book to learn more about ancient Mughal artifacts."

"The shop doesn't have books, but you can find something online, for sure."

I shook my head. "I wanted something older, something more . . . authentic."

"Why?"

How could I explain this without making her wonder what was going on? Maleeha was super smart, so she wouldn't be appeased by some silly excuse.

On the other hand, I could hardly tell her that I was searching for a way to heal her uncle using magical items. If—when—I got the spectacles back from Asaar, I still needed to know how the magic behind them worked.

Maleeha was looking at me with questioning eyes.

"Uh, my friend Nakia is writing an article about the Mughal artifacts," I stammered. "I thought I could bring her a gift that's truly authentic."

"Hmm." Maleeha thought for a minute. "I could take you to an outdoor market where old books are sold."

I grabbed her hand. "Right now?"

"No!" She laughed. "I have to go home soon, but maybe tomorrow."

"Tomorrow's good enough for me," I said cheerfully. "Now how about lunch?"

Some afternoons, a girl just wanted to sit alone and work on her fan fiction.

Sadly, I didn't have my notebooks, so I hunted for something to read. On a shelf in the closet, I found old knickknacks, dusty picture frames, and a couple of paperbacks. I picked out *In Other Rooms, Other Wonders* by Daniyal Mueenuddin and snuggled into the tufted chair with a blanket.

After a few pages, I realized I hadn't checked my phone in a while. I'd shut off the ringer in the art museum and then never put it on again.

There were four messages. I clicked on the ones from Bruno first.

Check your email. I created a new account for Ms. Marvel. You can send Deen a message through there.

I frowned. How was I supposed to do that?

Next message: *Oh, sorry, forgot to tell you that I found Deen's private contact info. Sent it via email too.*

Of course he did.

Also, I made a list of ancient artifacts that have recently been stolen. All of these are connected to Kingpin in some way.

I sighed happily, because Bruno Carrelli was seriously awesome. Quickly, I scanned the list he'd sent. A medieval ax, a bronze crown, a Viking-era chain, among others, just in the last six months. "Whoa, this is a lot of stuff," I muttered. "Who knew artifact theft was such roaring business?"

I read the list again, looking for patterns, wondering what Kingpin's connection to these artifacts was.

Just then, my phone buzzed in my hand. Bruno with another message, no doubt.

But actually, it was Kate Bishop: *Check this out!*

I clicked on the video link, and my heart lodged in my throat. Someone had taken a shaky video of Kate fighting with Delilah in a downtown area with big buildings. It wasn't Jersey City, but it looked familiar, like I'd been there a long time ago.

Kate and Delilah battled it out in the street, shouting and throwing each other around. I could see people crouched behind cars, hear their cries, feel their worry.

I watched with anxious eyes as Kate launched arrow after

arrow at Delilah, who laughed and batted them away as if they were sticks. Finally, Kate yelled and ran at Delilah.

Delilah waited until Kate was two feet away, then started punching my friend.

Kate punched back just as viciously. Once, then five times, then twenty. Back and forth, neither of them lagging. I felt myself lean forward as if I could jump into the video and help. Ms. Marvel and Hawkeye, together versus Delilah. That would be something incredible!

The video shook as it turned slightly to take in two security guards running at Delilah. They were youngish, with clean-cut looks and determination in their eyes. "Stop!" one of them shouted. "We've called the police!"

Delilah sneered and aimed her fists at one of the guards.

I watched in horror as Kate jumped in front of him and took the blow, right on her temple.

Kate crumpled to the ground in a daze.

Delilah laughed and, with a swipe of her fists, pummeled both guards into the wall behind, one after the other. They fell, eyes closed, heads bleeding. Whoever took the video zoomed into their faces, and I had to hold back a sob.

They were either dead or close to it.

In the background, Kate staggered up and reached for her bow. Delilah jumped up the wall and then to another one farther away, until she was just a speck. "You can't stop me,

Bishop!" she shouted. "This is part of something much bigger than you!"

I sat in my room, my phone in my lap, for a long time. The sun went down, and the sky outside my window turned pink and purple.

Dark thoughts swirled around me. I should've been there on that downtown street, instead of Kate. I should have fought Delilah myself and kicked her scrawny ass.

Nobody should have been hurt on my watch. Nobody.

I felt so . . . paralyzed. Unable to help Fahad Uncle, unable to save innocent people in my city.

Useless, that's what I was. Utterly useless.

Abu came to get me for dinner, but I told him I was too tired. I waited until he left to send a video request to Bruno and Nakia.

"Did you go shopping without me?" Nakia complained loudly as soon as she got on the call.

I tried to laugh. "Sorry, I couldn't help it. The mall was calling me!"

"The mall?" Nakia gasped. "You traitor!"

"Ahem," Bruno interrupted. "We have some serious business to discuss."

I tensed. "What serious business?"

"Another artifact was stolen," he said. "From the New Jersey History Collection this time."

The History Collection was privately owned, housed in an estate not far from downtown Jersey City. I'd patrolled there a few times months ago, but the area was mostly quiet.

"What was stolen?" Nakia asked. "Another Mughal item?"

"No, it was a shotel."

I just blinked and waited. Sometimes Bruno could be just as much of a know-it-all as Maleeha. It didn't happen often, but I knew what it meant. We needed to wait for his explanation.

Nakia wasn't so patient. "Uh, what's a shotel?"

"A curved sword from ancient Ethiopia," Bruno explained.

"Does it have any magical powers?" I asked urgently, thinking of what Delilah had said in the video. Then I saw Nakia frown and open her mouth to ask what the heck, so I added, "Myths of magical powers, I meant. Obviously."

"Yup," said Bruno. "The myth says whoever carries the sword into battle will not only win the battle but also rule the world."

Nakia scoffed. "Seriously, people and their legends!"

Bruno and I exchanged tense looks. "That's a dangerous power to have," I mumbled. "Theoretically."

"And get this," Bruno continued grimly, "Delilah was seen

outside the museum. She hurt a couple of security guards pretty seriously."

My heart sank. He'd either seen the same video I had or the news was spreading. With the number of onlookers, I guessed everybody knew by now. "Are the guards . . . alive?" I asked.

Bruno sighed. "Barely. They're both in the ICU with head wounds."

"That's horrible," Nakia exclaimed. "What's with all the villain activity around the artifact thefts? Do they really believe the myths about magical items are true?"

"Uh, maybe." In my heart, I knew what Delilah's presence at the scene meant. The shotel was definitely magical. And the humans she hurt? Ugh, I hated her guts. She was probably hiding out somewhere, laughing it up with Kingpin.

Nakia was furiously taking notes. "This is . . . Wow, this is awful. Maybe I can add it to my article. How this is just another reason to return artifacts to their places of origin. What else do museum staff expect? They can't blame anyone if their guards get hurt."

"Are you for real? How is that fair for people just trying to earn their living?" Bruno half yelled. "If anything, this proves we need to keep the artifacts wherever they'd be safest. With the most security. More guards, not less! Many of those countries don't even have the resources to maintain basic law and order."

My eyebrows jumped at his tone, but I kept silent.

Not Nakia. She scowled and leaned forward. "Those countries?" she said. "What exactly do you mean by *those countries?*"

Bruno sighed and lowered his voice. "I didn't mean . . . Countries with poverty, or lower economic status. . . ."

"You mean the previously colonized countries?"

"Well, yes, but . . ."

"How do you think they got that way, Bruno? Because of colonial theft! Because the Western countries came and stole everything from them! All the minerals and the jewels and the—"

I held up a hand. "Okay, you guys. Stop arguing. We've talked about this before. Nakia thinks artifacts should be returned to their original homes, even if violence is used to make that happen."

Nakia inhaled sharply. "Hey, I didn't say violence is okay!"

"Yes, you did," Bruno shot back. "You said you can't blame anyone if the museum staff get hurt!"

"Hush, please, I'm talking." I couldn't take my friends fighting like this, their faces red with anger, their voices harsh. "Bruno, you think it's better to keep the artifacts in a safe location, rather than return them to who knows what sort of situation?"

"Yup! It doesn't matter where they end up, as long as they're cared for."

"How convenient," Nakia grumbled.

I sighed. "Look, let's talk about something else for now."

Bruno shook his head angrily. "Two guards are in the hospital, Kamala! In critical condition! How can we just forget so easily?"

I stared at him. He didn't usually take such a harsh tone with me.

"Dude, chill," Nakia said.

He sighed. "I'm sorry, I didn't mean to snap. I'm just stressed out about Camp TechRo. The deadline for the registration fee is coming up, and I'm still short."

I gasped. I'd totally forgotten about the robotics summer camp Bruno wanted to go to. "What about that meeting in New York City?" I asked. "About the scholarship?"

"I didn't get it."

"Oh my God, Bruno!" Nakia whispered. "Why didn't you tell us?"

I sank down on my chair. "I'm so sorry. You should have led with that, Bruno!"

"No, the museum news was more important."

My eyes blurred. Nakia may not realize it, but this was Bruno talking to Ms. Marvel, not Kamala. We both knew everything related to her was the priority.

For both of us.

"You didn't find another job yet?" Nakia asked.

Bruno's shoulders slumped. "No. It's not the busy season."

I felt like a total ass for not asking him about all this earlier. "Maybe you can find something online," I offered. "Like tutoring or something. You're so good at teaching me physics."

He blinked. "Uh, that's because . . ."

I knew what he was going to say, so I pushed back my laptop and searched for a different topic. Anything to make him not admit to his feelings.

Feelings were stupid. Feelings had no place in our *strictly friends* relationship.

Nakia caught my eye and smirked. She could also guess what he was going to say. "Well, this article isn't going to write itself," she announced loudly.

"Yeah, I gotta go too," Bruno said quickly. "Back to my job search."

I watched silently as they both waved good-bye and logged off.

It was only when I was alone—lonely—in my room that I really thought about what Bruno had said. That private side conversation we'd had while Nakia listened wasn't all that uncommon. We'd become pros at talking about all things Ms. Marvel without anyone figuring it out.

But this time, it hit harder.

This time, he acknowledged that his own dreams and goals had taken a back seat to the museum theft.

Ms. Marvel had taken over his life, and not in a good way.

How long before he decided this wasn't worth losing his dreams for? That *I* wasn't worth losing his dreams for?

My guilt was like a living, breathing thing, so I went downstairs and spent the rest of the evening with Fahad Uncle and Abu in the living room. They talked about their teen years, about friends they hadn't seen in decades, and about family politics for both of them.

They also told me all about their motorbikes. Apparently Abu and Fahad Uncle had had matching ones, and they made for all sorts of fun times.

"Kamala, aren't you . . . bored . . . with all this grown-up . . . talk?" Fahad Uncle asked at one point, reaching over slowly to ruffle my hair. His fingers were thin and knobbly, making me want to weep.

I shook my head. "No, I want to spend time with you. That's what I came for."

"Where's that brother of yours?" Abu asked.

I shrugged. "Last I saw, he was helping Sumera Aunty with some books."

Fahad Uncle smiled softly. "Ah yes, her h-hadith collection. She's got all these . . . old books that she inherited from . . . her uncle. He used to be an imam . . . of one of the big mosques in Lahore, you know."

I didn't know that. But it made sense now why Aamir was hanging out with her so much. I'd seen them sitting in an old office off the front door the day before, piles of dusty books between them. Aamir had been excited, waving his arms about, making a point, while Sumera Aunty nodded.

Come to think of it, she'd also looked sort of happy. I guess she liked religious texts just as much as my brother did. She just wasn't so in-your-face about it.

"Fahad Uncle, can I ask you a question?"

"Sure, beti, anything."

"Why did you send me a picture of Minar-e-Pakistan that one time? Like, is there any significance to you, or you just saw a pretty picture and wanted me to have it?"

Fahad Uncle was quiet, thinking. I wondered if he was remembering when and why he bought the little picture. "I don't really know," he finally said. "I was at an art gallery and was thinking of . . . your father, how he wanted to study art . . . history . . . but never got the chance. And I thought you may . . . have shared the same passions. So . . . so I bought it for you."

Abu cleared his throat loudly. I knew he was trying to keep his emotions in check.

I leaned over and kissed Fahad Uncle on the cheek. His skin was cold and clammy, another stark reminder that he wasn't well. What I wouldn't do for the pair of emerald spectacles to heal all the pain this man felt.

"Thank you, Uncle," I said.

He smiled weakly, then motioned to the coffee table. "Bring me that photo album."

I went and got the album he was asking for. It was the kind you stuck printed pics in, thick with glossy black pages and clear plastic between them.

Fahad Uncle took the album and smoothed the cover with a trembling hand. "Did you know . . . we had a bucket list? Me . . . and your aunty Sumera?"

"Well . . ." I began, then stopped. His wife had spoken about their travels around the world on our first morning here, but I didn't want to shut him down. He had a little smile on his lips, like he was thinking of a small but lovely secret memory. "Tell me about it," I said.

"When I found out . . . about my cancer, several years ago, we decided to . . . make a list of all the places . . . we wanted to visit, and the . . . the experiences we wanted to have . . . before I . . ." He stopped to cough.

I gripped his hand, because I did not want him to finish

this sentence. "Is this album your pictures from your, uh, travel list?" I refused to call it a bucket list, like they were all waiting for him to kick the bucket. God forbid!

I was truly horrified that he'd talk like this about his impending death, but also a little impressed at his bravery. How many people could look death in the eye and decide to travel the world instead?

Fahad Uncle nodded and gave the album back to me. "Take a look."

I flipped the pages, my mouth open in wonder. Abu leaned over and looked at the pictures with me. I'd seen a few on the side table in the sitting room, but here were a bunch of others from EVERYWHERE! Indonesia, the Maldives, Japan, Norway, Germany, Ghana, Colombia . . . the album was full to the brim with pictures. Not just sceneries, but also experiences, like skydiving and mountain climbing. Watching a cultural dance in a village. Participating in ceremonies in temples.

And the best thing was the expressions on Fahad Uncle's and Sumera Aunty's faces.

I touched a picture with a finger. "You both look so happy."

"Yes, we were," he said, coughing again. "We are, I mean. This time brought us so close . . . together, Kamala."

"Really?" Abu frowned. "You must have been so stressed because of everything."

Fahad Uncle shook his head, trying to speak, but his coughing continued. Abu and I looked at each other, alarmed, but Fahad Uncle waved our concerns away. "I'm . . . fine. Don't worry." He took a deep, shaky breath. "Sumera and I . . . we became closer together during my illness. Yes, there is a lot of worry and . . . grief, even. But the memories we've made on these trips are so . . . incredibly special. I'd never want to lose them."

Gulping back my tears, I put down the album and gave him a tight hug. He patted my back again and again, coughing all the while.

"Fahad, maybe we should . . ." Abu began.

"No, no, I'm fine!"

But he wasn't fine. I could hear it in the wheezing and coughing that he needed help. I ran to get Sumera Aunty, and she clucked at her husband like he was a stubborn little boy. Then she called the doctor. He was a friend as well and made house calls especially for Fahad Uncle, even late at night.

"He'll be here in twenty minutes," Sumera Aunty said when the call ended. "With an oxygen tank."

I stood in the corner of the room, watching as my dear uncle lay back against the couch pillows, too weak and exhausted to protest.

When the doctor had come and gone, and Fahad Uncle was safely in bed with some strong pain meds, Sumera Aunty gave me a hug and asked, "Want a snack?"

I nodded. I'd missed dinner, and now I felt drained and hungry. Abu and Aamir had both gone up to their rooms, so it was just me and her.

We walked to the kitchen hand in hand. Sumera Aunty switched on the lights and pointed to a stool. "Sit, I'll make you something."

"You don't have to. . . ."

"I want to." She turned to the fridge and started taking things out. Bread. Tomatoes. A container of spicy shredded chicken. A block of cheese. "I didn't always have servants at my beck and call, you know."

"Really?"

"I grew up middle class. My father was a high school teacher, and my mother stayed at home to take care of me and my siblings. When I was twenty, my father passed away, and I had to start working to support the family."

"Wow." No wonder she looked so strong. Always smiling and patient. Never complaining. "Hope they appreciated it."

She gave me a knowing look, like she knew I was thinking of my own irritating family. The way Aamir and I squabbled wasn't lost on anyone here. "Family is important, Kamala. You can't let petty arguments ruin your relationship."

"Okay." I wasn't sure what Aamir and I had was petty, but I nodded. "So you got a job . . . ?"

"Yes, in the same school where my father had taught. It paid . . . peanuts, as you Americans say."

"You'd be shocked to know that teachers in the U.S. are also paid peanuts."

"It wasn't until I married your uncle that I saw wealth." Sumera Aunty laughed suddenly. "I remember my first few months as a young bride. One of the servants actually complained that I was in her way. She'd never met a begum sahiba who worked alongside them in the kitchen!"

"That's funny. You're still so . . . humble."

She looked in the direction of her room, where her husband lay sleeping. "God has a way of keeping us humble, Kamala."

I didn't really have anything to say to that, so I didn't. I sat silently and watched as she assembled a sandwich. She had soft brown hands with unpainted nails. Capable hands, like Ammi's.

Suddenly I missed my mother fiercely. My eyes blurred, and I swiped a finger at them.

Sumera Aunty looked at me with her eyebrows drawn together. "Something wrong, beta?"

I nodded wordlessly. What wasn't wrong at this point? And how was she, the wife of a terminally sick cancer patient, worrying about me right now? I wished so hard in that moment that I had those stupid emerald spectacles. Maybe they'd heal Fahad Uncle and obliterate the grief in Sumera Aunty's eyes. "How do you find courage when everything is going wrong, Aunty?"

She smiled so sadly, my eyes watered. "Kamala, my girl, it's not easy. Look at us, all waiting for a good man to die. All praying for something that the doctors have already told us cannot happen. His cancer is too advanced. It's not going to be cured."

"I'm sorry," I whispered. Her problems were way bigger than mine. What right did I have to complain?

She went back to the fridge to get a bottle of apple juice. "What can you do? It's God's will. We have to show patience during hard times, you know?"

I nodded, because yes, I did know. This was what Ammi had meant at the airport. Showing you could take anything and everything that the universe dished out to you. Patience and bravery, those were the key ingredients. "You two are so brave," I told her.

She shrugged. "We've had time to come to terms with it, say our good-byes, you know. This time we've spent together, traveling, seeing the world, has been so good for us. In a way, we owe the cancer a lot. We grew closer together, created this loving relationship that we never had before. . . . It is all somehow worth it. Love and closeness have come out of this horrible sickness, so how can I begrudge it?"

I was speechless. Fahad Uncle had said a similar thing, but she had a way with words that really brought home the message. I leaned over and kissed her softly on the cheek.

She smiled at me. "I'm so glad you all came. It's been so good for Fahad to spend time with your father."

"Me too," I whispered. "I'm glad we were able to visit."

Sumera Aunty slid my sandwich plate toward me, then held up a finger. "I'll be right back. I have something for you."

I took a bite of her delicious spicy-chicken-and-tomato sandwich while I waited. She came back in a few minutes, holding a dark green backpack with brown leather accents. "For you," she said. "Since you lost your other one."

I set down the sandwich and took the backpack carefully.

It was soft like butter, and I had to stop myself from rubbing it across my face like a weirdo. "It looks expensive," I murmured.

"It's my gift, so don't complain."

I laughed as I set the backpack aside. "Why would I complain? It's lovely. Thank you!"

"Good, I'm glad you like it." Sumera Aunty gave me another hug, then turned away. "I'm going to go sit with your uncle. Don't stay up too late."

I ate the rest of the sandwich and drank two glasses of apple juice while staring at the backpack in front of me. I hadn't been kidding; it was really lovely. It looked sturdy and functional but also very fashionable.

I went back to my room, happier than I'd been the whole day. I took a picture of my new backpack and sent it to Nakia. She'd get a kick out of it, for sure.

I tried not to think about Fahad Uncle and his cancer, but I kept returning to it like a scab I couldn't help picking at. This time, though, it wasn't with that crippling sense of grief.

This time, I realized all wasn't lost.

I just needed one thing: Shah Jahan's spectacles.

I logged in to my email to find the details Bruno had sent about Deen. His email address and the secondary one he'd created for Ms. Marvel. It was time to get the spectacles back and heal Fahad Uncle, for the sake of my family. It was the least I could do for my beloved uncle.

Dear Shareef Deen/Asaar, I am tired of fighting you, so I will say this once only. Return the emerald spectacles to me, otherwise I will have no choice but to expose your identity to the world. Let's see how the Pakistani public views you when they find out you're not the conscientious businessman you pretend to be. Contact me ASAP.

Your worst nightmare,

Ms. Marvel

"Hey, Kamala, what're you doing tonight?" Aamir asked, peering into my room.

I held up *In Other Rooms*. "Reading."

"I'm going to watch a movie and eat ice cream. Wanna hang out with me?"

I frowned. It was past midnight, and Aamir never stayed up this late. "Are you serious?"

"Yeah, why not? I've got nothing better to do."

What was happening right now? Maybe I'd teleported to another Earth (it had happened once or twice before) or hit my head and was in a coma. Aamir gave me an exasperated look and started to leave. I thought about what Sumera Aunty had said earlier. You can't let petty arguments ruin your relationship.

"Wait!" I jumped off the bed and followed him.

Aamir's room was next to mine but larger, with a big-screen TV on one wall and a cozy little couch in front of it. "Wow, you got the nice room, eh?"

Aamir shrugged. "I didn't ask for it."

I blinked again, because he looked . . . uncomfortable. I didn't think I'd ever seen my older brother like this.

"I know," I finally said. It was true. I knew he hadn't demanded a bigger room or expected it because of his age or gender or anything else.

Aamir might be a lot of things, but he was never demanding of things.

People, yes, especially me. But that was a different story.

We sat on the couch with a big tub of pistachio ice cream and two spoons between us. "We should probably get napkins," I mumbled around a huge bite of ice cream.

"We should probably eat like civilized human beings," Aamir grumbled, but he got up and went to get some paper towels from the bathroom.

We started the movie—a Pakistani blockbuster called *The Legend of Maula Jatt*. It was full of gore and violence and fight scenes better than anything I'd seen in real life. I loved it.

It was exactly what I needed.

"You okay?" Aamir asked suddenly.

I was too riveted to the screen to turn. "Yeah, why?"

"Sumera Aunty thought you seemed sad."

I shrugged, still not looking at him. We never had this kind of conversation. I wasn't sure how to deal. "It's just everything, you know," I replied vaguely, hoping he'd be satisfied.

"Hmm," he said as if he knew.

"Speaking of Sumera Aunty, since when did you become such good pals?"

He rolled his eyes. "Since we discovered we had something in common. Religion."

I snorted.

"What?" He pushed me a little with his arm. "It's true. I found her reciting the Quran one day, and we got to talking about our favorite reciters, and then she showed me those old hadith books, which honestly are such a treasure, and—"

I held up a hand. "Okay, okay. I understand."

Aamir continued like I hadn't said anything. "It's nice to have someone who doesn't mock or tease me about being religious, you know."

I smiled and went back to the TV. "Dude, I know."

He smiled at me, and we went back to watching the movie. It was only when the movie ended and I went back to my room that I realized that we hadn't argued even once the entire evening.

I got ready for bed and thought that maybe, maybe, my horrible relationship with my brother was finally mending.

Maleeha showed up mid-morning the next day. "We're going shopping!"

We were hanging out in the living room, all except for Fahad Uncle, who was still sleeping in his room. I'd brought my book down with me and was half reading, half watching the birds outside in the garden.

There was a gorgeous bluish-green parrot on a tree branch close to the window, staring at me.

"A-again?" I stuttered. I wasn't opposed per se, but the money Abu had given me at the start of this trip was seriously depleted.

Some might also think I didn't really need more clothes.

Some, such as Aamir.

"Maleeha ji," he began. "Our Jersey City imam Sheikh Abdullah delivered a lecture on avarice and greed recently. It was fascinating. I'm sure there's audio and transcripts, if you'd like them?"

"Stop." I kicked Aamir's leg, wanting to maintain the peace we'd established last night.

He shook his head and went back to the box he'd been rummaging through. It was full of old memorabilia Sumera Aunty's uncle had left behind.

Maleeha ignored Aamir and sank down next to me. Instead of her regular jeans and tunics, she was wearing the traditional shalwar kameez with a dupatta twisted around her neck. "Remember you were asking me for old books about the Mughals?"

I sat up straight. "Yeah?"

"My father said he knows a bookseller in Urdu Bazaar who may have some older manuscripts. It's a long shot, but we can go there and check it out."

"What's this?" Aamir asked, looking up. "Urdu Bazaar is not the sort of place you girls need to be going!"

Maleeha curled her lip. "Is he always like this?" she asked me.

I nodded. "Don't worry, Aamir, we'll be fine," I dismissed him, and turned to Maleeha. "When can we go?"

"Never!" Aamir inserted.

I kicked his leg harder this time. Why was he acting this

way again? I thought we'd bonded over violent movies and ice cream. I thought we had an understanding.

"Ow, Kamala!" he whined.

"Look, mister," Maleeha told him, "this is the twenty-first century. Girls are allowed to go places by themselves."

"I'm not saying you're not allowed. . . ."

"Abu!" I called out.

Abu looked up from the newspaper he was reading. "Kamala, Aamir's right. Open-air bazaars may not be safe for you."

I gasped, feeling totally betrayed. "Seriously?"

"And, Aamir . . ." Abu continued, totally ignoring me, "if you're so concerned about your sister's safety, then you go with her."

I laughed. Aamir's face was hilarious. Eyes popping out, beard trembling. Ha!

"Let's go." I stood up and pulled Maleeha behind me. She waited in the front entry while I quickly changed and piled my hair into a ponytail. To make Abu happy, I slung a dupatta around my neck like Maleeha. Seemed liked the dress code for old open-air markets was different than what one wore at a mall. Who knew?

At the last minute, I picked up my beautiful new backpack. I'd already put my Ms. Marvel costume inside, but there was still plenty of space. Maybe I'd end up buying a lot of books. I didn't want to have to carry things in plastic bags. Save the oceans and all that.

When we reached Maleeha's car, Aamir was already sitting in the front seat next to the driver. "Looks like I'm going with you today!" he said, his pompous, superior expression back on his face like it had never left.

"Perfect!" I said, gritting my teeth. I'd wanted to talk to Maleeha about Bruno and my stupid, complicated feelings about him. Only, there was no way I was doing that in front of my brother. He'd have a field day giving me lecture after lecture regarding modesty and propriety and blah, blah.

I'd rather throw myself out of this moving car.

I soon forgot my disappointment, though. Urdu Bazaar was awesome. It was a series of narrow streets lined on each side with tiny shops overflowing with books and stationery. Some shops faced the larger streets, so they were more "open-air," while others were in darkened corners of what looked to me like a labyrinth.

"Don't worry," Maleeha said as we walked into a narrow street, "despite what your brother thinks, it's pretty safe."

"I'm not worried, like *at all*." My eyes were huge as I tried to fit in all the sights around me. Books ranging from children's novels to encyclopedias, religious texts to racy romances, were all around me. Most were in Urdu—hence the name of the market—but some were in English. I even spied a few texts in French.

Or German. I really couldn't tell the difference.

Ammi would get a kick out of this, I thought. I stopped to take pictures for her.

"Addicted to your phone, I see?" Aamir whispered in my ear.

"Shush!" I glared at him. "I'm sending a message to Ammi."

Still, I sent the text and then put away my phone. I didn't need another lecture from Mr. Superiority.

It took us about ten minutes to reach the shop Maleeha's father had told her about. It was tucked between two much larger shops, old and quiet, as opposed to the new, brightly lit interiors of its neighbors. An elderly, bearded man in a gray shalwar kameez sat cross-legged on the counter, reading.

Maleeha cleared her throat. "Salaam alaikum, Uncle," she said loudly.

He looked up. "Ah, you must be Abdul Rahman's daughter. Walaikum salaam."

"How do you know who we are?" I asked, wondering what connection Maleeha's rich businessman father had to this dilapidated shop.

The shopkeeper smiled at me kindly. "Not many young people come to my shop, unfortunately," he said in English.

"I'm not surprised," Aamir said snarkily from behind me. "I'm not sure why we're here, to be honest."

"Nobody asked you to come with us!" Maleeha hissed at him.

"Somebody has to make sure you girls don't get hurt!" he hissed back.

I ignored them, despite my rising anger. "Uncle, do you have any books about ancient Mughal artifacts? Maybe something that would explain some of the myths and legends behind them?"

The shopkeeper stared intensely into my eyes. It was creepy, but I stared straight back, trying to tell him without words that I was trustworthy and didn't have any ulterior motives.

Well, I did, but nothing bad. I was trying to right some wrongs, get some answers that would ensure nobody else died or got injured on my watch.

The shopkeeper finally got up and brought out some books. "This first one is about the early Mughals and their love for art and architecture," he said, pointing to the bottom one. "And the next two are about the history of the Mughal Empire."

I nodded, uncaring. I didn't really need to know more about the history. I'd gotten enough history lessons in the last week to last me a lifetime.

The shopkeeper pointed to an old book on the top of the pile. It was so faded that you could hardly make out the cover. "This one is about some of the legends that abound regarding some of the precious artifacts."

Now we were talking! I leaned forward to grab the book, but the shopkeeper put his palm on top, guarding the pile. "It's in Urdu; you wouldn't understand it."

"I can read it," Maleeha protested.

"No." The shopkeeper scowled. "It's too old and tattered. I don't want people touching it."

I stopped myself from rolling my eyes. "Well, how do we know what's in it, then?"

"Ask me a question," he said. "I know this book inside out. I can answer whatever you need to know."

Both Maleeha and Aamir glared.

I stared at the shopkeeper again. His gaze was fixed, his eyes practically burning into me. Was he trying to give me a hint? Prompting me to ask specific questions? Guiding me?

Stop imagining things that don't exist, Kamala.

I racked my brain. Ammi had said that emeralds had healing properties. Maybe that was the angle I needed. "Does it talk about stones—precious stones—and their properties?" I asked.

The shopkeeper looked pleased. "Yes, that's an excellent question. Some stones were reputed to have important qualities. For example, emeralds were believed to possess healing powers, so they were often worn to repel illnesses."

"Ammi already told us all this," Aamir inserted helpfully. "You didn't need to come here."

The shopkeeper turned his intense eyes on my brother. "No effort ever goes wasted," he intoned. "You of all people should know this, O pious one."

Aamir squared his shoulder and smirked. "I suppose that's true."

I took a deep breath and decided to ask the question topmost on my mind. "Have you heard about the emerald spectacles that belonged to Shah Jahan?"

The shopkeeper turned away from my brother and went back to staring at me intensely. "How do you know about them?"

I shrugged. "I did some research."

He scoffed. "Your internet schminternet isn't going to give you anything except stories."

"That's why we've come to you, Uncle," Maleeha said with a cajoling smile. "Straight to the source!"

He ignored her too. He was so close to me now that I could see the hairs in his nostrils. "I've seen the spectacles work their magic, you know. I've been a witness to all the havoc they can cause."

Aamir made a loud, mocking sound, somewhere between a laugh and a scoff.

I gulped. "What do you mean?" I whispered. I was 50 percent sure this was just senile rambling, but the other 50 percent wondered if he was a hundred years old like the Barringtons.

"The spectacles can heal you, against all odds," he whispered back.

"Yeah, right," Aamir grumbled. "Come on, Kamala, time to go."

I didn't move. I looked deep into the shopkeeper's eyes and asked, "What have you seen?"

"My grandmother was very sick. Typhoid, I think it was. It had swept through the village and many of the people had died, but we were rich. My grandfather was the landowner, you see. He barricaded our family inside the doors of our haveli to make sure we didn't get ill. But my grandmother often went outside anyway, to assist the villagers. One of the village women was having a baby, and she went to help deliver it. She said it was her responsibility as the landowner's wife."

Aamir muttered something about landowners not having to sell books in old bazaars to make a living, but I tuned him out. There was a flare in the old man's eyes, a rich history that spoke of truth and grief and things he'd seen in his lifetime.

"How old were you?" I asked. "When your grandmother became ill?"

"Ten or eleven. I remember it like yesterday. My grandfather was distraught. He loved her very much, and he called all kinds of doctors and healers, even peers and mullahs, to try to help her. I used to stay in her room, rubbing her feet, telling her stories. I'd make up all sorts of imaginary tales in my mind, just to get her to smile. She said my stories made her feel better."

"I'm sure they did," I assured him. He looked so lost. So devastated.

He continued. "She got sicker and sicker, and in those days, they didn't have antibiotics and things to treat patients. In a couple weeks' time, she was at death's door."

"Then what happened?" Aamir asked, despite himself.

"A young man came one night, saying he was a descendent of the Mughals. That he had something in his possession that had been passed down from one generation to the next. And maybe it could heal my grandmother. He showed us a velvet pouch, and inside was a pair of glasses, sparkling with green and white."

"Emeralds," I breathed. "And diamonds."

The shopkeeper nodded. "Yes. The lenses were emeralds, and around the frames were round diamonds. It was so beautiful, it hurt my eyes. It shone even in the darkness of the room my grandmother slept in. He put the glasses on as we all watched, and kept rubbing his fingers along the frames, like he was soothing them. Or himself, I don't know. He kept at it for hours, so long that I fell asleep on the ground near the bed. When I woke up, it was morning. The mysterious man was gone, and my grandmother was awake."

"Was she . . . better?" Maleeha asked eagerly. Everyone had become entranced by the story.

"She was more than better," the shopkeeper replied with another intense look. "She was completely healed. No signs of the illness she'd been plagued with for the last two weeks."

"Wow," I squeaked. Here was the proof that Bruno's healed injury wasn't a fluke. It actually happened.

Which meant that it could happen with Fahad Uncle too. I just needed to get my hands on those magical, wonderful spectacles again.

Then I had a thought. "Wait, were there any side effects of the, uh, magic?"

"Are you really believing this nonsense, Kamala?" Aamir protested. "It's a nice story, but—!"

I shushed him with a hand. I really didn't care for all his silly interruptions. Nobody had told him to come with me.

The shopkeeper sagged against the counter like he was suddenly tired. With trembling hands, he picked up the pile of books in front of us and began to pack them up. "She forgot me," he admitted with a sigh.

"What do you mean she forgot you?" Maleeha asked, alarmed.

He shrugged in that *who knows* way that elderly people sometimes do, like they've seen the world and understood that some things remain mysteries forever. "My stories. She forgot all of them. She didn't even remember that I used to sit at her bedside day and night, talking to her, making her smile."

I started to say that didn't sound too bad, but he went on. "She forgot other things too. Important events, people she'd met those early days of her illness. Maybe the magic touched her head in some way. Maybe it was the typhoid. Nobody knows. But she forgot everything that had happened after the day that little girl was born, in the village."

"You mean, the day she went to help deliver the baby?" I asked, my stomach filling with dread. "The day she caught those typhoid germs, probably?"

The shopkeeper nodded sadly, just a short, succinct movement of the head, as if his entire body hurt. "I never really got my grandmother back, even though she was healthy again."

"What an odd man," Aamir remarked as we walked the streets of Urdu Bazaar. "That story was . . . total fantasy, obviously."

I gave him a sideways glance. This was my brother, only seeing the black and white in everything. No grays allowed in his perspective. "He seemed to believe it," I replied quietly.

Aamir scoffed. "So, like, magical glasses are real? How do we still have people getting sick and dying every single day, then? How come Fahad Uncle is dying, Kamala?"

My eyes burned with unshed tears. "I don't know. I don't have all the answers."

Maleeha reached over and squeezed my hand. "That's okay. Nobody has all the answers."

I laughed tearfully. "Not even you?"

"Nope, especially not me." She looked stunned, like her entire worldview had changed in the past half an hour.

I blinked to clear away the paralyzing grief that always rose in my chest whenever I thought about Fahad Uncle. I could admit that the shopkeeper's story had shaken me. I'd never really believed that the spectacles could heal to that extent. Or that the side effects could be so . . . monumental.

But the intense truth in the old man's eyes couldn't be denied. He had seen them at work as a child, and it had left an impression forever.

The worst part: the side effects. Bruno had lost a few moments of memories. No biggie, to him. But the shopkeeper's grandmother had lost weeks. She'd forgotten meaningful time spent with her own flesh and blood. Important things that had happened. Events, experiences.

So what would happen to all of Fahad Uncle's memories if—when—I healed him with the spectacles? If I ever got them back from Asaar and was able to use them on my uncle, what would he forget?

The question left me almost breathless with worry.

"You okay, Kamala?" Maleeha asked, nudging my shoulder with hers.

"Uh, yeah, I'm fine."

We left Urdu Bazaar and walked over to another famous outdoor market called Anarkali Bazaar. We saw little shops selling colorful hanging decorations made with glass and beads. *Would Nakia like this?* I wondered. I should get her—and Bruno—some gifts before we left Lahore.

Maleeha started telling us the legend of Anarkali, the supposed concubine lover of the Mughal emperor Jahangir when he was just a prince named Saleem.

I pushed away all my swirling thoughts about magical spectacles. "Concubine lover?" I demanded. "They had those back then? I thought Desis were supposed to be all serious and decent."

"We're talking about the Mughals. They had all kinds of vices in their court." Maleeha gave me an *Are you kidding?* look. "Nobody really knows who Anarkali was. Maybe a prostitute in the court. Maybe a dancing girl."

"What happened to her?"

"Well, Saleem's father, the great emperor Akbar, was enraged when he discovered the, uh, relationship. He threatened to disown Saleem, punish him, et cetera. Finally, he had Anarkali entombed behind a wall."

"What?" I gasped. "Why?"

Maleeha shrugged. "She was highly unsuitable. No money, no prospects. No royal lineage."

Horrific. No matter how creative, these rich rulers were also pretty barbaric, if you asked me.

"It's just a story, Kamala," Maleeha assured me, squeezing

my hand once again. "No need to look ready to fight for Anarkali. Nobody's sure if she actually existed."

"Another fantastical story," Aamir said, shaking his head. "Complete bakwas."

I sighed and rubbed my forehead wearily. I'd hoped Aamir would have calmed down, but he was back to his annoying, holier-than-thou behavior. I just needed a break from him. I pointed toward a shop that had brightly colored prayer rugs hanging from the ceiling. "Look, Aamir! Ja namaz!"

Aamir whirled around and immediately headed that way. "Oh, those would make perfect gifts!"

Maleeha shook her head. "Wow, how do you stand him?"

An image of Ammi at JFK airport rushed to my mind. "Patience has a magical effect, Maleeha dear," I told her. "Remember what John Q. Adams said?"

"Well, look who's being wise," she retorted. "Fountain of—what did you call it? Information?"

"Ha." I began walking. "Fountain of knowledge."

We stopped near a little cart selling brightly colored bracelets. "Ooh, they're so pretty," Maleeha exclaimed.

From the corner of my eye, I saw familiar gray clothing I'd seen just a little while ago. "You go ahead," I muttered. "I need to sit down for a bit."

Without waiting for a response, I hitched my backpack

higher on my shoulder and walked quickly away. Behind a bicycle shop, I found who I was looking for.

The shopkeeper from Urdu Bazaar, only his beard was now unkempt and his shalwar kameez torn in places. "What happened to you?" I whispered, aghast.

He sighed and leaned against the wall. "A woman came to my shop and tore it apart."

"A woman? Who was she? What did she want?"

"I don't know who she was," he admitted. "She didn't look like anything I'd ever seen. She had an American accent like you, but she was dressed . . . differently. A lot less clothing, for one. And her hair was in a long—how do I say this?—tail."

My heart stuttered. It was obvious that the woman was Delilah. What on earth was she doing in Lahore, in this little bazaar? Why had she attacked the bookstore?

"She said she was looking for the magic spectacles," the shopkeeper said. "I . . . I haven't seen those since I was ten years old. I don't have them!"

I patted his hand. He looked so scared and desperate. "I'm sorry. This woman is . . . evil. She's trying to get the spectacles so she can become more powerful."

He shook his head sadly. "Those spectacles are the real evil. They may give life, but they take away everything good too. She must be careful what she wishes for." He looked at me in that intense way of his, so it felt almost like he was warning me, not Delilah.

"Thank you for telling me," I said. I wasn't sure why he'd sought me out. Maybe he connected the dots because I was also American, and also asking about the spectacles. "Please go home. Try and get some rest."

"What will you do?"

Grimly, I hefted my backpack onto my shoulder. It's a good thing I'd brought it along. "I'm gonna find that evil woman and punish her."

The shopkeeper begged me to be careful and left. I asked the bicycle shop owner if he knew where the public restrooms were, and he pointed them out only a few yards away. Bingo!

Delilah was probably around somewhere. She'd still be looking for the spectacles, putting innocent people in danger. I had to stop her. I had to.

Blood pumping, I went into a restroom, locked the door, and changed into my Ms. Marvel costume. I might be anywhere in the world, and this costume made me feel stronger. More confident.

Basically, the opposite of Kamala Khan.

I slunk out of the restroom, ready to find Delilah. I could already hear shouts and crashes not far away, and that's where I headed. Sure enough, Delilah was standing in the middle of an alley lined with shops, throwing punches left and right. Some people were huddling together inside, while others stood frozen near the walls. "Where are the spectacles?" Delilah screamed. She was holding a small round object.

Yup, she'd lost it. Did she really think these randos on the street knew what she was talking about?

Time to take this crazed villain down.

"Why don't you fight someone your own size?" I called out. Then, without waiting for a reply, I made my right arm big and long and punched her in the head. *Yowza!*

She went down with a yell but bounced back in the next second. "Ms. Marvel! I knew I'd find you here!" She seemed almost cheerful, like all this chaos was a ploy to bring me to her.

I wouldn't put it past her. It was a decent strategy to trap me.

I brought my arm back to my body and gave her a mocking slow clap. "Good job! You get ten points for excellent deduction!"

Delilah's face contorted. "Are you making fun of me, you . . . you punk?!"

She ran at me with lightning speed, slapping me with her open palm, then kicking me in my stomach so hard that I reeled backward.

Oof! Every breath in my body flew out my mouth.

Pain gushed in.

Delilah chortled like it was funny.

Shaking my head to get rid of the ringing, I made my arm long and punched her back. Twice. Three times.

She took it like the super-strong evil rat she was. "You think you can embiggen me to death?" She laughed and took a long silver weapon from her back. "My energy blaster will pulverize you!"

Shoot. An energy blaster?

I hated those.

I hardly had time to react before Delilah let loose with a red energy shot that missed my head by inches. People scattered around, trying to get away from us.

My heart was beating so fast, it felt like it would leap out of my chest and attack Delilah.

I crouched and sent a long, slinky arm to grab the energy blaster. "I'll take that!"

I threw the weapon far away, then sent the other arm to punch her over and over. Over and over. "This is for those security guards you hurt!"

Delilah batted my long arms and giant fists away from her without much fear. "Ah, you heard?"

It infuriated me, her lack of care. Her disregard for human life. I punched harder. Faster.

She fell backward into a shoe display but got up in a flash. Drat. She didn't seem to be slowing down at all.

Me on the other hand? I was flagging, big-time. I felt stupid and useless and just . . . not enough. How was this woman always able to get the upper hand? How?

With another scream, I threw all my anger and frustration into my fist and punched her hard.

Or at least, I tried.

She ducked, and my fist landed on a wooden sign behind her. It splintered and fell to the side.

"Give up," she sneered, just before grabbing the energy blaster and blasting me to the ground.

I was exhausted. I needed a few seconds to breathe, but Delilah was striding up to me fast.

Ammi, Abu, I'm sorry for everything, I prayed frantically. *Aamir, don't be such an ass. Try to do better now that you're the only child. Nakia and Bruno, stay safe. There are so many monsters out there. Maleeha, don't ever lose that encyclopedic brain of yours; it's as lovely as the rest of you.*

Oh God, let there be a special heaven for super heroes who've saved lives and tried to be good daughters. I may not go to the mosque regularly, but my heart is in the right place.

Oh, and don't let Bruno end up with that Brittany gal. She's awful.

My head swam, and my breath stuttered in my throat. Darkness flooded the corners of my eyes.

This was it. This was the end of Ms. Marvel.

I waited for the next blast of energy, but it didn't come. Instead, I heard the crackling of a familiar light, then saw the green and white colors zap right into Delilah's back.

Delilah roared and went down like a sack of bricks.

Behind her stood Asaar, grinning at me. "Need some help?"

I groaned as I stood up. "Why are you here?"

"There's a shopkeeper in Urdu Bazaar whom I've been keeping an eye on," Asaar said. "He called me and asked me to come rescue you."

I scowled. "I don't need help. What I do need are my spectacles back!"

"*Your* spectacles?" He lost his grin, but the superior, cocky expression was still on his face.

I prowled closer, panting, trying to get my heartbeat under control. I was so sick of everyone treating me like a little girl, thinking I needed help. Thinking they could hoodwink me and steal from me. "Yes, mine. I had them in my backpack, which you stole."

"They belong to my family." Asaar backed away, holding up his hands. I noticed that the light on his fingertips was gone, but I knew it could come back any second. I'd seen it happen before. "Not to you, or the Jersey City Art Museum, or the Barringtons, or anyone else. Not to Kingpin or Delilah or the Avengers."

I didn't care. I was past caring. All I wanted was to get the spectacles from him somehow and take them back to Fahad Uncle. Even after hearing about the shopkeeper's grandmother, I wasn't willing to give up.

If there was even a small chance that Fahad Uncle would get better, I was taking it.

Asaar was still backing away. "Look, I don't want to fight with you," he said placatingly. Maybe he saw how upset and determined I was. Maybe all my emotions showed on my face.

Like I said, I was past caring.

I clenched my hand into a giant fist. Then I crashed it down on his head.

Or at least, I tried.

Asaar leapt to the side, then jumped on top of a cart covered by a tarp. He balanced himself on the uneven surface, one of his legs wobbling a little, and shouted, "Stop!"

"Never!"

He held up his hands, where his green-and-white light was already crackling away. *Zzap!* He threw it right at me, then jumped down and ran.

I shook off the electricity and rushed after him at full speed. I didn't think about Delilah, or Aamir and Maleeha. I just wanted to catch this pain in my butt and make him turn the spectacles over.

Asaar ran down a narrow street, then another, where the shops were mostly closed. He was fast, but I could be faster. With a grin, I made my legs longer and longer, until I overtook Asaar. "Going somewhere?" I mocked as I got ahead of him and stopped.

He came to a screeching halt. "I don't want to fight you!"

"Too bad," I replied. "I want to fight *you*."

"Very well," he said, taking a deep breath, then throwing light zaps. Right. On. My. Face.

I groaned as they fell on my skin, my hair, my face. Rationally, I knew he wasn't sending full-power blasts my way. I'd felt those, and they weren't fun.

This was Asaar being a gentleman villain, and that meant I had a chance to defeat him.

As Abu often quoted from one of his oldie movies: *Jo dar gaya who mar gaya*. He who gets scared dies.

I screamed to get Asaar's attention, like the little girl he assumed I was. "AAAH, that hurts! Help!"

He stopped zapping me immediately. His hands lowered and he stepped backward, the stupid man.

I grew my arms big and long, then shoved him away from me. Hard.

"Hey!" he shouted as he toppled to the ground.

In a flash, I was standing over him and throwing a clenched fist to his head. Once, twice, three times. I pummeled him while he groaned.

"That's right, buddy. I'm not a little girl," I told him furiously as I stood over him. "I'm a badass super hero, and the faster you accept it the better."

He grunted with each hit but kept standing. Ugh, how strong was this guy?

"I can't believe I came here to help you," he roared. "Should've just left you to Delilah!" Light shot out from his fingertips, and without warning, he crashed it all over my body. This time, the blow was fully powered. One hundred percent strength.

I felt like a sizzling barbecue.

My knees buckled, and my head swam. I crashed down, my eyes closing before I even hit the ground.

I woke up groggy. The market was still mostly empty, but I saw people here and there, staring at me.

I needed to change out of my costume, pronto.

Quickly I ducked into an empty stall, dragged a box to keep the door closed, and changed. My heart beat wildly at the thought of being caught. At the thought of Asaar coming back and discovering my identity.

In the street, I took deep breaths and looked around. My brain was a blank, and I didn't know what to do next.

I just needed a minute to think.

"Kamala!" yelled a familiar, annoying voice.

I whirled around to see Amir stomping toward me with a scowl. Maleeha trailed behind him, smiling apologetically.

"I can't believe you just disappeared by yourself!" Aamir exclaimed. "After everything I told you about sticking to my side! What were you thinking?"

I gritted my teeth, trying not to smack him.

Yeah, he was my brother, and family was important, and good Muslims didn't hate the sinner, only the sin, et cetera, et cetera. But the way Aamir was acting was beyond ridiculous. It was insulting. He was treating me like a little girl again, despite our peaceful evening the day before.

Despite me thinking he understood me better.

"It's a good thing you still had the FindMe app on, Kamala. Otherwise, we'd never have found you. . . ."

I blinked back tears from my eyes. I wasn't sad; I was angry. He didn't know me. He didn't trust me. His arrogance was unbelievable.

Maleeha squeezed my hand. For once she didn't have a

snappy comeback for my brother. I guess she'd been worried.

At least she wasn't lording it over me, telling me I didn't know anything, couldn't protect myself, should have stayed with her because I couldn't handle things myself.

Me. Ms. Marvel. Super hero with cool powers most people didn't even dare dream about.

We walked back to Maleeha's car. The ride home was quiet, thankfully.

As soon as we reached home, I spilled out of the car, grabbed my backpack, and rushed inside. I'd text Maleeha later to apologize; I just needed a hot shower, some food, and some peace and quiet.

First, though, I climbed on my bed and checked my email. Not my regular account, but the one Bruno had created for Ms. Marvel. I was going to write Deen another scathing email, telling him what I thought about his attack in the market.

I sat up quickly when I saw a new email notification. Nobody had this address except Bruno . . . and Shareef Deen.

I clicked on the email to open it.

Dear Ms. Marvel,

Please see the invitation to a party tomorrow night. I will answer all your questions there.

Sincerely, Shareef Deen

Blood pumped through my veins so loud I could almost hear it. Was he finally accepting defeat? Would he give me the spectacles at this party?

Or maybe it was a trap to finally annihilate me.

I clicked on the attachment, half worried it was a virus, but it was a fancy digital invitation requesting my presence at half past eight (British culture alive and well in postcolonial Pakistan, apparently) at an address that the internet told me was close to Fahad Uncle's house.

I read the fine print at the bottom of the invitation. I could bring two guests with me. I had to dress in formal wear. I was to carry no cell phones or recording devices.

I stared at the screen for a minute, then closed the email application and reopened it. The email was still there, waiting patiently.

I read the invitation again and again, until the words were burned into my retinas. I tried to find a trap or code or something. Anything for Deen to discover my identity.

There was nothing special about the invite. It looked plain and generic and ordinary.

Still, in my heart I knew it didn't matter if this was a trap. I was going.

I picked up my phone and texted Maleeha. *Wanna go to a party tomorrow night?*

"You look fabulous!" Sumera Aunty gushed, admiring me in the mirror of her bedroom.

Fahad Uncle smiled weakly from his bed. "Yes, she's grown into such a beautiful lady, MashAllah!"

I flushed. "Uh, thank you. Especially for the stylist, you know?"

Sumera Aunty tucked back a tendril of hair that had escaped from my elegant updo. "It's no trouble, child," she murmured. "You're like my own daughter."

I eyed the couple I loved like my own parents. "Do people know . . . ?"

"That I'm dying?"

I cringed. Maybe I should have kept my mouth shut.

"Well, we haven't announced it . . . in the papers or

anything." Fahad Uncle coughed and leaned back against the pillows.

"I guess I'm wondering how things would have been different if you had a large family," I admitted. I wasn't sure if it was insensitive to talk about how they didn't have any kids. All I knew was that I worried about them.

Sumera Aunty closed her eyes briefly, like she was in pain. "Life without a large family can be very lonely," she said softly. "But we aren't alone, you know. I have my siblings. I have Maleeha."

"And your parents . . . you and Aamir . . . mean so much to us," Fahad Uncle added.

I sniffed before I started bawling. "I'm glad we could be here for a few days, even if I'm out sightseeing every day!"

Sumera Aunty smiled a watery smile. "You're young, enjoying yourself. There's no harm in that."

"It makes me happy . . ." Fahad Uncle added, "to have you here, acting normal."

"That's good, then." I smoothed my fancy shalwar kameez, the one I'd bought from the mall a few days before and thought was a waste of money. It was black, with red roses embroidered all over the bodice and sleeves. Gold thread was intertwined with the red, making the whole outfit sparkle subtly. Around my neck was the fabulous necklace I'd bought on the same trip, the one I'd thought I'd never wear in a million years.

Well, I was wearing it now and looking awesome!

"Ready?" Abu peeked into the room. "Your friend is here."

I hugged Sumera Aunty and followed Abu out to the living room. He was dressed in a dark gray suit he'd borrowed from Fahad Uncle, but I only had eyes for Maleeha. "Girl, you look awesome!" I squealed.

Maleeha twirled around. "You like it?" Her white kameez was long, like a ball gown, so long I could only see a hint of white leggings underneath. It was some silky material that swished around her. The neckline was gold, and so were the edges of the sleeves.

"We're going to be late," Abu said, heading out.

"What about your brother?" Maleeha asked. "Are we safe from him, or is he accompanying us to act like an ass again?"

Abu frowned.

I laughed outright. "Sadly, I could only bring two guests with me."

"He must be devastated."

It took Maleeha's driver less than ten minutes to drive us to the address in the invitation I'd received. Cars were lined up to drop off guests, and we waited outside for a while. "We have to leave our phones," I suddenly remembered.

"What kind of party is this?" Abu grumbled.

"Uh . . ." I looked around wildly. "They don't want photos of the celebrities. . . ."

"Which celebrities?" Abu perked up. "Will Hamza Ali from *Maula Jatt* be there?"

I shrugged like that was a very real possibility. "You never know."

I met Maleeha's eyes. She was looking at me carefully, like she didn't know what to think of this entire situation.

"Can't wait to meet that Hamza dude," I said lightly.

"Sure, me too."

I bit my lip nervously. Maleeha didn't know what my interest in Shareef Deen was, only that I'd reached out to him via email and asked some questions, so he'd invited me—us—to this event. She'd been suspicious, of course. So had Abu, frowning heavily and muttering under his breath when I'd told him.

It wasn't every day a notoriously private millionaire, A.K.A. a beloved benefactor, invited a random stranger to meet with them.

Abu accepted it once I told him Deen was part of the Jersey City Mughal exhibit. Maleeha was a tougher sell, but the best thing about her was she didn't pester you with questions. Her intelligence was off the charts. If she didn't understand something right away, she'd frown and turn it over in her mind again and again, trying to figure it out. But she wouldn't press you to give answers you didn't want to.

I worried about the day she figured out my secret. Hopefully, I'd be long gone by then.

Our car slowly moved forward until we were at the head of the line. We left our phones in the console under the driver's care, Abu still grumbling about rich people and their idiosyncrasies, and climbed out.

"Whoa!" My mouth dropped open as I laid eyes on the house. Mansion? Estate? Palace? It was white stone with balconies on the upper floors, armed guards at the entrance, and a fountain in the middle of the circular driveway. Big cars and SUVs snaked in a line, letting out their passengers and then moving on slowly.

We had to walk up several small steps to reach the front doors, which were stained glass and huge.

"I've heard about this place," Maleeha whispered. "Mr. Deen holds these lavish parties where the average Pakistani is never allowed. It's all celebrities and politicians and fellow millionaires."

"Hey!" I smacked her arm lightly. "We're not average today! Look at us!"

"You know what I mean."

Maleeha looked starstruck, and Abu looked dazed. I took it upon myself to walk briskly up the steps, hoping the two would follow. A guard checked my invite, then opened one of the huge doors for us.

I smiled a thank-you, but he didn't even look at me. Rude.

Together, we entered the mansion and took deep breaths. Sure, I was acting like the perfect starry-eyed teenager blown away by riches, but underneath it I was determined. If this was Deen's primary home, then chances were I'd find the emerald spectacles hidden here somewhere.

"Come on, Kamala," Maleeha urged. "Let's see the inside."

The inside was even more gorgeous. Shining black and white tiles throughout, paintings on the walls, chandeliers dripping from the ceilings. People milled about, dressed in clothes and jewelry that screamed *Look at me, my owner is filthy rich!* The guests had drinks in their hands and bored, pouty looks on their faces. Most of them were older, but I saw a few kids my age or maybe in their early twenties. They looked the most bored, and I wondered if they'd been dragged to this party by their parents.

They were dressed fabulously, though, and I saw one teenage girl wearing a diamond necklace with rubies dripping down her very low neckline. I wished I had my phone to take a picture for Nakia. She would freak at the elitism on display.

"Welcome to another side of Lahore," Maleeha muttered. "Not the best side, but it's there, hidden from the masses."

"I feel underdressed," I muttered back.

"Same," Maleeha replied in a low voice.

It wasn't like her to be uncertain about her looks. "Are you okay?" I asked. "I know I dragged you here. . . ."

Maleeha straightened her spine. "Just a headache. I'll be fine once I eat something."

"Must be the heat," Abu told her kindly. "I got one too, the day Kamala and I went sightseeing. Be sure to get plenty of rest, beta."

"I will, Uncle," she replied.

"Oh, look, it's Yusuf Khan!" someone exclaimed. It was a man Abu's age, looking absolutely delighted to see us. "Where have you been all these years, yaar? We totally lost touch with you!"

Abu held out his arms. "Mahmood? Is that you? I didn't recognize you with all that hair."

Mahmood Uncle grinned and passed a bony hand over his head. "Hair transplant, yaar. Best decision of my life!" He beckoned and said, "Come, let me introduce you to my friends."

Since Mahmood Uncle hadn't acknowledged us girls, I didn't know if we should go with him. "How do you know this dude, Abu?" I whispered.

"He was in my college," Abu replied. "Rich kid. Father was a minister in the government, but he got embroiled in some bribery scandal and had to leave the country. Last I heard they'd settled in Dubai."

"Well, they're back," Maleeha said sarcastically. "With more hair than he left with, apparently."

I snickered.

Mahmood Uncle joined a group of men and then turned back to us. "Are you coming, Yusuf?" he shouted. "Hurry, my man. There's so much to catch up on."

Abu squeezed my hand and joined the group. I could tell he was excited about this new experience, these new surroundings. I'd been hesitant when I'd told him about the invitation, and he'd insisted he join me. *Don't want you going to parties on your own, whether it's in Pakistan or America,* he'd grunted.

But now, seeing him here, in his element despite how different it was from his everyday life, I was happy. *I gave my father something cool. It was me, Kamala, not Ms. Marvel.*

Plus, he looked great in a suit.

"I'm hungry," Maleeha announced, obviously getting over her self-consciousness. "Let's go find the food. It's bound to be out of this world."

We wound through the crowds, smiling politely at the people around us. I kept my eyes peeled for Shareef Deen, not sure if I'd even recognize him if I saw him. The only time I'd seen him in real life was at the exhibit in New Jersey, when he'd stood next to Kingpin at the press lectern. Every other time had been through pictures or videos.

What if he didn't even show up?

What if he did?

Don't be stupid, Kamala. I shook my head to rid myself of negativity. *He invited all these people to his house. He's not going to bail.*

"Ooh, look, sushi!" Maleeha found the buffet table and grabbed a plate.

The food lineup was . . . impressive. There were tables for different cuisines, including Japanese, Italian, and Mexican. At one section, servants were grilling Desi barbecue. Slightly apart was the dessert table, laden with brownies, cakes, pies, parfaits, and God knew what else.

This was ridiculous. Who needed this much food, especially when half the world starved daily?

Me, that's who. A greedy little monster inside me insisted that I needed to gobble up all this food, ASAP! It smelled delicious and looked gorgeous.

Just then, my mind flashed back to Sheikh Abdullah's lecture about avarice. I finally got it. Finally.

An hour later, stomach full of delicious food, I sat on the

edge of a couch in a room off the main hall, where the party raged. Maleeha sat with me, massaging her temples.

I wasn't feeling too great either. This place sucked all the energy out of you. Made you feel like you were lacking.

It wasn't like I hated the party overall. The food was incredible. Plus, we'd had a lot of fun the past hour, people-watching. Maleeha had pointed out some celebrities who I didn't know even existed. I'd told her a little about the ones I'd seen at the Jersey City Art Museum.

I'd also told her about Bruno's Camp TechRo woes and how he didn't have a job yet. She thought he wasn't trying hard enough to get a job because he wanted to spend every waking minute with me. "Just like Romeo would," she'd reminded me.

I'd told her to shut up, because that was a thought I didn't want or need.

Just then, I looked up to find Shareef Deen walking by, toward the grand winding staircase in the big hall. It wasn't the first time I'd seen him tonight. I'd caught glimpses of him more than a few times, surrounded by admiring fans.

It was definitely him. Tall, lean, graying temples. Muscles. Sharp-looking white tux with a black bow tie.

He sorta looked like a different version of Asaar, but you'd never guess they were the same if you didn't know it.

I felt a little smirk tugging my lips. I knew who he was, but he didn't know me, Kamala Khan. He'd invited Ms. Marvel to his party, so maybe it was time she showed up.

The only question was, when and how would our meeting take place?

My dilemma was solved when Maleeha groaned and staggered to her feet. "I'm not feeling too well. I think I'll head home."

I sprang up too. "What? Why? Your headache's that bad? Surely you're used to the heat in Lahore!"

"No, I just didn't get much sleep last night, and now I have a full-blown migraine. I'd rather go lie down in my dark room."

This was perfect. I'd get a chance to sneak around the mansion and look for the spectacles. Plus, Abu was still chatting it up with his old friends, a plate of food in his hand, a smile on his face. I really didn't want to interrupt him.

Then I had a sinking thought. "But we came with you. . . ."

Maleeha patted my hand. "Don't worry, Kamala. The driver will drop me home and come back for you."

Still, I hesitated. "Are you sure?"

"Yes, please stay and have fun."

"Okay, sounds good." I hugged her tightly. "Text me when you're feeling better."

"I will."

I didn't wait once Maleeha left. Determinedly, I walked out of the room and turned into the direction I'd seen Deen go. There were fewer people around near the staircase, but I wandered nearby for a few minutes, making sure nobody was paying me any attention. Then, with quick feet, I went up the stairs and down the first hallway on the second floor.

First things first, I needed a restroom to change in. I'd worn my Ms. Marvel costume under my clothes, knowing I'd be doing some investigating sooner or later.

Upstairs, it was darker and much quieter. The halls were covered with soft carpeting, and paintings lined the walls. I leaned forward and inspected a painting. It was a Mughal-style piece.

Of course.

These days, it seemed like I was discovering Mughal art at every corner.

The halls twisted this way and that, rooms on either side. I tried a small door, more like a linen closet, right at the top of the stairs. Bingo!

It opened easily, and I slid among blankets, pillows, cleaning supplies, and the biggest vacuum I'd ever seen. In a flash, I unzipped my clothes and stepped out of them. I balled them in my hands, then stopped. I still had to walk out of this mansion as Kamala Khan. Wrinkled clothes would really raise eyebrows among the picture-perfect crowd. Reaching for a hanger, I hung my clothes on the closet rod.

Perfect.

Then, as silently as I'd entered, I tiptoed out and closed the door softly behind me.

Now to find the spectacles.

The hallway was full of rooms on either side. Some were bedrooms, empty and sparely furnished. The others were bathrooms, all black tile and gold fixtures. Ew.

I was positive the spectacles weren't there. If I were in Asaar's place, I'd keep them close to me, in my bedroom or office or somewhere else that was very personal.

After a few minutes of walking, looking at expensive paintings, and trying not to cringe at the shadows around me, I came to a set of double doors. They were made of a solid wood like teak or mahogany, delicately patterned in the corners with a flowery design.

I was 99 percent sure these doors would also be locked. The knob was silver and round. I was prepared to stretch and shrink my hand to pick the lock—one of the first things I'd learned as Ms. Marvel—but there was no need. When I reached out and twisted, the knob turned smoothly.

I opened the door, then pulled it shut very gently behind me.

I was in an office. Bookshelves lined the walls, all except one, where a huge window overlooked the fountain in the driveway outside. Big leather armchairs were placed around the room, and lamps in the corners gave out soft yellow light.

In the middle of the room, facing me, was a desk of solid wood in the same style as the door.

My eyes widened. If the spectacles were in this room, that's where they'd be hidden. I just knew it! All I needed to do was go through the drawers and—

A floorboard creaked behind me, and I whirled around.

Across the open window, a shadowy figure came into view. The next second, the lights in the room switched on, making me blink.

"Hello, Ms. Marvel. Welcome to my home," said Shareef Deen.

I froze.

I'd known, as I snooped through the halls, that there was a chance I'd find Deen. Now that he was face-to-face with me, though, I didn't really know how to act. Most regular people got scared when they saw the Ms. Marvel costume. Villains scowled and threatened me.

This dude, though, seemed mildly entertained. He smirked at me like he knew all my secrets.

"Thanks for inviting me to your party," I said. "And for replying to my email in the first place."

"I was sure you'd show up. You want answers, don't you?"

"I want the spectacles more," I replied. "But sure, let's have Q and A first."

Deen pulled the leather chair behind the desk and sat down gracefully. "Go ahead—ask me."

I took a deep breath. Where to start? "Why were you at the exhibit opening in Jersey City?" I demanded. "Are you working with Kingpin?"

Deen's smirk grew into a full-blown grin. "I'd never work with scum like that."

I frowned. "But you were standing at the lectern with him, and you sponsored his exhibit. . . ."

The grin faded. "It's not Kingpin's exhibit. He doesn't own those artifacts."

"True, but—"

"I sponsor a lot of things related to Mughal art all over the world," he continued. "It's part of my mission."

Something about his arrogant attitude rubbed me the wrong way. He needed to be taken down a notch, and I was the person to do it. "Ah, yes, what did you call yourself? A repatriation warrior?" I mocked.

Deen didn't take the bait. He nodded calmly. "Yes, exactly that. I just let Kingpin—Fisk—think I'm in it for the publicity, but it's a good way to keep an eye on him."

My entire body relaxed. I hadn't realized I'd been holding a tension inside myself for so long, worrying about the connection between Asaar and Kingpin. For some reason, I'd never thought Asaar was truly evil, unlike Kingpin and Delilah.

"So you're not working together," I said slowly. "But he's

still working on something nefarious. Something to do with magical artifacts."

Asaar's face became dark and grim. "He's trying to amass power by collecting all sorts of magical objects. Some he keeps in a warehouse; others he disposes of."

"How do you know all this?"

He barked out a laugh. "I know a lot more than you, little girl. I've been keeping tabs on him for a long time now."

Little girl? My heart sank.

Ugh, Asaar was no different than the others. Treating me as a teenager, disrespecting my powers. I *hated* that.

"At least I'm not a common thief, stealing things that don't belong to me!" I stated harshly.

Deen stood up, shoving the chair back so hard that it fell to the floor with a muffled thud. "Stealing? I told you before, I didn't steal anything. I simply took back what was stolen from me. From us!"

"Isn't that just vigilante justice?" I asked. "What's to stop someone else from doing the same thing? What's to stop people from getting hurt?"

My breath hitched as I remembered the security guards at the New Jersey History Collection.

Deen smiled cruelly. "It did work. It's been working for years. The spectacles aren't the first item I've taken back from their original thieves, and they won't be the last. I spend a lot of time and money on this passion project of mine."

"Money?" I scoffed. "What money do you spend on it? It's all stolen, just like Kingpin's stash."

"Ah, you haven't done your research, have you, Ms. Marvel? Not all the pieces I bring back are stolen. Some I buy from collectors. Others are traded on the black market. It's only the ones in museum exhibits that I can't access otherwise. So I must sneak in and take them away."

My jaw dropped. "You think that's a good thing? You sound so . . . proud of yourself."

"I am," he replied. "The colonial powers did the same thing, didn't they? Sneak into our nations and steal away all that was valuable. Looting, that's what they did. Do you know where the word *loot* comes from?"

"Uh, no . . ."

"It comes from *lut* in Hindi. Means the spoils of war, or robbery. When the British came to India, they stole and plundered all in their path. Soon, the word entered British slang."

I did not, in fact, know this. It was fascinating and reminded me of Nakia's discussion about spoils of war. "Thanks for the history lesson, but I've got more important things to think about." I turned my arms into long tentacles and clasped both sides of the desk. "The spectacles."

Deen stepped back, eyeing the desk in a careful way that made me think the spectacles were inside. I hugged the desk harder with my tentacle arms. I wasn't going to let go, no matter what.

"They're not there, Ms. Marvel," he said with gritted teeth. "No need to—"

"Oh, there's every need!" Heaving, I flipped the desk over, then smashed one hand into the middle of it. With a crash it tore apart, things bursting out from the drawers and spilling everywhere.

I saw a glint of sparkling emerald and grabbed it before Deen could even move. "Aha!" I held up the precious, beautiful spectacles in triumph.

Deen swallowed. "What will you do with them?"

I took pity on his horrified expression. "I just need them to heal my uncle, who's sick with cancer," I said, bringing both arms back to my body. "After that . . . you can have them back, I guess. I don't care where they end up, as long as I can save Fahad Uncle."

"That's preposterous!" Deen's face twisted in horror. "You don't know about the consequences of using this magic. Your uncle will lose his memories. Everything he's done and all the people he's loved since the time his cancer first attacked. It will all be lost, forever."

I shook my head emphatically. That wasn't going to

happen. It just wasn't. "No," I said quickly. "There's always a way to make things right."

I was Ms. Marvel, after all. I could use the spectacles safely, and without any of those stupid consequences Deen was harping on about.

"There isn't!" Deen insisted. "Believe me, I've tried. Other people over the years have tried."

I shook my head rapidly. "I don't care," I whispered. "I . . . I'll give them back to you once I've healed my uncle. I promise."

He looked sad and disappointed and angry and frustrated, all at the same time. "Ms. Marvel . . ."

The next instant, a crash of glass and a rushing wind from the windows dropped me to the ground next to Deen. "Oof!"

I made my arms huge pillows to cradle the spectacles. Twisting my head, I saw a sleek figure rising from the floor, shaking off pieces of broken glass. "Well, well, if it isn't Ms. Marvel," Delilah said in her signature sultry voice.

I gritted my teeth so hard my jaw hurt. "I'd say it's a pleasure, but I'd be lying."

"How did you find us?" Deen demanded.

She held up a round object—the same one she'd been holding the day she'd attacked me at Urdu Bazaar. "See this compass? It's magical. Leads me straight to all the other magical objects in its vicinity."

"Very cool," I mocked. "Did you steal that too?"

She ignored me and tucked the compass carefully into a pocket. "Just one of the hundreds of nifty artifacts we've been collecting the past few months."

"Let me guess," I said dryly. "By *we*, you mean Kingpin and his rats?"

She bared her teeth at me. "Who're you calling a rat?"

I shrugged. "If the shoe fits . . ."

Delilah scowled. "Watch this rat destroy you," she said, then punched me right in the face.

Oh. My. God. That hurt so freaking much. "What . . . what're you made of?" I gasped. "Rocks?"

She didn't bother with a response. She pummeled me with her fists until I fell backward on the remnants of the desk. Then she whirled away and punched fists into the furniture, the bookshelves, even the walls. Deen yelled at her to stop, but she was on a roll.

I wondered briefly whether the guests below could hear the commotion. I guessed the mansion was big enough to keep sounds from filtering through. Still, I couldn't afford to have more innocent people hurt.

I tucked the spectacles into my left elbow and sent my right arm hurtling toward Delilah when her back was to me.

She turned at the last minute and caught my arm with both of hers, twisting it cruelly.

"Ow!" I yelled.

Deen roared and tried to pull her off, but he was no match for her superhuman strength. She shook him off like he was a puppy and then flipped me around and around, until I was a rag doll in the air. When she dropped me onto the floor, I didn't even have enough breath to groan.

I watched with blurry eyes as the emerald spectacles, glinting in the light, fell from my grip. Delilah grabbed them from me with a broad smile. "Thank you," she said, and jumped back out the broken window.

Deen ran at her, but she pushed him back with a flying kick that made him grunt.

Then she was gone.

I sagged against the desk. "Freaking perfect," I whispered.

"I can't believe you're leaving already!" Sumera Aunty said, sighing.

I lugged my suitcase into the living room and set it down in the corner next to Abu's and Aamir's. It was our last night in Lahore, and our flight back home was super early in the morning. I couldn't believe a week had passed so quickly! They say time flies when you're having fun, but in this case, our visit was a mixture of grief and pain and worry.

And fun. Definitely fun too.

"I know. I'm sad." I hugged Sumera Aunty and then sat down next to Fahad Uncle on the couch. He'd stayed in his room the past two days, ever since the horrible coughing incident that had called the doctor to the house.

Tonight, though, he was out of bed, looking weak but still smiling.

Actually, he and Sumera Aunty were smiling at each other, and their faces were so full of love and—was that happiness? I couldn't understand how they could be happy when he was obviously in pain and near the end.

"What's on . . . your mind, Kamala?" Fahad Uncle breathed.

I sighed. "Nothing, just praying for you to get better, somehow."

He chuckled, even though it cost him a lot. Every movement seemed to cost him a lot these days. "That . . . would be a . . . miracle, my child."

I gulped as I thought of the miracle spectacles I'd had in my possession just two days ago. If Delilah hadn't grabbed them, I could have healed my uncle quicker than you could say *What the heck?*

"What if there *was* a miracle?" I asked, sitting up. "Like, a magic button you could press, and voilà, you'd be healed?"

Sumera Aunty sat down on his other side. "That sounds too good to be true," she murmured. "With a magic like that, there would definitely be a catch."

"Still thinking about that shopkeeper's stories, Kamala?" Aamir scoffed.

I honestly didn't know why I was asking. The spectacles were gone, to Kingpin, no doubt. I'd definitely search for them when I got back to the U.S., but that wouldn't help Fahad Uncle in any way.

"Suppose there was a mysterious cure that could kill all your cancer cells," I said slowly, "but it also killed your memory. All the things you'd done and seen since you were first diagnosed. Gone, along with the cancer."

"Oh, I know," Abu exclaimed. "This is like those *would you rather* games kids play these days. Our neighbor's son showed me last month. Would you rather swim in a pool of Nutella or a pool of maple syrup?"

"How funny!" Sumera Aunty said, laughing a little. "What was your answer?"

Abu shrugged. "I told him we Desi people have chutney, why would we bother with this Nutella or syrup, eh?"

"Good one, Abu!" Aamir snickered.

"Or chili garlic sauce," Sumera Aunty added. "I love that with my pakoras!"

I ignored the conversation around me. "Would you do it?" I urged Fahad Uncle. I wanted—needed—him to answer me. Assure me I'd not been wrong in trying to help him.

He finally shook his head sadly. "No, I wouldn't."

Um, what? Was he serious?

"Don't you want to be done with this pain and weakness?" I demanded. "Don't you want to live?"

He patted my hand. "Of course, Kamala. Who . . . doesn't want to live? But . . . not at the cost of . . . all the years I've already . . . *lived*, you know?"

"Whoa," Aamir said. "That's deep."

"You mean all your trips and things?" I asked. "But you could make new memories, right? You could go back to all those incredible places again, this time without the cancer invading your body!"

Fahad Uncle coughed loudly, again and again. I felt so, so bad for making him talk to me. "I'm sorry, Uncle. . . ."

Sumera Aunty handed her husband a glass of water. "I think what Fahad's trying to say is that he'd miss out on the relationship we built while he was sick. All the love and companionship that came out of his illness—was a direct result of it, actually—would also disappear."

He nodded as he took a sip of water. "Yes, that's it."

"You see, we had an arranged marriage later in life," Sumera Aunty continued. "We liked each other, of course, but it was a surface level of companionship based on our culture. But when Fahad got sick, we both realized that we didn't have much time together. We spent the next several years actively building our love and trust and friendship."

Fahad Uncle smiled weakly and patted his wife's hand. "Don't want to mess with that."

"No, we don't," she agreed softly, then put her head on his shoulder.

The conversation moved on to other topics. I saw Sumera Aunty's eyes fill with tears, but her face also had a sort of peace I'd never seen before on any human being.

I sat silently among my family, feeling like a huge load was finally off my shoulders. The weight of my guilt at having lost the spectacles not once but three times had been so crippling. The fact that I couldn't heal Fahad Uncle had made me totally miserable.

Now, with everything he and Sumera Aunty just said, I was surprisingly okay. This incredible couple was okay with their future. Who was I to insist otherwise?

After dinner, I texted Bruno to debrief him about Deen's party. Because of the time difference, Bruno was probably still asleep, but I asked him to search for warehouses where Kingpin could possibly be hiding the loot. Or lut, whatever.

Maleeha showed up to say good-bye just as I put my phone away.

"I'm going to miss you so much," she declared, her eyes glassy.

"Same," I told her. "Who's gonna tell me all the weird facts I don't need to know?"

She handed me a gift bag with crumpled-up tissue paper inside of it. "How's this for a fact?"

With a grin, I dug inside. It was a small painting in the miniature Mughal style of a woman dancing in a garden. There was a gazebo behind her, with a peacock sitting in the middle. "Gorgeous!" I gasped.

"Everyone's into this Mughal stuff these days," Aamir complained. "There are other important dynasties too, you know. The Safavids, the Ghaznavids. The Ottomans—hasn't anyone ever heard of those dudes?"

"The Mughals encouraged the arts, I'll have you know," Abu told him. "Especially Akbar, who was a great patron of all arts, including portraits, architecture, and book illustrations."

"Really? I didn't know about illustrations."

"That's the problem, my son. You think you know everything, but in reality, you know very little beyond your own self."

Maleeha and I giggled together. *"Shukriya,"* I told her. "I'll hang it up next to my picture of Minar-e-Pakistan. Right over my desk!"

We went back upstairs to my room for one last gossip sesh. "So are you dying to see your precious Romeo again?" she teased as we climbed onto my bed.

I gave her my best *Don't be stupid* look. "He's not my precious," I said. "Do I look like Gollum to you?"

Maleeha went into peals of laughter. "I can just imagine you . . ." she gasped, "with no hair!"

I rolled my eyes. "Gee, thanks."

When she stopped laughing, she looked at me expectantly. "Joking aside, have you spoken to him again? Do you know if he's got another job yet? I know you've been worried about him."

Ha. She didn't even know all the things I'd been worried about lately. "He hasn't really been texting me, so hopefully it means he's found a job."

"It'll be fine. He'll be really happy to see you when you get back."

"Let's hope so." I paused. "You know, you're so different than what I thought when we met."

Maleeha wrinkled her nose. "How so?"

I smirked. "Well, you seemed like this arrogant girl who knew everything."

"I do!"

I understood that she was joking, but it brought back something that was on my mind ever since I became Ms. Marvel. "I wish I knew everything," I told her. "Sometimes I feel like I'm just this kid with these big responsibilities, and no clue at all."

"You've got no need to worry, Kamala. You're really cool." Maleeha pointed a finger at me. "Which, by the way, I always knew. The minute we met, I thought, this is a cool girl I want to be friends with!"

"Good to know."

"It was like that quote from Maya Angelou," she continued. "'A friend may be waiting behind a stranger's face.'"

"Okay, enough with the quotes!" I groaned.

"You do know who Maya Angelou was, right, Kamala?" Maleeha smirked. "She was a poet, an activist, oh, even a Grammy Award winner . . ."

I threw a pillow at her face. "Seriously, shut up. I'm rethinking this friendship business with you."

She laughed. "Never! I'll text you at two a.m. your time every night and remind you of our friendship."

I groaned again, but in my heart that was perfectly fine with me. That was when I was usually out patrolling the streets of Jersey City. Maleeha's texts would be more than welcome.

"So tell me all about your trip, woman!" Nakia exclaimed.

The cafeteria was as noisy as ever, and kids jostled us as we wound over way between crowds to find a table. My tray rattled a little, but I steadied it. There were a few empty seats at the far end of the room, and I headed toward them. I was so tired of all the noise. I'd gotten used to Sumera Aunty's quiet house with the soft, lilting adhaan from the corner mosque and the birds chirping merrily in the back garden.

"Kamala?" Nakia urged once we'd sat down.

"What?" I took a bite of my chicken strip. Dry. Bland. Tasted like paper.

Zero stars.

"How was your trip to Lahore?" Nakia asked again. "You've been back three days and you haven't said anything. Or been around much either."

"Yuck." I made a face at my chicken and threw it back on the tray. "Sorry, bestie, I've been swamped with all the schoolwork I missed. Physics is brutal, and Mr. Harper thinks it's a personal insult or something that I left for a week mid-semester. He's been giving me extra-hard assignments to make it up, I swear!"

"Sorry." She smiled at me sympathetically.

"Try the chicken," I tell her, scowling. "It's horrible, right?"

She took a dainty bite and shrugged. "It's okay. It's high school cafeteria food—what do you expect?"

I picked up the apple on my tray instead. "Ow, why is this so hard? And not at all juicy! Pakistani apples are so soft and juicy, dude!"

Nakia smile faded. "One week in Pakistan and now you're hating on our food?"

"Maybe." I put down the apple and turned to her. "Okay, what do you want to know?"

"Everything! How's your dad's friend? What did you do? Did you sightsee? What about that girl you met—what was her name? Maleeka?"

"Maleeha." I smiled softly. "She's amazing. She took me around to so many places, showed me the real Lahore, you know?"

"That's good." Nakia wrinkled her nose. "I'm a bit jealous, but that's okay."

I shook my head. "No need to be jealous—she's thousands of miles away."

Nakia narrowed her eyes. "What? I didn't mean jealous of her, I meant jealous of your overall experience, jet-setting halfway across the world in the middle of school, visiting exotic locations . . ."

"Never say *exotic* again."

". . . but it's weird because you don't seem happy or excited. Getting you to tell me about your vacation has been like pulling teeth, literally."

I scowled again. "It wasn't a vacation! I went to see someone who means a lot to me, before he dies."

Her face fell, and she looked ready to cry. "I'm sorry, I know! I didn't mean . . ."

"It's fine—I know what you meant." It wasn't Nakia's fault, anyway. My trip to Lahore had definitely felt like a vacation, despite the sadness that permeated throughout Fahad Uncle's house. The sightseeing trips, the restaurants, the gossip sessions with Maleeha, had been incredible.

But the truth was, I hadn't been busy because of homework—well, not too busy, although Mr. Harper's vendetta was very real. Since I'd returned, I'd spent hours rewatching the video Kate Bishop had sent me. I'd stared at the two young men, lying broken and bleeding on the ground.

Daniel Mendoza and Tucker Lampert. Those were their names. They were both still in the ICU at the hospital. Tucker had a four-year-old kid and a young wife who looked bone-tired as she stood outside the hospital being interviewed by reporters.

Daniel was younger. He wasn't married, but he had a mother who stayed in the hospital day after day, hoping he'd wake up.

It was my fault Tucker was in a coma, and Daniel had to breathe through a tube. It was my fault, because I was supposed to defeat Delilah and make sure the Jersey City Art Museum was safe and secure.

To make sure the stolen artifacts were secure in their glass cabinets, far, far away from their homelands . . .

Wait, what? Big-time record scratch here!

I shook my head, trying to dislodge that last thought. Their homelands? The artifacts weren't people. They didn't have a home. They just stayed where they were put.

Ugh. Nakia and Deen's talk of stolen artifacts had infiltrated my mind, I guess, and made some inroads into my feelings.

"What are you stressing about?" Nakia asked, taking note of my frown.

"My trip to Lahore really made me think," I said slowly. "It was impactful."

"Made you think about what?"

I sighed, because it was difficult to explain. She'd ask questions that I couldn't answer because of Ms. Marvel. "About family, how important it is," I finally said.

"Even your brother?"

"The jury is still out on that," I joked. "But yeah, I guess family is something you have to cherish and own, you know, even if they're not perfect. Even if you don't agree with their decisions."

Nakia nodded sympathetically like she knew I was talking about Fahad Uncle. She ate some more of her dry, bland chicken, and muttered, "Mmm."

"How's your article going?" I asked suddenly. I hadn't asked her about it in days.

She swallowed. "So far, so good. I still have to do some revisions, but it's coming along well."

"I'm sorry I couldn't help more with, you know."

"No worries, I know you were busy."

I opened my mouth to say something, but just then, someone slammed their tray on the table next to me. It was Bruno Carrelli, although now I kept thinking of him as Romeo.

"Hey, what's up?" He slid into the seat beside me. "Why didn't you girls wait for me?"

"'A hungry man can't see right or wrong. He just sees food.'" Nakia winked. "Pearl S. Buck said that."

My heart skipped a beat. She looked and sounded just like Maleeha in that instant.

"Not sure who that is, but okay." Bruno turned to me, grinning. "Miss me, world traveler?"

I blushed and tried to tell myself that it was because the cafeteria was overheated. "I saw you yesterday."

"For a minute." He dug into his food. "You were watching something on your phone and told me you'd catch me later, remember? But you never did."

I did remember. I was just hoping he didn't. "Physics is kicking my ass."

His grin slipped a little. "Why didn't you come to me? I'd have helped you out."

Nakia snickered in front of us. "Did you miss her too, Bruno pie?"

Bruno ducked his head, acting like his chicken was a gourmet meal. "Sure. Whatever."

Nakia laughed, and I kicked her under the table. "Shut up, dude."

"What?" She looked so innocent, sitting there eating her bland chicken.

Bruno looked up. "I did miss you, you know. It was weird not having someone to make fun of Harper's goatee."

I heaved a sigh of relief. I knew he'd missed me—it was in his eyes, the soft curve of his smile—but he was still making jokes to make me feel comfortable. That was Bruno to a T. "Oh my God, that goatee!" I said with the same put-on enthusiasm. "Did you see how long it's grown since last week? Maybe he lost his razor or something!"

"Ha! Or he's just trying out for some off-Broadway role."

Bruno and I met again after school.

"Where's Nakia?" he asked as we walked outdoors.

"In the library," I replied. "She's doing some last-minute research for her article."

"Good. I need to show you something." He pulled me to a bench and held up his phone. "Check this out."

It was a grainy black-and-white video feed of a warehouse, with people coming and going with wooden crates. Bruno pressed a button and the video sped up, showing the time in minutes, then hours.

I frowned as I watched, because none of it made sense. "What . . . ?"

"Wait for it."

I watched for another minute before a large figure in a suit came on the screen. Bruno stopped the video.

I squinted. "Is that . . . Kingpin?"

"Yup."

My eyes widened. In all my sadness over the last few

days, I'd half forgotten what Deen had told me about Kingpin's plans. "You found it?" I whisper-yelled. "You found the warehouse where Kingpin's hiding all the artifacts?"

"Yup." Bruno pocketed his phone and grinned. "I scoped out all the warehouses in the museum area, researched their owners, and found one that was owned by Fisk Industries."

I deflated a little. Fisk Industries owned a crap ton of buildings. What were the odds that this one housed stolen artifacts? "Only one?"

"In Jersey City, yes. The bulk of Fisk Industries real estate is in large cities like New York." Bruno grinned even wider. "There are some holdings in Jersey City, but they're mostly office buildings and the occasional hotel. This is the only warehouse."

"This has to be it!" I said excitedly.

"I agree!" Bruno nodded. "That's why I hacked into their security system and copied video recordings from the last six months."

"Is that the only time Kingpin showed his face here?"

"No. Every time there's an artifact theft, he shows up within the next few days." Bruno waved his phone in my face. "This video clip is from last week, the day after the shotel was stolen."

I jumped up from the bench, ready to rush to the warehouse right now and confront Kingpin. Heck, if Delilah was there too, the more the merrier. I wanted to bash that whole operation straight to the ground. Take revenge for the pain and suffering those two had been causing.

Would that change the whole issue of ancient artifacts and where they belonged?

No, but that was a problem for future Kamala.

Bruno grabbed my arm. "Hey, where are you going? You need a plan."

"Plan, schman, who cares?" But I sat back down, because of course he was right. I didn't even know where this mysterious warehouse was. And it was broad daylight. The video showed Kingpin coming in at night.

I took out my phone to check the time, figure out how long until sundown, when I saw an email notification.

It was from the Ms. Marvel account, which only one person knew about, apart from me and Bruno.

"Who is it?" Bruno asked, leaning over my shoulder.

"Deen," I replied. "Or Asaar, I suppose."

Tonight 10:30 p.m.

5300 West 36th Street

Bruno checked his phone. "That's the address of the warehouse."

"And he's telling me to be there tonight."

Bruno looked alarmed. "You're not going, right? It's gotta be a trap!"

I shook my head. Nothing about Asaar's actions—or Deen's, for that matter—had proven him to be an enemy. Every time he'd fought me, it had been after I practically forced him to. "I have a feeling he's on my side."

"He's a thief!"

"But he's not stealing for money or power," I argued. "Only to put things back in their proper place. To right some wrongs, as Nakia would say."

"I'd still feel more comfortable if you stayed away. Let Asaar fight this battle by himself."

I gritted my teeth. Bruno treating me like a fragile creature in need of protection would tear my world apart. He was the only person in my personal life who looked at me like a super hero. Who saw Kamala and realized there was a strong person in there, even without the costume.

There was no way I was letting him forget that. "Look, Asaar's been fighting this battle alone for a long time. It's time someone else helped him. It's my heritage too, you know. I've got plenty of skin in the game."

Bruno sighed. "I guess."

"Besides, if Kingpin is there, I really want to be the one to hammer his bald head with one of my giant fists." I laughed at the image. "Maybe both. A fist sandwich, with Kingpin's head in the middle!"

Bruno laughed too. "Don't forget to take a picture of that as evidence!"

We started walking again. I needed to go home and strategize about tonight. Make sure I was ready.

"Sorry for doubting you, Kamala," Bruno said. "I know you're more than capable of beating those dirtbags."

I smiled my thanks. "But I hear what you're saying about safety." I switched to my messages and opened the thread with Kate Bishop. "We can always call for reinforcements."

"And I'll hack into their security system," he added. "Make sure you and Asaar can get inside without any issue."

I tucked my phone back into my pocket and clapped my hands in glee. "Now that's what I call a plan!"

A little before ten o'clock, I changed into my Ms. Marvel costume and slipped on a tunic and loose pants over it.

"Kamala, where are you going?" Aamir called from his room. The door was half open, and I could see him sitting on his prayer mat.

"Nowhere," I mumbled.

He scrambled to his feet and followed me down the stairs. "There's been a lot of theft in the city recently," he warned. "A few people have been hurt too."

"Really," I said dryly. *As if I don't know.*

"It's better to stay indoors after dark."

I tucked my phone into my pocket. "Relax. I'm just going to Bruno's."

"You shouldn't go out right now! It's not safe!"

I walked out of the house and slammed the door in his face. *That's what I think about your safety speech, brother dear.*

I slipped into the garage and eyed my bike. I didn't have much time to reach West 36th Street and scope out the area before Asaar arrived. Bikes, buses, trains, or even old-fashioned walking wouldn't do the trick.

Quickly, I pulled off my outer clothes, revealing the red-and-blue Ms. Marvel suit underneath. I walked out of the garage with my shoulders pulled back and a little smile playing on my lips. *Ms. Marvel, reporting for duty.*

I stretched out my legs, then my entire body, until the street and houses were specks on the ground. I took giant, careful steps, heading toward downtown. The wind ruffled my hair, and I chuckled. I should travel this way more often; it was seriously fun!

The warehouse was part of an industrial complex on the far side of downtown. The area was full of identical buildings with big black doors and no windows. Everything looked eerie and abandoned.

I whooshed back to my normal size and looked around stealthily. Number 5300 was right at the back, shrouded with darkness at this time of the night. Most of the streetlights in the parking lot were out.

"Glad you could make it." Asaar walked toward me

casually, his suit making him seem more like a runway model than a vigilante.

I brisk-walked until I was at his side. "So what's the plan? Defeat Kingpin and Delilah, and grab the spectacles?"

"Pretty much." He smirked. "Should be a piece of cake."

"Aargh!" I groaned. "You're just as bad as my brother! So annoying!"

There was a rumbling noise up ahead, and we stiffened. Quickly, Asaar pulled me behind a tall bush at the edge of the parking lot, near the boundary wall.

I shrugged him off and peeked out. A delivery truck at the warehouse entrance. Two figures were unloading what looked like heavy wooden crates. A third figure emerged from inside the warehouse. He was bigger and rounder and held a cane.

Kingpin.

"We should catch him right now!" I whispered furiously. "What are we waiting for?"

Asaar rolled his eyes. "First of all, there are three of them and two of us. And we don't know who else is hiding inside."

"So?" I didn't think those odds were bad. I could take Kingpin and his goons any day of the week.

"Second," Asaar continued like I hadn't spoken, "he's probably unloading priceless artifacts. I'd rather they didn't get shattered to pieces while we fight."

"Oh, good point."

"Third of all, once Kingpin goes back inside, he'll have less space to fight, so we can corner him easier."

I held up a hand. "Okay, I get it. We'll wait."

We stayed leaning against the wall silently. The tension spiked until I couldn't stand it.

"You mentioned your brother earlier. Is he a super hero too?" Asaar asked.

"What? No!" I didn't know if I should be amused or horrified. "He just . . . thinks he can tell me what to do, because he's older."

"And your parents?"

I shrugged. "Same, mostly. Overprotective. On my case all the time."

"On your case about what?"

"I don't know. Getting As. Not going to a boy's house at night. Getting enough sleep." I shuddered. "Like I said, annoying."

"Family is all you have at the end of the day. If they stick by you—do they?"

"Yes."

Asaar nodded. "If they stick by you, if they want to take care of you and protect you and spend time with you, that's the biggest blessing you can have. More than any super hero powers, more than money. More than fame."

I thought about Abu taking me sightseeing in Lahore, talking with me about his childhood. I thought of Ammi going with me to the mosque, and Aamir lecturing me frantically about the dangers on the street. "You're right," I whispered. "Family is everything."

"Of course I'm right. I'm much older than you. And wiser."

I scoffed. "Debatable."

Asaar turned to stare at me. "Family is everything, Ms. Marvel. You're lucky you have people who care about you enough that they're—what did you call it?—on your case. Some of us aren't as lucky."

I stared back, nonplussed. He wasn't wrong. If there was anything I'd learned in Pakistan, it was that family and heritage were priceless. Even more so than diamonds and emeralds. "You're speaking from experience?"

He turned away. "I made a lot of mistakes when I was younger. Too busy building my companies. Too busy making money. Even the search for artifacts took up so much of my time. My wife left me. My children hardly talk to me anymore. They say I was never really a father to them."

"And now you're alone?"

"Now I'm alone."

Wow. This was becoming a regular therapy session. I cleared my throat. "What about your powers? When . . . how . . . did you get those?"

"I fell into a factory overflow eight years ago, in Lahore. It was one of my own factories, but I'd had news that something strange was going on, so I'd visited to investigate."

I remembered reading about this in one of my internet searches. "What kind of strange?"

"Unusual readings on the output charts, weird power fluctuations, that sort of thing. I closed the place down for a few days and went in alone. When I fell into the waste overflow, my first thought was *I'll ruin this Armani suit*."

"Well, those *are* expensive."

"Anyway, I got out, went home, showered, but then I got ill. High fever, that sort of thing. I was in the hospital for a few days. When I woke up, my fingers were emanating the green-and-white light you've seen."

"Wow. You never found out what happened at the factory?"

"No. By the time I got out of the hospital, everything had gone back to normal again."

I frowned. "So you didn't try to dig deeper, find out why those weird things had been happening? And why they stopped?"

Asaar sighed. "I tried to. There weren't really any answers. I'm still working on it, but it's old news now. And my priorities have changed."

I smirked. "The reparations!"

He didn't respond. Maybe he didn't really need to. Instead, he stuck his head out of the bushes. "The truck's driving away."

I followed him out. The truck was almost gone now, and when I turned back to the warehouse, Kingpin's figure was disappearing inside. He slammed the door shut loudly.

"Let's go!" I jogged toward the warehouse.

"Wait!" Asaar said. "They're bound to have a good security system, to protect all those artifacts."

"On it." I pulled out my phone and texted Bruno. *Did you disable the security?*

Bruno replied in two minutes. *All done. Good luck.*

"Okay, we're good." I put my phone back in my pocket and motioned for Asaar to move forward.

We hugged the boundary wall as we advanced to the warehouse. Asaar tried the door, and it opened easily.

I had a moment of panic. What if Bruno hadn't disabled everything? Kingpin wasn't a fool. He probably had several layers of security for his precious warehouse.

What if it's a trap?

Asaar stepped in and looked over his shoulder. "Ready, Ms. Marvel?"

Somehow, his strong, deep voice calling me Ms. Marvel made me remember who I was right now. Kamala might be scared, but Ms. Marvel was fearless.

Bruno had faith in me.

So did Asaar, apparently.

I nodded, then stepped in and closed the door quietly behind us.

The inside of the warehouse was a huge, cavernous space, dimly lit by little lights set in the walls at regular intervals. Shelves taller than me made rows and rows of aisles, filled with crates.

Nothing interesting, unless those crates contained priceless ancient treasures.

We walked farther in, trying to keep as quiet as possible. "I should go first," I whispered to Asaar.

"Why? Don't think I can protect you?"

"I don't need protection! You . . ."

There was a crack behind us; then the warehouse flooded with lights. Asaar and I paused in our tracks. Kingpin and Delilah stood in front of us, identical sinister smiles on their ugly mugs.

"Hello, Ms. Marvel," Kingpin said politely, tapping his cane at the ground. "Fancy meeting you here."

Asaar kept silent. I wondered if he'd ever met Kingpin face-to-face in his costume.

"Kingpin," I said just as politely. "Just the person I wanted to see."

"Really?"

"Yup," I replied, popping my lips to emphasize the *p* sound. "I heard you've been amassing ancient artifacts here for some nefarious purposes."

"How did you find this place?" Delilah asked suspiciously.

There was no way I was telling her about Bruno. I shrugged and lied. "Followed you here the other day. You fight pretty hard, but nobody's a match for my stretchy limbs!"

Delilah snarled and stepped forward. "You little . . ."

Kingpin held out a hand to stop her. "No need, Delilah. These two are powerless around here."

"So confident." Asaar finally spoke, his tone mocking.

Kingpin focused on him for the first time since we'd entered. "Asaar, am I correct? I've heard about you, prowling for artifacts, talking about national pride, heritage, blah, blah, blah." Kingpin grimaced, as if he'd swallowed a pickle without meaning to.

"Heritage is everything for some people," I said through a clenched jaw.

"But not for you, Ms. Marvel." Delilah smirked. "The first Muslim super hero? What is that, an oxymoron?"

I saw red. "What's that supposed to mean?" I bit out. "Muslims can be super heroes. Brown people too. What century are you living in?"

"Sorry, my bad," she said, not at all convincingly.

I pointed to the open crate at Kingpin's feet. I could see packing bubbles inside, but nothing else. "What's all this? Your delivery came to the wrong address?"

Kingpin's eyes gleamed. "Ah, this. Let me show you." He tucked his cane under his arm and reached down to pull out a small ax. It had a rough stone head and a thin black handle that looked worn with age.

I tensed. Was he going to try to bash my head in?

Kingpin smirked again. "Relax, Ms. Marvel. This ax is from medieval Europe. It's way too precious to dirty with your blood." He passed a hand lovingly over it.

I blinked at the display. It was disturbing. "What's so special about it?"

"It has magical powers," Kingpin explained. "Whoever wields this ax gains a crown."

"Sounds vague," I quipped. "And a bit old-fashioned. I mean, are there even crowns anymore? Most countries have democracy now, or dictatorship."

"Dictatorship is a form of crown too."

Delilah reached down and picked up a curved sword. "Pretty, no?"

"The shotel," I breathed. Bruno had said that whoever carried the sword into battle won the battle and ruled the world. So, basically, even more powerful than the ax Kingpin was holding.

"Where are the Mughal artifacts?" Asaar demanded. "I know you have them. Delilah stole the emerald spectacles twice."

Kingpin tsked. "Impatient much, Asaar? I've got them here somewhere."

Delilah smirked again and walked to another crate. Reaching inside, she took out an object and cradled it in her hands. It was bright, glowing, green, and most definitely the emerald spectacles.

I let out an involuntary gasp.

Next to me, Asaar took a step forward.

"Aren't they pretty?" Kingpin smirked. "They can heal the worst illness. The emperor Shah Jahan used them to heal his eyes after all his crying over his dead wife."

"Yes, I know!" How dare he try to tell me about my own history?

Kingpin went on as if I hadn't spoken. "He wasn't very smart, that Shah Jahan. He could have used the power of the emeralds to save his wife from dying, but he didn't."

"Perhaps he came upon them too late," Asaar muttered angrily.

"Or maybe he knew about the consequences of using such powerful magic," I added bitterly, thinking of Fahad Uncle.

Kingpin shrugged. "Doesn't matter. I don't care about history, unless it tells me more about the value of an artifact."

I shook my head. The brilliance of the emeralds was giving me a headache. Or maybe it was just this entire effed-up situation. "What I don't understand is why you need healing powers," I said. "The ax and sword, I understand. The spectacles, not so much."

Delilah laughed and put the spectacles back in the crate. "That's because you're young and stupid. You know nothing about strategy."

"Okay, then, enlighten us about your strategy," Asaar said. He was looking at the open crate with the spectacles. It was the look of a starving man gazing at a feast he couldn't quite reach.

I realized he was distracting Kingpin with his questions. Planning a strategy of his own to take the spectacles back.

Kingpin made a little swipe in the air with the ax. "Owning magical artifacts is a powerful thing, my dear super heroes. Their power gives you power, because you own it. Amassing the world's magic in my warehouse is going to give me ultimate power. I can barter, I can trade, I can threaten, all without lifting a finger."

I felt a chill go down my spine at his words. He was absolutely freaking right. He would be immensely powerful if he owned all that magic. "The value of these artifacts is way more than just power," I insisted roughly. "They're a symbol of culture and history. They mean something."

Delilah and Kingpin burst into laughter.

"Aw, poor baby," Delilah mocked me. "Did your feelings get hurt?"

From the corner of my eye, I saw Asaar's nostrils flare and fists clench, getting ready to emit his green-and-white light. It was time to attack, but in a way that kept the two villains distracted.

Luckily, I was the queen of distraction.

"You . . . What do you care about getting hurt?" I yelled at Delilah. "You hurt innocent people! I saw the video! It was horrible!"

Kingpin and Delilah exchanged amused glances and began laughing again. If I hadn't been yelling at them on purpose, I'd be so upset at this blatant disrespect.

I was Ms. Marvel, after all. It was time I proved that.

I nodded at Asaar, and he roared, taking the two villains by surprise. The next instant, he'd shot his fiery light straight at Kingpin's upper body.

Kingpin held up his arm to deflect.

"Embiggen," I yelled, and with a giant fist pushed Delilah deep into the shelves behind her.

She crashed against the crates, eyes wide with shock.

Kingpin's arm bore the worst of Asaar's energy. It rattled his frame, and his cane clattered to the floor. "You dare attack me?" he shouted.

"I dare much more!" Asaar shouted back, launching another energy bolt.

I kept my eyes on Delilah, who had straightened up by now. Her face was fearsome. "I'll teach you a lesson you'll never forget!" she hissed.

I rolled my eyes. "What a clichéd phrase. Did you learn it in villain school?"

Delilah screamed and jumped at me, arms forward as if she couldn't wait to pummel me to the ground. I knew her strength, though, and didn't want to be anywhere near it. I made my legs so long that my head touched the ceiling of the warehouse. Delilah's momentum pushed her clear through the huge gap in my legs.

"Ha!" I called down to her. "Poor baby! Did your feelings get hurt?"

She glared at me, but before she could move, I turned and kicked her very, very hard with one of my giant legs. She screamed as she flew all the way across the warehouse, right into some metal shelving.

"Good job!" Asaar told me, panting.

I nodded my thanks. I knew Delilah wouldn't stay down for long, but it was still a win. It meant I could help Asaar take out Kingpin.

"You think you can defeat me?" Kingpin shouted from

where Asaar had shoved him face down on the ground. "When I have magical artifacts giving me power?"

"Um, maybe?" I said, coming back to normal height. "What do you think, Asaar? Can we do it?"

"Not maybe," Asaar replied. "Definitely!"

With another shout, Kingpin rolled over, his eyes glinting with . . . was that excitement?

Uh-oh, he was up to something.

Sure enough, Kingpin held the ancient ax in his hand. With another shout, he buried it in the ground next to us. A blast of sparkling red light sprang from it, shattering the concrete like it was glass.

I yelped and jumped away, but not before I felt the quake from my head down to my toes. "Whoa."

"Whoa, indeed." Kingpin stood up slowly, grinning in that evil way of his. "Now you see my artifacts are not to be messed with."

"They're not yours!" Asaar grunted, and threw more light at Kingpin, pushing him back to the ground.

"Finders keepers," Kingpin whispered.

"What is it with clichéd phrases today?" I shook my head at Kingpin, then made my arm long to grab the ax. It was burning hot and would have scalded a human. I stretched my arm back and tucked the ax behind some crates near me. I'd have to figure out what to do with this weapon of medieval destruction later.

"Look out, Ms. Marvel!" Asaar yelled from behind me.

I turned around just in time to see Kingpin reaching for his cane. He pressed a button, and almost too late, I remembered that the blasted thing carried a laser. I jumped to the side a millisecond before the laser hit me, falling right into the crates behind me. My head was jarred with the impact. "Ow!"

Kingpin threw another laser in my direction, and it smashed the crate next to my head in spectacular fashion. Splinters of wood showered me like spiky rain. Yikes! If I let that thing hit me, it might just pulverize my very being.

Asaar ran toward me, but Kingpin's laser stopped him in his tracks. One powerful beam, and Asaar was pushed into a pile of crates. The noise as he went down was loud and horrifying.

"I think there were some World War I hand grenades in there," Kingpin mused. "Cursed by the ghosts of soldiers who died in the trenches, so they pack a punch."

I stared at where Asaar had gone down but couldn't see anything.

Kingpin got to his feet and prowled closer to me. "Where are your embiggen powers now, little girl?"

Before I could disentangle my limbs from the mess of

crates and shelving and broken wood, he stood over me, his cane pointed right at my chest. "Say your final prayers, Ms. Marvel," he uttered, so arrogant and calm. Like threatening to kill someone was no biggie.

My eyelashes fluttered. *This is it, Kamala. You didn't even get to hug your family one last time.*

"Not so fast, Kingpin."

I recognized the girlish voice behind me.

"Hawkeye!" Kingpin snarled. "What are you doing here? Is there a super hero convention nobody told me about?"

He sounded so disgruntled, a little laugh bubbled out of my chest. "Hey, Kate, thanks for dropping by."

Kate smiled back. "No problem, friend. I was patrolling outside just like you asked, but then I heard some loud noises and couldn't help myself. You know I love a good fight."

Kingpin tried to move toward Kate, but I sent a long, heavy arm to lift him and hold him in place like a lasso. "Let me go!" he said.

"Sure!" I shrugged and dropped him to the ground.

Movement from the far end of the warehouse reminded me that Delilah was going to be a problem soon. I nodded to Kate. "Think you can take care of her?"

"My pleasure," Kate said, fitting an arrow into her bow. "I have a score to settle with that mean girl."

I kept an eye on Kingpin as I rushed to Asaar. He was sitting up, a little dazed but not injured as far as I could see. "Are you okay, old man?" I teased.

He scoffed and stood. "I need those spectacles."

"Go for it." I pointed to the open crate where Delilah had placed them. "I'll take care of Kingpin."

"Stop!" Kingpin shouted, incensed. He dragged himself and his cane behind a nearby shelf. "Don't touch those spectacles!"

Asaar picked up the emerald artifact gingerly. "They're my heritage. They belong to my people."

"Again with the heritage, you foolish man!" Kingpin said furiously. "Who cares about that when you can have power?"

"If the Mughals taught me one thing, it's that power is fleeting. Someone else always comes along with more guns, more weapons, more smarts." Asaar looked sideways at me, his face drawn. "But who you are, what you stand for, is never up for grabs."

Kingpin sneered. "And what do you stand for?"

"For my homeland. For my people. My history."

Kingpin's face turned red. With a disgusted roar, he pointed his cane at Asaar and let loose a laser blast with enough heat to singe a person's eyebrows off.

Asaar ducked to protect the spectacles in his hands. I blocked the laser at the last minute by shoving a nearby shelf in the way.

"Aargh!" Kingpin roared again in disgust.

Asaar and I heaved a sigh of relief. Kingpin was now blocked in by two huge metal shelves full of his own stolen goods. He could get out by blasting his laser, but it would only destroy his own precious artifacts.

Perfect.

I looked toward Kate. She had Delilah cornered and was advancing with a rope. "Looks like Delilah's gonna be tied up soon," I joked breathlessly.

"Yeah," Asaar replied, standing to check on the spectacles. "Phew. That was close."

My lips turned at the corners, ready to smile. Almost.

The warehouse door opened and banged shut so loudly, the sound echoed around us. "Hello, Kamala? Where are you?"

My heart jumped straight into my throat. I blinked the sweat from my eyes to make out—*oh my God!*—Aamir's blurry shape just inside the warehouse door.

Is this real? Did I hit my head in all the fighting?

"Kamala? Are you in here?"

Okay, so definitely real. Utterly, horribly, real.

The question was, what was my stupid, stupid brother doing here?

Asaar frowned. "Who is that? What's he doing?"

Aamir came closer warily until he stood only a few feet away. "Uh, I'm looking for my sister, Kamala. She's a teenager, and I can't find her. . . ."

He trembled at the sight of me—Ms. Marvel—and Asaar, but when his eyes flicked to Kate dragging a tied-up Delilah, he backed up a little.

"Your sister isn't here, dude," Kate called out as she left.

"That's not possible. I tracked her with the FindMe app on her phone. She's here somewhere." Aamir looked around the warehouse, his eyes widening even further as he took in the chaos. "She may be in danger. I have to protect her."

"You need to leave," Asaar said in warning. "You're the one in danger right now."

I gulped harshly. I didn't know whether to be angry at Aamir for thinking I needed protection again, or to be angry at him for tracking me on that ridiculous app, or to be angry that he had now put himself in danger.

So basically, I was angry. Who cared what the reasons were?

"I'll take care of this," I hissed. I walked forward until I was close enough to see the fear in his eyes. I wasn't gonna lie—it was nice to have the upper hand with my older brother, even if he didn't know who I was.

"Hello, Ms. Marvel," Aamir croaked, backing away some more.

"You know who I am?"

"Of course. You're Muslim. I'm Muslim. We have a lot in common."

I raised a disbelieving eyebrow. This dude who once told me I was a bad Muslim because I forgot to take off my nail polish before praying wanted to connect with me on religion? "I'm not your kind of Muslim," I told him.

"You shouldn't judge people before getting to know them."

I barked out a laugh. Aamir, the most judgy person on the planet, was preaching to me? "Wow," I said. "You . . ."

"Enough!" Kingpin roared from behind his metal barrier. "I can't stand all this chitchat. Let me out of here!"

He shoved at the metal barrier, and it rattled ominously. A jade vase trembled in place. A small fish-shaped metallic ornament fell to the floor.

"Careful, Kingpin," Asaar growled in a low, threatening voice. "You don't want to destroy those magical items, do you?"

Kingpin roared even louder, sounding like a tortured bear. "You think you can contain me?"

"Uh, what's going on?" Aamir asked shakily. "Did you say K-Kingpin?"

The back of my neck prickled. Much as I hated to admit it, Kingpin was right. He was too strong and cunning to be contained. The only thing standing in his way were the artifacts. If he stopped caring about them, even for a second, he'd crash out and cause mayhem, right in front of my brother!

No matter how mad I was at Aamir, I'd never want him to be faced with the slimeball Kingpin. That was an experience best left to the experts.

"You need to leave!" I told Aamir sternly.

"Not until I find my sister!" He squared his shoulders. "She's my resp—"

With another terrifying roar, Kingpin shoved the metal shelves so hard, they crashed to the ground.

Asaar and I gaped at the mess. The magical artifacts, all utterly destroyed.

Before we could react, Kingpin emerged with a furious expression on his face. "I told you, I will not be contained!"

He pointed his cane at me—at us—and *zzap!* A bolt of laser shot out and struck Aamir right in the chest.

Time stopped.

My breathing stopped. From the corner of my eye, I saw Kingpin grin viciously and run for the door.

Asaar cursed under his breath and ran after him.

I didn't care even a little. All I cared was my brother, with a laser shot to his body.

Aamir shuddered and then fell in slow motion.

"No!" I screamed, and ran to catch him. With trembling hands, I held him close to me and sank down to the ground. Blood was seeping from his chest and soaking my hands, my clothes, my everything. "Aamir, Aamir! Oh my God!"

Aamir just lay there, eyes closed, breaths shallow. I tore off my mask so I could see better. Aamir was bleeding out. My brother was bleeding out, and I didn't know what to do. *"Ashfi wa antash-shaafi,"* I whispered over and over, even though my brain told me that wasn't going to help.

My heart told me I had to pray.

Aamir opened his eyes and saw me, a strange mixture of Kamala and Ms. Marvel. I didn't even care. I was just happy he was conscious. Maybe his injury wasn't too severe.

"Hey, how're you feeling?" I asked, pressing my bloody hands over the wound in his chest.

Aamir winced. "Like I was hit by Kingpin's laser."

"You saw that, huh?"

"Yes." He tried to nod. "Also, Kate Bishop, Delilah, that other dude . . . and you. Ms. Marvel."

"Oh." I didn't really know what to say. I kept repeating *Ashfi wa antash-shaafi* over and over, my lips moving, my heart thundering so loud I could practically hear it.

"I'm glad you remember that prayer, Kamala," he murmured. "I'm the one who taught you that, you know."

I laugh-cried. "No, it was Sheikh Abdullah."

"But I was there, helping the younger students. You were throwing a tantrum, so I told Sheikh Abdullah that I'd teach you."

I sort of remembered that. I smiled through my tears. "You're a good brother, Aamir. I can't believe you came here to find me."

Aamir's face was pale, and sweat dotted his forehead. "It's my job, little sister," he whispered, and for the first time, I didn't mind being called little.

Aamir sighed and closed his eyes. For some reason, that sound, that action, reeked of finality. An ending I wouldn't be able to accept. Ever.

Footsteps hurried nearby, and I tugged my mask back on, sniffling.

It was Asaar, panting a little. "I lost Kingpin," he said, then looked down at Aamir. "How's he doing?"

I shook my head, trying to act like Aamir was just another innocent Jersey City resident caught in the cross fire. "What do I do?"

Asaar pursed his lips in thought. Then he put his hand in his pocket and took out Shah Jahan's emerald spectacles. "Heal him."

Oh Lord! How could I have forgotten the magical healing powers of that thing? I stared at the spectacles. "Are you sure . . . ?"

"Not really. I've never seen them in action." Asaar shrugged. "But it's worth a try, no?"

I nodded, my breath steadying a bit. If I healed him right away, Aamir would only forget the last few minutes since he'd been hit. He'd forget he saw Ms. Marvel. My secret would be safe.

Most importantly, he'd be safe.

I wiped a hand on my shirt to get the blood off, then took

the spectacles and slid them on. Everything turned green and hazy, but this time I was ready for it. I rubbed the little bump on the bridge, and the frame vibrated.

"It's glowing," Asaar said in awe.

I kept rubbing and praying until Aamir opened his eyes again. "Where . . . where am I?"

I checked his chest. The wound had vanished. There was blood on the floor, but none on Aamir's body. I had a slight headache, but it was nothing in the face of my joy. "Oh my God, you're okay!"

"Ms. Marvel? Why are you holding me in your lap?"

Asaar snickered.

Aamir jumped up. "I . . . How did I get here? What's going on?"

I stood up slowly. "You don't remember? You wandered in looking for someone named Kamala."

Aamir nodded slowly. "Yes, I remember that. But nothing after it."

Asaar pointed to the door. "Maybe check outside?"

"Oh, yes, good idea." Aamir frowned as he walked away. "Is this blood? Ya Allah, or did I spill ketchup again?"

This time, Asaar's laugh was a straight-out bellow.

"No need to worry," I called after my brother. "It's probably paint. There's wet paint all over this warehouse."

"911. What's your emergency?"

"I found a warehouse with stolen items," I said into the security phone on the wall. "Can you please send some police officers out here to seize them?"

"Who is this?"

"Ms. Marvel."

The guy at the other end laughed incredulously. "Yeah, right."

I ignored that and kept talking. I had to name-drop Ms. Hibbert and the Jersey City Art Museum before they took me seriously.

"They're coming," I told Asaar when I hung up.

"Good."

I chewed my lip. Asaar had been seen on video fighting me. The police would think he was a villain. "You should go."

"Go?" He raised an eyebrow. "You want to get rid of me already?"

"Yes," I deadpanned.

"Wow, way to hurt a guy's feelings."

"The police think we're enemies," I told him. "Technically I should tie you up, have them take you into custody."

"Why don't you?"

I threw up my hands. "I don't know! I guess because we're both vigilantes, fighting for justice?"

"Is that all?" He held up a hand. There was no light on his fingertips right now, but I remembered it vividly. How it seared through my flesh countless times. How it acted as a buffer between me and Delilah. How it kept Kingpin away from me. "No, that's not all," I admitted. "I guess . . . we're friends? Sort of?"

Asaar grinned. "Only sort of?"

I grinned back. "Don't push your luck."

"It's okay—I'm only teasing," he said. "I know you're right."

"You do?"

"Yes, I should leave before the authorities extradite me to Pakistan. It'll ruin my reputation."

"Good point. Nobody will come to your lavish parties."

He scoffed. "Good riddance. I never enjoy those."

I looked at the crates lying in shambles around us. "Wish

I'd caught Kingpin, though. I hate the thought of him running around stealing more artifacts."

"I think we've set him back," Asaar mused. "He'd need to start from scratch to get such a big hoard again."

"Speaking of artifacts." I held out the emerald spectacles. "You should take these with you."

"Are you sure?"

"Yes," I replied firmly. "They belong in Pakistan. You can make sure they're well protected."

"I will." Asaar took the spectacles and put them carefully in his pocket. Even with his mask, I could tell he was exhausted. "Maybe I can start a local traveling exhibit. Make sure our countrymen see their heritage in all its glory."

"Great idea."

I could hear the sound of sirens approaching, so I gave him a little push. "You should go now."

He patted me on the head in true Desi uncle fashion. "Look me up next time you visit Lahore," he said when he let me go.

I thought of Fahad Uncle and swallowed. Who knew if I'd ever see him again? "Not sure I'll be going there any time soon."

At night, lying in bed, I flipped through all my memories of Lahore. I hadn't been kidding earlier. I didn't think I'd be able to visit Lahore again. At least not for a long time.

Feeling all sorts of weepy, I texted Maleeha. *Did you forget all about me?*

Absolutely not, girl!!! Was just waiting for you to rest up after your trip.

How's everything? How's Fahad Uncle?

Not good. He was taken to the hospital last night.

For good?

Maybe. All we can do now is pray.

My eyes filled with tears. I knew I'd done the right thing by letting the spectacles go. But the world would be missing a great person when Fahad Uncle passed away.

The next day in school, I met up with Nakia in the hallway before class.

"Guess what?" she squealed, hiding her hands behind her back.

"You got tickets to the Taylor Swift concert?"

"What? No!" She held out the school newspaper. "My article is on the front page!"

I snatched it from her. "No way!"

"Yes, way."

Jersey City Exhibit Straddles the Line Between Art and Theft. "Spunky headline. I love it!" I read the first few lines quickly. "'A new exhibit of Mughal-era artifacts has raised protests and eyebrows in the local Jersey City South Asian population. Critics wonder why these priceless artifacts are not showcased in their original homelands, and how they got to Europe and North America in the first place. . . .'"

"Read more," she urged, pointing to the third paragraph.

"'NYC businessman Wilson Fisk's sponsorship of the exhibit also raises serious questions about his involvement in the exhibit. With most of his corporate concerns in the state of New York, some question why he has crossed the Hudson to invest in a charitable cause he's never shown interest in before.'"

"Cool, huh?" Nakia grinned.

"Very." I scanned the rest of the piece before handing the newspaper back to Nakia. "Looks like you really dug into the colonial looting angle. Aren't you worried about repercussions?"

"From who?"

"I dunno. The museum. The public." My eyes widened. "Maybe even Kingpin himself, since he was such a big, ahem, supporter of the exhibit."

Nakia scowled. "Bring it on! I'm not scared of that douchebag."

I let out a startled laugh. "Good for you, my bestie!"

She was stuffing the newspaper in her backpack when a group of kids walked past. "Hey, Nakia, great article today!" one girl called out.

"Yeah, I liked how you wrote so bravely about colonialism," a boy added. "The British did that to South Africa too, you know."

"And the Caribbean," a third kid said.

When the kids left, Nakia raised her eyebrows. "You were saying? About repercussions from the public?"

"Shut up." I nudged her. "I'm glad."

She squealed again. "Me too!"

By the end of the day, everyone in school was talking about Nakia's article. The principal made a special announcement about it, praising Nakia's commitment to journalism. Nakia blushed so hard I thought her cheeks would catch fire. "Having fun, Miss Celebrity?" Bruno asked her as we walked home.

She groaned. "It's just school, Bruno."

It wasn't. When I reached home, Ammi met me in the entryway. "Did you know your friend Nakia wrote a scathing piece in the newspaper today?"

"Um, yes." I put down my backpack and turned around. "How did you know?"

"A sister from the mosque called me."

"What? How did she know?"

Ammi gave me a withering look. "It's all over the internet, Kamala. It was shared in four of my WhatsApp groups."

I ran up to my room and texted Nakia. *You're WhatsApp famous, dude.*

She sent back a GIF of a woman screaming hysterically.

"Invite Nakia for dinner. I'm making kofta," Ammi yelled from downstairs. "I want to ask her about her journalism career."

"Can I invite Bruno too?" I yelled back.

"Sure. Better to call him here than go over to his house again."

Okay, then.

Nakia and Bruno were more than happy to come over for dinner. Ammi's koftas were legendary. We ate and talked—mostly about Nakia's article—then went to the living room to chat some more. Abu pulled out his phone to show Nakia and Bruno the pictures he'd taken from Pakistan. "Ooh, Kamala, you look incredible in that dress," Bruno said.

I flushed.

Then he realized what he'd said, and he flushed too.

Ammi and Abu frowned at both of us. "Bruno, don't give my daughter compliments," Abu grumbled.

"Sorry, Mr. Khan."

I giggled, feeling like a fool.

"That was uncomfortable," Nakia whispered to me.

I shrugged. It was, but it also wasn't. I'd known that nothing more could grow from Bruno's and my friendship. It just wouldn't be acceptable to my parents, and as Asaar had said, family was everything. I would never hurt them, or disappoint them, for my own desires.

Not that I had any desires regarding Bruno, no, sirree. "Ahem." Nakia nodded to Aamir, sitting quietly in the corner armchair. "What's up with him?"

I laughed a little. Aamir had been waiting for me when I'd come home the night before. I'd expected loud scolding and name-calling, but all he'd done was say "I'm glad you're safe" before going up to his room.

And now here he was, a day later, sitting quietly, watching everyone like he was glad we were all here, together. "I have this ache in my chest," he complained.

I smiled to myself. I hated my brother's guts sometimes, but I was so grateful he was alive and well. "Probably indigestion."

"Oh, I forgot to watch the news," Abu exclaimed suddenly. "The jet lag has really messed up my timings."

He switched on his tablet and pulled up a local news video. Nakia, Bruno, and I leaned forward to watch.

"Hundreds of stolen artifacts have been retrieved from a local warehouse believed to be owned by New York City businessman Wilson Fisk," the reporter said. "Authorities are concerned that this is just the tip of the iceberg for a crime spree of epic proportions."

"Epic proportions, huh?" Abu repeated, shaking his head.

"Look!" Aamir pointed. On the screen, a tied-up Delilah was being pulled away by two police officers. "I remember seeing her last night. And Kate Bishop!"

I held my breath, but nobody paid attention to Aamir. Abu was complaining loudly about the crime in our city, while Ammi was bringing out chai and cookies for everyone.

"So have your views about reparations changed at all, Mr. Carrelli?" Nakia asked Bruno in a low voice.

Bruno rolled his eyes. "Yes, I agree with you. Colonial theft is a real scourge in society, and we need to give those precious artifacts back to their original countries."

Nakia smiled triumphantly. "Glad I could change your mind."

Bruno shrugged. "You're an excellent writer. I really learned a lot from your article."

"Aww," I whispered. "My two friends are finally on the same page!"

Bruno's phone rang. "It's Brittany," he said, surprised.

I frowned. "Like, museum Brittany?" Why the heck was she calling Bruno in the middle of the night?

Okay, eight o'clock. Which was still kind of late.

Bruno put the call on speaker. "Hello, Bruno," came a familiar, gratingly cheery voice. "This is Brittany Myers from the Jersey City Art Museum."

"Hey, Brittany, you're on speakerphone," Bruno replied. "What's up?"

"Ms. Hibbert read your friend's article, and let me tell you, she's not happy. It's caused quite a PR nightmare for us."

"Oh." Nakia's eyes grew big. "Sorry?"

Brittany gave a husky laugh, which made me grit my teeth. "It's fine," she said gaily. "Ms. Hibbert actually reminded me that the exhibits in our museum are often looted from somewhere else."

There was that word again, *looted*. Now that I knew, thanks to Asaar, that *loot* was derived from the Hindi word, I couldn't unhear its connotations every time it was spoken. Loot. Plunder. Steal.

None of it was right. None of it was just.

Brittany continued. "Anyway, I wanted to let you know that the board members of the museum have met to discuss what we can do to, uh, make things right."

"And what have they decided?" Nakia sat up. "Will they return all the Mughal artifacts to their rightful place in South Asia?"

There was a silence that spoke volumes. "Well, that's not really, uh, possible," Brittany said cautiously. "Where would they even go? The Indian government? The Pakistanis? Private museums or benefactors like our very own Mr. Deen?"

I wanted to jump in and say *Yes! That last one.* Because Deen—Asaar—definitely deserved to have his heritage returned.

I leaned forward, but Nakia pinched my arm. "Ow," I whispered.

"So what can you do?" Bruno asked.

"The board has decided to donate all our exhibit ticket sales to the Asia Society," Brittany announced happily. "And they'll be able to borrow the artifacts to showcase them in all their locations next year."

"Borrow," I said flatly. "Wow, they must be ecstatic."

"They are." Brittany sighed. "Look, I know this isn't much, but believe me, Ms. Hibbert fought really hard to get the board to agree with this. One article and a bit of bad publicity can't change hundreds of years of colonial ideology, you know. One can only try."

Ugh, I hated when people like Brittany Meyers made sense. What was the world coming to?

"Okay," Bruno said. "Thanks for letting us know."

"Anything for you, cutie!"

I grimaced, and Nakia laughed. "Jealous?" she whispered in my ear.

I watched as Bruno took the call off speakerphone and

chatted some more with Brittany. I didn't get any awfully angry feelings, which was surprising but also really perfect. I might have a little bit of a crush on my best friend, but I didn't want to ruin the friendship we had, ever. "No, not really," I finally replied.

Nakia sighed. "Well, that was exciting. Even the board of directors read my article."

Ammi patted her hand. "We're proud of you, beta."

"Thank you, Aunty."

Bruno ended his call and stood up, his eyes gleaming "Guess what? Ms. Hibbert is giving all the opening day workers a bonus! That means I can afford the TechRo fees after all!"

I let out a little shriek of joy. "Yay!"

"We should go out for ice cream to celebrate!" he continued, his entire body vibrating with excitement.

I froze. Abu was scowling, and Ammi looked irritated. Now Bruno had done it. The lectures about girls going out with boys would commence in three, two, one. . . .

"Good idea," Ammi replied. "If you go to that falooda place around the corner, bring some back for me too."

"Sure, Mrs. Khan."

"Thank you, Ammi!" I hugged her, then went over to kiss Abu's head. "I'll be back soon, don't worry."

Abu sighed. "We will always worry, Kamala. You're our child. It's our job as parents."

"But that doesn't mean you don't get to have fun," Ammi added, shooing me away. "Now go, bring me back some falooda."

I eye Aamir in the corner. "You're not gonna say anything?"

He rolled his eyes. "Say the prayer for protection before you leave. In fact, I'll text it to you so you don't forget. I'm pretty sure you don't even remember it."

There he was, my annoying brother. I was so happy he was alive, I didn't even feel insulted that he thought I'd forgotten the Ayatul Kursi. Sheikh Abdullah had made all the kids memorize it when we were eight years old.

Or maybe I'd forgotten who taught me, and it was actually Aamir.

Who knew? Almost every idea, opinion, and preconceived notion I'd held until a couple of weeks ago had now been destroyed.

I'd figured out something new. Something even more magical than a pair of emerald spectacles.

Family, heritage, love. All those were bigger than the super heroes and villains of the world.

When the first Kamala Khan/Ms. Marvel comic was announced, written by the amazing G. Willow Wilson, my kids were in elementary school. As a Pakistani American immigrant mom, I was excited for them to have this role-model figure, a super hero sharing more than one aspect of their identity. As time went on, we'd bring home the comics from the library and sometimes read them together. Sometimes I'd read them by myself.

I realized that maybe these stories—this character and her family—were for me too.

I cannot thank the creators enough for this gift they've given the world in the form of Kamala Khan, a first-generation Muslim and South Asian American teen struggling with not just villains, but also her own self. Trying to fit in, trying to find her place, trying to do good in a world that often doesn't encourage that.

I'm grateful for the opportunity to add to this canon with *Ms. Marvel: Remnants of the Past*. I'm fangirling so hard as I write these words! I cannot wait for this story to reach all those kids, like mine, who need it, who will enjoy it and treasure it and pass it on. Who will be proud of their heritage and their complicated hyphenated identity. Like Kamala. Like me.

Thank you so much to Kim Anderson and John Morgan at Disney/Marvel for their guidance and patience as I worked on this novel. Thank you to my agent, Kari Sutherland, who is always my rock. Thank you to my family for being my biggest cheerleaders. And lastly, but most importantly, thank you to my readers, young and old, who've supported me throughout the years. This book is for all of you!